ALSO BY GORE VIDAL

Novels:
Williwaw
In a Yellow Wood
The Season of Comfort
A Search for the King
Dark Green, Bright Red
The Judgement of Paris
Messiah
Julian
Washington, D.C.
Myra Breckinridge
Two Sisters
Burr
Myron
1876
Kalki
Creation
Duluth
Lincoln
Myra Breckinridge and Myron
Empire
Hollywood
Live from Golgotha

Plays:
An Evening with Richard Nixon
Weekend
Romulus
The Best Man
Visit to a Small Planet

Essays:
Rocking the Boat
Reflections upon a Sinking Ship
Homage to Daniel Shays
Matters of Fact and Fiction
The Second American Revolution
Armageddon?
Screening History
United States: Essays, 1952–1992

THE CITY AND THE PILLAR

AND

SEVEN EARLY STORIES

GORE VIDAL

THE CITY
AND
THE PILLAR

REVISED, WITH A NEW PREFACE BY THE AUTHOR

AND
SEVEN EARLY STORIES

RANDOM HOUSE
NEW YORK

The City and the Pillar was originally published in 1948 by E. P. Dutton
& Co., Inc., New York, in the United States, and in 1949 by John
Lehmann in Great Britain. A revised edition, entitled The City and the
Pillar Revised, was published by E. P. Dutton & Co., Inc., New York, in
1965. A reprint edition was published in 1994 by Andre Deutsch Ltd.,
London.

The seven short stories included in this edition were originally pub-
lished separately in the following journals betwen 1948 and 1956:
Encounter, New Directions No. 12, New World Writing No. 1 and No.
4, and Tomorrow. They were published as a collection entitled A Thirsty
Evil by Zero Press, New York, in 1956, and by William Heinemann
Ltd., London, in 1958. This work was reprinted in 1974 by Panther
Books, Granada Publishing Ltd., London, in 1981 by Gay Sunshine
Press, San Francisco, and in 1994 by Andre Deutsch Ltd.

Library of Congress Cataloging-in-Publication Data
Vidal, Gore.
[City and the Pillar]
The city and the pillar and seven early stories.
p. cm.
Contents: Consists of the novel The city and the pillar and seven
short stories originally published under title: A thirsty evil.
ISBN 0-679-43699-5
I. Vidal, Gore. A thirsty evil II. Title. III. Title: A
thirsty evil.
PS3543.I26C5 1995
813'.54—dc20 95-3805

Manufactured in the United States of America on acid-free paper
2 4 6 8 9 7 5 3
First Edition

For the memory of J.T.

For the memory of L.L.

But his wife looked back from behind him
and she became a pillar of salt.

GENESIS 19:26

PREFACE

Much has been made—not least by the Saint himself—of how Augustine stole and ate some pears from a Milanese orchard. Presumably, he never again trafficked in, much less ate, stolen goods, and once this youthful crime ("a rum business," snarled the unsympathetic American jurist Oliver Wendell Holmes, Jr.) was behind him, he was sainthood bound. The fact is that all of us have stolen pears; the mystery is why so few of us rate halos. I suspect that in certain notorious lives there is sometimes an abrupt moment of choice. Shall I marry or burn? Steal or give to others? Shut the door on a life longed for while opening another, deliberately, onto trouble and pain because . . . The "because" is the true story seldom told.

Currently, two biographers are at work on my sacred story, and the fact that they are trying to make sense of my life has made me curious about how and why I have done—and not done—so many things. As a result, I have begun writing what I have said that I'd never write, a memoir ("I am not my own subject," I used to say with icy superiority). Now I am reeling haphazardly through my own youth, which is when practically everything of interest happened to me, rather more soon than late, since I was force-fed, as it were, by military service in the Second World War.

My father once told me, after reviewing his unpleasant period in public office, that whenever it came time for him to make a crucial decision, he invariably made the wrong one. I told him that he must turn Churchill and write his own life, demonstrating what famous victories he had set in motion at Gallipoli or in the "dragon's underbelly" of the Third Reich. But my father was neither a writer nor a politician; he was also brought up to tell the truth. I, on the other hand, was brought up by a politician grandfather in Washington, D.C., and I wanted very much to be a politician, too. Unfortunately, nature had designed me to be a writer. I had no choice in the matter. Pears were to be my diet, stolen or homegrown. There was never a time when I did not make sentences in order to make those things that I had experienced cohere and become "real."

Finally, the novelist must always tell the truth as he understands it while the politician must never give the game away. Those who have done both comprise a very short list indeed. The fact that I was never even a candidate for the list had to do with a choice made at twenty that entirely changed my life.

At nineteen, just out of the army, I wrote a novel, *Williwaw* (1946): it was admired as, chronologically, at least, the first of the war novels. The next year I wrote the less admired *In a Yellow Wood* (1947). Simultaneously, my grandfather was arranging a political career for me in New Mexico (the governor was a protégé of the old man). Yes, believe it or not, in the greatest democracy the world has ever known—freedom's as well as bravery's home—elections can be quietly arranged, as Joe Kennedy liked to explain to you.

For someone twenty years old I was well situated in the

world, thanks to two published novels and my grandfather's political skills. I was also situated dead center at a crossroads rather like the one Oedipus found himself at. I was at work on *The City and the Pillar.* If I published it, I'd take a right turn and end up accursed in Thebes. Abandon it and I'd turn left and end up in holy Delphi. Honor required that I take the road to Thebes. I have read that I was too stupid at the time to know what I was doing, but in such matters I have always had a certain alertness. I knew that my description of the love affair between two "normal" all-American boys of the sort that I had spent three years with in the wartime army would challenge every superstition about sex in my native land—which has always been more Boeotia, I fear, than Athens or haunted Thebes. Until then, American novels of "inversion" dealt with transvestites or with lonely bookish boys who married unhappily and pined for Marines. I broke that mold. My two lovers were athletes and so drawn to the entirely masculine that, in the case of one, Jim Willard, the feminine was simply irrelevant to his passion to unite with his other half, Bob Ford: unfortunately for Jim, Bob had other sexual plans, involving women and marriage.

I gave the manuscript to my New York publishers, E. P. Dutton. They hated it. One ancient editor said, "You will never be forgiven for this book. Twenty years from now you will still be attacked for it." I responded with an uneasy whistle in the dark: "If any book of mine is remembered in the year 1968, that's real fame, isn't it?"

To my grandfather's sorrow, on January 10, 1948, *The City and the Pillar* was published. Shock was the most pleasant emotion aroused in the press. How could our young war novelist . . . ? In a week or two, the book was a best-seller in the United States and wherever else it could be published—not exactly a full atlas in those days. The English publisher, John Lehmann, was very nervous. In his memoirs, *The Whispering Gallery*, he writes, "There were several passages in *The City and the Pillar*, a sad, almost tragic book and a remarkable achievement in a difficult territory for so young a man, that seemed to my travellers and the printers to go too far in frankness. I had a friendly battle with Gore to tone down and cut these passages. Irony of the time and taste: they wouldn't cause an eyebrow to be lifted in the climate of the early sixties." But only twenty years ago the book was taken from Dennis Altman as he arrived at the airport in Sydney, Australia. Altman challenged the obscenity law under which the book had been seized. The judge in the case acknowledged that under the law that he must administer the book was obscene, but then, in a famous obiter dicta, he wrote that he thought the law absurd: in due course, it was changed. Meanwhile, even today, copies of the book still fitfully blaze on the pampas and playas of Argentina and other godly countries. As I write these lines, I have just learned that the book will at last appear in Russia, where a Moscow theater group is adapting it for the stage.

What did my confreres think? I'm afraid not much. The fag writers were terrified; the others were delighted that a competitor had so neatly erased himself. I did send copies to two famous writers, fishing, as all young writers do, for endorsements. The first was to Thomas Mann. The second was to Christopher Isherwood, who responded enthusiastically. We became lifelong friends. Through Joseph Breitbach I was told that André Gide was planning to write an "appreciation," but when we finally met he spoke only of a handwritten, fetchingly illustrated pornography that he had received from an English clergyman in Hampshire.

At fourteen I had read Thomas Mann's *Joseph* books and realized that the "novel of ideas" (we still have no proper phrase in English for this sort of book or, indeed, such a genre) could work if one were to set a narrative within history. Later, I was struck by the use of dialogue in *The Magic Mountain,* particularly the debates between Settembrini and Naphta, as each man subtly vies for the favors of the dim but sexually attractive Hans Castorp. Later, there would be complaints that Jim Willard in *The City and the Pillar* was also dim. But I deliberately made Jim Willard a Hans Castorp type: what else could someone so young be, set loose in the world—the City—that was itself the center of interest? But I did give Jim something Hans lacked: a romantic passion for Bob Ford that finally excluded everything else from his life, even, in a sense, the life itself. I got a polite, perfunctory note from Thomas Mann, thanking me for my "noble work": my name was misspelled.

Contemplating the American scene in the 1940s, Stephen Spender deplored the machinery of literary success, remarking sternly that "one has only to follow the whizzing comets of Mr. Truman Capote and Mr. Gore Vidal to see how quickly and effectively this transforming, diluting, disintegrating machinery can work." He then characterized *The City and the Pillar* as a work of sexual confession, quite plainly autobiography at its most artless. Transformed, diluted, disintegrated as I was, I found this description flattering. Mr. Spender had paid me a considerable compliment; although I am the least autobiographical of novelists, I had drawn the character of the athlete Jim Willard so convincingly that to this day aging pederasts are firmly convinced that I was once a male prostitute, with an excellent backhand at tennis. The truth, alas, is quite another matter. The book was a considerable act of imagination. Jim Willard and I shared the same geography, but little else. Also, in the interest of verisimilitude I decided to tell the story in a flat gray prose reminiscent of one of

James T. Farrell's social documents. There was to be nothing fancy in the writing. I wanted the prose plain and hard.

In April 1993, at the State University of New York at Albany, a dozen papers were read by academics on *The City and the Pillar*. The book has been in print for close to half a century, something I would not have thought possible in 1948, when *The New York Times* would not advertise it and no major American newspaper or magazine would review it or any other book of mine for the next six years. *Life* magazine thought that the greatest nation in the country, as Spiro Agnew used to say, had been driven queer by the young army first mate they had featured only the previous year, standing before his ship. I've not read any of the Albany papers. For one thing, it is never a good idea to read about oneself, particularly about a twenty-one-year-old self who had modeled himself, perhaps too closely, on Billy the Kid. I might be shot in the last frame, but I was going to take care of a whole lot of folks who needed taking care of before I was done.

There were those who found the original ending "melodramatic." (Jim strangles Bob after an unsuccessful sexual encounter.) When I reminded one critic that it is the nature of a romantic tragedy to end in death, I was told that so sordid a story about fags could never be considered tragic, unlike, let us say, a poignant tale of doomed love between a pair of mentally challenged teenage "heteros" in old Verona. I intended Jim Willard to demonstrate the romantic fallacy. From too much looking back, he was destroyed, an unsophisticated Humbert Humbert trying to re-create an idyll that never truly existed except in his own imagination. Despite the title, this was never plain in the narrative. And of course the coda *was* unsatisfactory. At the time it was generally believed that the publishers forced me to tack on a cautionary ending in much the same way the Motion

Picture Code used to insist that wickedness be punished. This was not true. I had always meant the end of the book to be black, but not as black as it turned out. So for a new edition of the book published in 1965 I altered the last chapter considerably. In fact, I rewrote the entire book (my desire to imitate the style of Farrell was perhaps too successful), though I did not change the point of view or the essential relationships. I left Jim as he was. He had developed a life of his own outside my rough pages. Claude J. Summers recently noted that of the characters

> only Jim Willard is affecting, and he commands sustained interest largely because he combines unexpected characteristics. Bland and ordinary, he nevertheless has an unusually well-developed inner life. Himself paralyzed by romantic illusions, he is surprisingly perceptive about the illusions of others. For all the novel's treatment of him as a case history, he nevertheless preserves an essential mystery. As Robert Kiernan comments (*Gore Vidal*), Jim Willard is Everyman and yet he is l'étranger . . .* the net effect is paradoxical but appropriate for it decrees that, in the last analysis, we cannot patronize Jim Willard, sympathize with him entirely, or even claim to understand him. Much more so than the typical character in fiction, Jim Willard simply exists, not as the subject of a statement, not as the illustration of a thesis, but simply as himself.

Not long ago I received a telephone call from the biographer of Thomas Mann. Did I know, he asked, the profound effect that my book had had on Mann? I made some joke to

---

*Claude J. Summers in "The Cabin and the River" (*Gay Fictions,* New York: Continuum, 1990) quotes from Robert F. Kiernan's book *Gore Vidal* (New York: Frederick Ungar, 1982).

the effect that at least toward the end of his life he may have learned how to spell my name. "But he didn't read the book until 1950, and as he read it he commented on it in his diaries. They've just been published in Germany. Get them." Now I have read, with some amazement, of the effect that Mann's twenty-one-year-old admirer had on what was then a seventy-five-year-old world master, situated by war in California.

> Wednesday 22, XI, 50
> . . . Began to read the homo-erotic novel "The City and the Pillar" by Vidal. The day at the cabin by the river and the love-play scene between Jim and Bob was quite brilliant.—Stopped reading late. Very warm night.
> Thursday 23, XI, 50
> . . . Continued "City and Pillar."
> Friday 24, XI, 50
> . . . In the evening continued reading "The City and the Pillar." Interesting, yes. An important human document, of excellent and enlightening truthfulness. The sexual, the affairs with the various men, is still incomprehensible to us. How can one sleep with men—[Mann uses the word *Herren,* which means not "men" but "gentlemen." Is this Mann being satiric? A rhetorical question affecting shock?].
> Saturday evening 25, XI, 50
> . . . in May 1943, I took out the *Felix Krull* papers only to touch them fleetingly and then turn to *Faustus.* An effort to start again must be made, if only to keep me occupied, to have a task in hand. I have nothing else, no ideas for stories; no subject for a novel. . . . Will it be possible to start [*Felix Krull*] again? Is there enough of the world and are there enough people, is there enough

knowledge available? The homosexual novel interests me not least because of the experience of the world and of travel that it offers. Has my isolation picked up enough experience of human beings, enough for a social-satirical novel?

Sunday 26, XI, 50

Busy with [the *Krull*] papers, confusing.

Read more of Vidal's novel.

Wednesday 29, XI, 50

. . . The *Krull* papers (on imprisonment). Always doubts. Ask myself whether this music determined by a "yearning theme" is appropriate to my years. . . . Finished Vidal's novel, moved, although a lot is faulty and unpleasant. For example, that Jim takes Bob into a Fairy Bar in New York.

I am pleased that Mann did not find the ending "melodramatic," but then what theme is more melodramatically "yearning" than *Liebestod*? In any case, the young novelist who took what seemed to everyone the wrong road at Trivium is now saluted in his own old age by the writer whom he had, in a certain sense, modeled himself on. As for Mann's surprise at how men could sleep with one another, he is writing a private diary, the most public act any German master can ever do, and though he often refers to his own "inversion" and his passions for this or that youth, he seems not to go on, like me, to Thebes but to take (with many a backward look) the high road to Delphi, and I am duly astonished and pleased that, as he read me, he was inspired—motivated—whatever verb—to return to his most youthful and enchanting work, *Felix Krull*.

Some of my short stories are almost as lighthearted as Thomas Mann in his last work. One of them, "The Ladies in the Library," is an unconscious variation on *Death in Venice*. Three variations on a theme: Mann's Hans Castorp; then my own, Jim Willard; then a further lighter, more allegro version of Jim in the guise of a character whom he appropriately called Felix—the Latin for "happy."

CONTENTS

THE CITY
AND
THE PILLAR

▼

CHAPTER

1

THE MOMENT WAS STRANGE. There was no reality in the bar; there was no longer solidity; all things merged, one into the other. Time had stopped.

He sat alone in a booth, listening to the music which came out of a red plastic box, lighted within. Some of the music he remembered from having heard it in other places. But the words he could no longer understand. He could recall only vague associations as he got drunk, listening to music.

His glass of whiskey and water and ice had slopped over and the top of the table was interesting now: islands and rivers and occasional lakes made the top of the table a continent. With one finger he traced designs on the wooden table. He made a circle out of a lake; he formed two rivers from the circle; he flooded and destroyed an island, creating a sea. There were so many things that could be done with whiskey and water on a table.

The jukebox stopped playing.

He waited a long time for it to start again. He took a swallow of the whiskey to help him wait. Then after a long time, in which he tried not to think, the music started. A record of a song he remembered was playing and he allowed himself to be taken back to that emotional moment in time when . . . when? He tried hard to remember the place and the time, but it was too late. Only a pleasant emotion could be recalled.

He was drunk.

Time collapsed. Years passed before he could bring the drink to his mouth. Legs numb, elbows detached, he seemed to be supported by air, and by the music from the jukebox. He wondered for a moment where he was. He looked about him but there were no clues, only a bar in a city. What city?

He made a new island on the tabletop. The table was his home and he felt a strong affection for the brown scarred wood, for the dark protectiveness of the booth, for the lamp which did not work because there was no bulb in the socket. He wanted never to leave. This was home. But then he finished his drink, and was lost. He would have to get another one. How? He frowned and thought. A long time went by and he did not move, the empty glass in front of him.

At last he came to a decision. He would leave the booth and go talk to the man behind the bar. It was a long voyage but he was ready for it.

He stood up, became dizzy, and sat down again, very tired. A man with a white apron came over to his table; he probably knew about liquor.

"You want something?"

Yes, that was what he wanted, something. He nodded and said slowly so that the words would be clear, "Want some whiskey, water, bourbon, water . . . what I been drinking."

The man looked at him suspiciously. "How long you been here?"

He didn't know the answer to that. He would have to be sly. "I have been here for one hour," he said carefully.

"Well, don't go passing out or getting sick. People got no consideration for others when it comes to doing things like that for other people to clean up."

He tried to say that he did have consideration for others but it was no use. He could not talk anymore. He wanted to get back home, to the tabletop. "I'm OK," he said, and the man went away.

But the top of the table was no longer home. The intimacy had been dispelled by the man with the apron. Rivers, lakes, islands, all were unfamiliar; he was lost in a new country. There was nothing for him to do except turn his attention to the other people in the barroom. Now that he had lost his private world, he wanted to see what, if anything, the others had found.

The bar was just opposite him and behind it two men in white aprons moved slowly. Four five six people stood at the bar. He tried to count them but he could not. Whenever he tried to count or to read in a dream, everything dissolved. This was like a dream. Was it a dream?

A woman wearing a green dress stood near him, large buttocks, dress too tight. She stood very close to a man in a dark suit. She was a whore. Well well well. . . .

He wondered about the other booths. He was at the center of a long line of booths, yet he knew nothing about the people in any of them. A sad thought, to which he drank.

Then he stood up. Unsteadily, but with a face perfectly composed, he walked toward the back of the barroom.

The men's room was dirty and he took a deep breath before he entered so that he would not have to breathe inside. He saw himself reflected in a cracked distorted mirror hung high on the wall. Blond hair, milk white, bloodshot eyes staring brightly, crazily. Oh, he was someone else all right. But who? He held his breath until he was again in the barroom.

He noticed how little light there was. A few shaded bulbs against the walls and that was all, except for the jukebox, which gave not only light but wonderful colors. Red blood, yellow sun, green grass, blue sky. He stood by the jukebox, his hands caressing the smooth plastic surface. *This* was where he belonged, close to light and color.

Then he was dizzy. His head ached and he could not see clearly; stomach contracted with sharp nausea.

He held his head between his hands and slowly he pushed out the dizziness. But then he pushed too hard and brought back memory; he had not wanted to do that. Quickly he returned to the booth, sat down, put his hands on the table, and looked straight ahead. Memory began to work. There had been a yesterday and a day before, and twenty-five years of being alive before he found the bar.

"Here's your drink." The man looked at him. "You feeling all right? If you don't feel good you better get out of here. We don't want nobody getting sick in here."

"I'm all right."

"You sure had a lot to drink tonight." The man went away.

He had had a lot to drink. It was past one and he had been in the bar since nine o'clock. Drunk, he wanted to be drunker, without memory, or fear.

"You all by yourself?" Woman's voice. He didn't open his eyes for a long time, hoping that if he could not see her she could not see him. A basic thing to wish but it failed. He opened his eyes.

"Sure," he said. "Sure." It was the woman in the green dress.

Her hair was dyed a dark red and her face was white with powder. She too was drunk. She leaned unsteadily over his table and he could see between her breasts.

"May I sit down?"

He grunted; she sat opposite him.

"It's been an awfully hot summer, hasn't it?" She made conversation. He looked at her, wondering if he could ever assimilate her into the world of the booth. He doubted it. For one thing, there was too much of her, and none of it simple.

"Sure," he said.

"I must say you're not very talkative, are you?"

"Guess not." The intimacy of the booth was gone for good now. He asked, not caring, "What's your name?"

She smiled, his attention obtained. "Estelle. Nice name, isn't it? My mother named all of us with names like that. I had one sister called Anthea and my brother was called Drake. I think Drake is a very attractive name for a man, don't you? He's in women's wear. What's your name?"

"Willard," he said, surprised that he was giving her his right name. "Jim Willard."

"That's a nice name. Sounds so English. I think English names are attractive. In origin I'm Spanish myself. Oh, I'm thirsty! I'll call the waiter for you."

The waiter, who seemed to know her, brought her a drink. "Just what the doctor ordered." She smiled at him. Under the table her foot touched his. He moved both feet under his chair.

She was not distressed. She drank rapidly. "You from New York?"

He shook his head and cooled his forefinger in the half-empty glass.

. "You sound sort of Southern from the way you talk. Are you from the South?"

"Sure," he said, and he took his forefinger out of the glass. "I'm from the South."

"It must be nice down there. I've always wanted to go to Miami but I never seem to get away from the city. You see, all my friends are here and I can't very well leave them. I did have a friend once, a man," she smiled privately, "and he always went to Florida in the winter. He had beautiful luggage. He invited me to go down with him and I almost went, once." She paused. "That was ten years ago." She sounded sad, and he didn't pity her at all.

"Of course it must be terribly hot there in the summer. In fact, it's so hot *here* that I think sometimes I'll *die* from the heat. Were you in the war?"

He yawned, bored. "I was a soldier."

"I'll bet you look good in a uniform. But I'm glad it's finally over, the war."

He moved his glass around the table, listening to the satisfying noise it made as it hit scars and cracks. She watched him. He wished she would go away.

"Why're you in New York?" she asked. "And why are you getting drunk? You got everything and still you're sitting here all by yourself, getting drunk. I wish *I* was you. I wish I was young and nice-looking. I wish . . ." Quietly she began to cry.

"I got everything," he said, sighing. "I got everything, Anthea."

She blew her note in a piece of Kleenex. "That's my sister's name, Anthea. I'm Estelle."

"And you have a brother named Drake."

She looked surprised. "That's right. How did you know?"

Suddenly he felt himself in danger of becoming involved in her life, hearing confessions, listening to names that meant nothing to him. He shut his eyes, tried to shut her out.

She stopped crying and took a small mirror out of her handbag. Tenderly she powdered the pouches under her eyes. Then she put the mirror away and smiled. "What're *you* doing tonight?"

"I'm doing it. Drinking."

"No, silly, I mean later. You're staying in a hotel somewhere, maybe?"

"I'm staying right here."

"But you can't. It closes at four."

Alarm. He had not thought what he was going to do after four o'clock. It was her fault. He had been happily listening to music, until she came along and changed everything. It had been a mistake, not assimilating her.

She menaced him with reality. She must be destroyed.

"I'm going home alone," he said. "When I go home, I go home alone."

"Oh." She thought a moment, decided on injury and hurt. "I suppose I'm not good enough for you."

"Nobody is." He was mortally weary of her, and sick at the thought of sex.

"Pardon me," said Estelle, sister of Anthea and Drake. She stood up, arranged her breasts, and returned to the bar.

Now he was alone and he was glad, with three glasses before him on the table: two empty, one half full with lipstick on it. He arranged the glasses to form a triangle, but then when he tried to arrange them to form a square, he failed. Why? Three glasses ought to be able to form a square. He was distressed. Fortunately, reality began to recede once more. And Jim Willard sat at his table in his booth in his barroom and made lakes, rivers, islands. This was all that he wanted. To be alone, a creature without memory, sitting in a booth. Gradually, the outline of fear grew blurred. And he forgot entirely how it began:

CHAPTER
2

I

ON THE WARMEST AND greenest afternoon of the spring, the high school's commencement exercises ended, and boys and girls, parents and teachers, streamed out of the brand-new Old Georgian school building. Separating himself from the crowd, Jim Willard paused a moment on the top step and looked out, searching for Bob Ford. But he could not make him out in the mob of boys in dark jackets and white trousers, girls in white dresses, fathers in straw hats (this year's fashion in Virginia). Many of the men smoked cigars, which meant that they were politicians—this was the county seat and singularly rich in officeholders, among them Jim's father, the courthouse clerk.

A running boy struck Jim's arm playfully. Jim turned, expecting Bob. But it was someone else. He smiled, struck back, and exchanged cheerful insults, secure in the knowledge that he was popular because he was the school's tennis champion and all athletes were admired, particularly those who were modest and shy, like Jim.

At last Bob Ford appeared. "This year me. Next year you."

"I sure wish it was me who just graduated."

"I feel like they opened the prison door and let me out into the great big world. So how did I look up there on that stage wearing that black potato sack?"

"Great."

"Don't you know it?" Bob chuckled. "Well, come on. We better play while we still got some light." As they moved through the crowd to the door to the locker room, a dozen girls greeted Bob, who responded with an easy grace. Tall, blue-eyed, with dark red curling hair, he was known throughout the school as Lover Man, a phrase somewhat more innocent than it sounded. "Love" meant little more than kissing. Most girls found Bob irresistible, but boys did not much like him, possibly because girls did. Only Jim was his friend.

As they entered the dim locker room, Bob looked about him with a delighted melancholy. "I guess this is the last time I'll be coming in here."

"Well, we can still use the courts this summer. . . ."

"That's not what I meant." Bob took off his coat and hung it up carefully. Then he took off his tie. These were his best clothes and he handled them with respect.

"What do you mean?" Jim was puzzled. But Bob merely looked mysterious.

The two boys walked the half mile to the tennis courts without speaking. They had known each other all their lives but it was not until this last year that they had become close friends. They had been on the baseball team together and they had played tennis together, even though Jim always won, to Bob's chagrin. But then Jim was the best player in the county, and one of the best in the state. Games had been particularly important to both of them, especially for Jim, who found it difficult to talk to Bob. The hitting of a white ball back and forth across a net was at least a form of communication and better than silence or even one of Bob's monologues.

They had the red-clay courts to themselves. Bob spun a racket and Jim, the loser, took the side facing the sun. The game began. It was good to hit the white ball evenly, making it skim the net. Jim played his best, obscurely aware that this was a necessary ritual enacted for the last time.

They played while the sun set and the shadows of tall trees lengthened, darkening the court. A cool breeze stirred. After the third set, they stopped. Jim had won two out of three.

"Nice going," said Bob, and gave him his hand briefly, as though they were in a tournament. Then they both stretched out on the grass beside the court and breathed deeply, tired but comfortable.

Twilight and the day ended. Chattering birds circled among the trees, preparing for night.

"It's getting late." Bob sat up, brushing away the twigs and leaves that had stuck to his back.

"It's still light." Jim did not want to go.

"I hate to leave, too." Bob looked about, again the mysterious sadness.

"What're you talking about? You been hinting around all day. What're you up to?" Then Jim understood. "You're not going to ship out on a boat, are you? Like you said last year?"

Bob grinned. "Curiosity killed the cat."

"OK." Jim was hurt.

Bob was contrite. "Look, I can't say anything just now. Whatever it is, I'll tell you before Monday. That's a promise."

Jim shrugged. "It's your business."

"I got to get dressed." Bob stood up. "I'm taking old Sally Mergendahl to the dance tonight." He winked. "And tonight I mean to do myself some good."

"Why not? Everybody else has." Jim disliked Sally, a dark aggressive girl who had been after Bob all year. But then it was none of his business what Bob did.

As they walked through the blue twilight to the school, Bob suddenly asked, "What're you doing this weekend?"

"Nothing. Why?"

"Why don't we spend it down at the cabin?"

"Well, sure. Why not?" Jim was careful not to show too much pleasure; it was bad luck. The cabin had been the home of a onetime slave, recently dead. It stood deserted now, in thick woods close to the Potomac. Once they had spent a night there; more than once Bob had brought girls to the cabin. Jim was never certain exactly what happened because Bob's stories varied with each telling.

"OK," said Bob. "Meet you at your house, tomorrow morning."

An irritable janitor let them into the locker room.

II

BREAKFAST WAS INVARIABLY UNPLEASANT, possibly because it was the only meal the Willard family always had together.

Mr. Willard was already at the head of the table when Jim came into the dining room. Small, thin, gray, Mr. Willard tried to appear tall and commanding. It was the family's opinion that he would have had no trouble at all being elected governor, but for one reason or another he had been forced to allow lesser men to go to Richmond while he remained at the courthouse, a bitter fate.

Mrs. Willard was also small and gray but inclined to fat; after twenty-three years of her husband's stern regime, she had assumed the melting look of the conscious martyr. Now wearing a white frilled apron which did not become her, she cooked breakfast in the adjoining kitchen, looking from time to time into the dining room to see if her three children were down.

Jim, the firstborn son, was first to appear. Since this was a special day, he was cheerful, glad to be alive.

"Morning, Father."

His father looked at him as though he could not quite place the face. Then he said, "Good morning," and distantly started to read the paper. He discouraged conversation between himself and his sons, especially Jim, who had made the error of being tall and handsome and not at all the sort of small, potentially gray son Mr. Willard ought to have had.

"You're down early." Mrs. Willard brought him his breakfast.

"Beautiful day, that's why."

"I don't think a quarter to eight is such an early hour," said his father from behind the *Richmond Times*. Mr. Willard had been brought up on a farm and one of the reasons for his life's success had been rising "at the crack of dawn."

"Jim, you didn't hear any funny noises around the house last night, did you?" Like Joan of Arc, his mother was always hearing funny noises.

"No, ma'am."

"Funny, I could've sworn someone was trying to get in the window; there was this tapping. . . ."

"I should like some more coffee, if I may." Mr. Willard lowered his newspaper and raised his chin.

"Of course, dear."

Jim ate his cereal. Mr. Willard rearranged his newspaper.

"Good morning." Carrie came into the room. A year older than Jim, she was pretty but pale, and disliking paleness, painted her face with a bold and imaginative hand, which sometimes made her look whorish and infuriated her father. She had graduated from high school the year before, at seventeen, a fact which the family impressed on Jim. Since then, she helped her mother in the house while encouraging the attentive courtship of a young realtor whom she expected to marry just as soon as he had "put something by."

"Morning, Carrie." Mr. Willard looked at his daughter with wintry approbation. Of his children, she alone gave him pleasure; she saw him great.

"Carrie, will you come in here and help me with breakfast?"

"Yes, Mother. How was the graduation, Jim?"

"OK."

"I wish I could have gone but I don't know why it is, I'm so busy all the time, on the go. . . ."

"Sure, sure."

Carrie joined her mother in the kitchen and Jim could hear them arguing in low voices; they always argued. Finally, John entered. At fourteen, he was thin, nervous, potentially gray, except for black eyes.

"Hi." He sat down with a crash.

"Glad to have you with us," said his father, continuing the war.

"It's Saturday." John was a skilled domestic warrior, master of artillery. "Everybody sleeps late."

"Naturally." Mr. Willard looked at John and then, satisfied in some strange way with what he saw, returned to his paper.

Carrie brought her father more coffee and then sat down beside Jim. "When do you start work in the store, Jimmy?"

"Monday morning." He wished she wouldn't call him Jimmy.

"That'll be nice. It's sort of dull, I guess, but then I suppose you have to be *qualified* to do more skilled work, like in an office, typing."

He didn't answer her. Neither Carrie nor his father could irritate him today. He was meeting Bob. The world was perfect.

"Hey, they're playing baseball today over at the school. You going to play?" John struck his fist against his palm with a satisfactory sound.

"No, I'm going down to the cabin. For the whole weekend."

Mr. Willard struck again. "And who, if I'm not asking too much, are you going with?"

"Bob Ford. Mother said it was all right."

"Is that so? It is amazing to me why you want to sleep away from your own home which we have tried at such expense to make comfortable. . . ." His father slowly unfurled the domestic banner, and charged. Jim refused to defend himself, beyond promising himself that one day he would throw a plate at this bitter old man he was forced to live with. Meanwhile, he simply stared at his future weapon while his father explained to him how the family was a Unit and how he owed all of them a Debt and how difficult a time Mr. Willard had had making the Money to support them and though they were not rich, they were Respectable, and Jim's going around with the son of the town drunk did them no good.

During her husband's tirade Mrs. Willard joined them, a demurely pained expression on her face. When Mr. Willard had finished, she said, "Well, I think the Ford boy is nice and he does get good marks in school and his mother *was* a friend of ours no matter what we think of the father. So I don't see anything wrong with Jim seeing him."

"*I* don't mind," said Mr. Willard. "I just thought *you* would mind having your son exposed to that sort of a person. But if you don't, I have nothing more to say." Mr. Willard, having embarrassed his son and disagreed with his wife, ate fried eggs with unusual gusto.

Mrs. Willard murmured something soothing and Jim wished that his father were like Bob's father, drunk and indifferent.

"When are you going to the cabin?" his mother asked, in a low voice, so as not to disturb her husband.

"After breakfast."

"And what are you doing about food?"

"Bob's getting stuff from the store where he works."

"That's nice," said Mrs. Willard, obviously thinking of something else; she had a difficult time concentrating for very long.

Carrie and her younger brother started arguing and soon breakfast was finished. Then Mr. Willard rose and announced that he had business at the courthouse, which was not true. The courthouse never did business on Saturday. But his wife did not question this and, with a reserved nod to his children, Mr. Willard put on his straw hat, opened the front door, and stepped out into the bright morning.

Mrs. Willard watched him a moment, expressionless; then she turned and said, "Carrie, come help me clean up. Boys, you better fix your room."

The boys' room was small and not very light. The two

beds, close together between two bureaus, made the room crowded. Pictures of baseball and tennis players covered the walls, early idols of Jim's.

John had no idols. He was intense and studious and he was going to be a Congressman, which pleased his father, who often gave him talks on how to be a success in politics. Jim had no plans beyond college. It all seemed a long way off.

Jim made his bed quickly; John took longer.

"What're you and Bob going to do down by the river?"

"I don't know." Jim straightened the patchwork quilt. "Fish. Loaf."

"That sounds like a waste of time." John echoed his father.

"Isn't that too bad?" Jim mocked as he opened the closet and took down two blankets from the shelf, his contribution to the weekend.

John sat on the bed and watched. "Bob sees a lot of Sally Mergendahl, doesn't he?"

"I suppose so. She sees a lot of people."

"That's what I mean." John looked knowing and Jim laughed.

"You're too young to be hearing such things."

"Like hell I am." John proved his virility with an oath.

"Sure, you're a real lover and you keep track of all the girls."

John was angry. "Well, that's more than you do and you're older than me. You don't ever go out with girls. I heard Sally say once she thought you were the best-looking guy in school and she couldn't understand why you didn't go around more. She said she thought you were afraid of girls."

Jim flushed. "She's full of crap. I'm not afraid of her or

anybody. Besides, I do my traveling on the other side of town."

"Really?" John was interested and Jim was glad he had lied.

"Sure." He was mysterious. "Bob and me go over there a lot of times. All the baseball team does, too. We don't want to mess around with 'nice' girls."

"I guess not."

"Besides, Sally isn't so fast."

"How do you know?"

"I just do."

"I'll bet Bob Ford said that about her."

Jim fixed the top of his bureau, ignoring his brother. He was ill at ease and he didn't know why; it was seldom that John could irritate him.

Jim looked in the dusty mirror above his bureau and wondered if he needed his weekly shave. He decided that he could wait till he got back. Absently he ran his hand over his short blond hair, glad that it was summer, the season of short hair. Was he handsome? His features were perfectly ordinary, he thought; only his body pleased him, the result of much exercise.

"When's Bob coming by?" John was sitting on his bed, balancing his brother's tennis racket in his hand.

"Right now."

"Must be nice down there. I was only to the cabin once. I guess anybody can go there."

"Sure."

"They say the guy who owns the land lives in New York and he never comes down here. I'm playing baseball this afternoon and then I'm going to a meeting of the Democratic Party in the back of the drugstore." John's mind was quick and unsettled.

"That must be a lot of fun." Jim put his racket in the closet. Then he picked up the two blankets and went downstairs.

Carrie was in the sitting room, lazily dusting furniture.

"Oh, *there* you are, Jim."

He stopped. "Anybody looking for me?"

"No, I just said there you were." She put the duster down, glad of an excuse not to work. "Are you going to the high-school dance tonight?"

He shook his head.

"That's right," she said, "you and Bob are going to the cabin. I'll bet Sally is jealous of you for keeping him from coming to the dance."

Jim didn't let his face change expression. "It was his idea," he said evenly. "Maybe you'll find out *why* later." Mystery was clearly the order of the day.

Carrie nodded. "I think I know. I've been hearing stories about Bob's going away. Sally said something about it not so long ago."

"Maybe he is, maybe he isn't." Jim was surprised that Carrie and Sally knew; he wondered how many other people Bob had told.

Carrie yawned and began to dust again. Blankets under his arm, Jim went to the kitchen. His mother was not yet finished cleaning.

"Now be sure you're back by Sunday night. Your grandfather's coming over and your father will want you to be here. Are those the good blankets you're taking?"

"No, old."

Through the kitchen window Jim saw Bob carrying a large paper bag.

"I'm on my way."

"Look out for water moccasins!"

The morning sun was hot, yet the air was cool. The day was green and blue and very bright. Jim Willard was meeting Bob and the weekend was not yet lived. He was happy.

III

THEY STOOD ON THE edge of the cliff and looked down at the brown river, muddy from spring rains and loud where it broke up on the black rocks in midstream. Below them, the cliff dropped steeply to the river, a wall of stone, dark green with laurel and wild grapevines.

"Must be a flood upstream. That old river looks mean," said Bob.

"Maybe we'll see a house come floating down."

Bob chuckled. "Or a privy." Jim sat on a rock and plucked a piece of long grass and chewed on the white sweet-tasting stem. Bob squatted beside him. Together they listened to the roar of the river and the noise of tree frogs and the rustle of bright new leaves in the wind.

"How was Sally?"

Bob growled. "Prick-teaser, like all the rest. Leads you on so you think, *now* I can lay her and then, just as you get all hot, *she* gets scared: Oh, what're you doing to me? Oh, stop! You stop that now!" Bob sighed with disgust. "I tell you it makes a man so horny he could lay a mule, if it would just stand still." Bob contemplated mules. Then: "Why didn't you come to the dance last night? Lots of girls asked for you."

"I don't know. Don't like dancing, I guess. I don't know."

"You're too bashful."

Bob rolled up a trouser leg and removed a large black

ant, which was crawling up his calf. Jim noticed how white Bob's skin was, like marble, even in the sun.

Then, to break the silence, they threw stones over the edge of the cliff. The sound of rock hitting rock was entirely satisfying. Finally Bob shouted, "Come on!" And they crawled over the edge of the cliff and cautiously worked their way downward, holding on to bushes, finding toe-holds in the rock.

The hot sun shone in a pale sky. Hawks circled while small birds flashed between trees. Snakes, lizards, rabbits all scuttled for cover as the boys made their noisy descent. At last they reached the river's muddy bank. Tall black rocks jutted from brown sand. Happily, they leapt from rock to rock, never once touching earth, stepping only on the relics of a glacier age.

Shortly after noon they came to the slave cabin, a small house with a shingled roof much perforated by weather. The interior smelled of rotted plaster and age. Yellow newspapers and rusty tin cans were scattered over the rough wood floor. On the stone hearth there were new ashes: tramps as well as lovers stayed here.

Bob set down the paper bag he had been carrying while Jim put the blankets on the cleanest part of the floor.

"Hasn't changed much." Bob looked up at the roof. The sky shone through holes. "Let's hope it don't rain."

Close to the cabin there was a large pond, bordered by willows and choked with lilies. Jim sat on the moss-covered bank while Bob undressed, throwing his clothes into a nearby tree, the trousers draped like a flag on one branch while his socks hung like pennants from another. Then he stretched happily, flexing his long muscles and admiring himself in the green smooth water. Though slim, he was strongly built and Jim admired him without envy. When

Bob talked of someone who had a good build, he invariably sounded envious; yet when Jim looked at Bob's body, he felt as if he were looking at an ideal brother, a twin, and he was content. That something was lacking did not occur to him. It seemed enough that they played tennis together and Bob spoke to him endlessly of the girls he liked.

Cautiously Bob put one long foot in the water. "It's warm," he said. "Real warm. Come on in." Then, hands on knees, he leaned over and studied his own reflection. As Jim undressed, he tried to fix the image of Bob permanently in his mind, as if this might be the last time they would ever see one another. Point by point, he memorized him: wide shoulders, narrow buttocks, slim legs, curved sex.

Naked, Jim joined Bob at the water's edge. The warm breeze on his bare skin made him feel suddenly free and curiously powerful, like a dreamer who is aware that he is dreaming.

Bob looked at him thoughtfully. "You got a good tan. I sure look white. Hey!" He pointed at the water. Below the dark green surface, Jim could see the blunt slow-moving shape of a catfish. Then, suddenly, he was falling and there was a rush of water in his ears. Bob had pushed him in. Choking, he came to the surface. With a rapid movement, Jim grabbed Bob's leg and pulled him in. Grappling, they turned and twisted in the water, making the pond foam. As they wrestled, Jim took pleasure in the physical contact. So, apparently, did Bob. Not until both were exhausted did they stop.

For the rest of that day they swam, caught frogs, sunned themselves, wrestled. They talked little. Not until the light began to fail did they relax.

"It's sure nice here." Bob stretched out full length. "I guess there isn't any place as nice and peaceful as this place is." He patted his flat stomach and yawned.

Jim agreed, totally at peace; he noticed that Bob's belly quivered with the regularity of a pulse. He looked at himself: the same phenomenon. Before he could comment on it, he saw a tick heading toward his pubic hair. He pinched it hard until it popped.

"I got a tick."

Bob jumped to his feet. Ticks gave you a fever, so they examined themselves carefully, but found nothing. They got dressed.

The air was gold. Even the gray walls of the cabin looked gold in the last light of the sun. Now they were hungry. Jim built a fire while Bob made hamburgers in an old frying pan. He did everything easily, expertly. At home he cooked for his father.

They ate their supper, sitting on a log facing the river. The sun had gone. Fireflies darted like yellow sparks in the green shadow of the woods.

"I'm going to miss this," said Bob finally.

Jim looked at him. In the stillness there was no sound but the rushing river. "My sister said Sally said you were going to leave right after graduation. I told her I didn't know anything about it. Are you going?"

Bob nodded and wiped his hands on his trousers. "Monday, on the Old Dominion Bus Line."

"Where are you going to go?"

"To sea."

"Like we always talked about."

"Like we always talked about. Oh, I tell you I'm fed up with this town. The old man and I don't get along at all and God knows there isn't anything to do around here. So I'm going. You know I never been out of this county, except to go over to Washington. I want to see things."

Jim nodded. "So do I. But I thought we were going to

go to college first and *then* we would . . . well, you would go off on this trip."

Bob caught a firefly in his hand and let it climb up his thumb, and fly away.

"College is too much work," he said at last. "I'd have to work my way through and that means a job, which means I'd never get a chance to play around. Besides, there isn't a thing they could teach me that I want to know. All I want is to travel and to hell around."

"Me too." Jim wished that he could say what he wanted to say. "But my father wants me to go to college and I suppose I got to. Only I'd hoped we could go together . . . well, team up in tennis doubles. We could be state champions. Everybody says so."

Bob shook his head and stretched out. "I got to get moving," he said. "I don't know why but I do."

"I feel the same way, sometimes." Jim sat beside Bob on the ground and together they watched the river and the darkening sky.

"I wonder what New York is like," said Bob at last.

"Big, I guess."

"Like Washington. That sure is a big town." Bob rolled over on his side, facing Jim. "Hey, why don't you come with me? We can ship out as cabin boys, maybe even deckhands."

Jim was grateful Bob had said this, but he was cautious by nature. "I think I ought to wait till next year when I get that high-school diploma, which is important to have. Of course my old man wants me to go to college. He says I should . . ."

"Why do you pay any attention to that bastard?"

Jim was shocked and delighted. "Well, I don't really. In fact, I'd just as soon never see him again." With surprising ease, he obliterated his father. "But even so, I'm scared, going off like that."

"Nothing to it." Bob flexed the muscles of his right arm. "Why, a guy like you with brains and a good build, he can do most anything he wants. I knew these guys, they were sailors out of Norfolk, and they said there was nothing to it; easy work and when you're onshore you have a good time all the time, which is what I want. Oh, I'm tired of hanging around this town, working in stores, going out with *nice* girls. Only they're not really so damned nice, they're just afraid of getting knocked up." Fiercely he struck the ground with his fist. "Like Sally! Why, she'd do anything to you you want except the one thing you got to have. And that sure makes me mad. She makes me mad. All the girls around here make me mad!" Again he struck the dark earth.

"I know how it is," said Jim, who did not know how it was. "But aren't you scared you'll catch something from somebody you meet in New York?"

Bob laughed. "Man, I'm careful!" He turned over on his back.

Jim watched the fireflies rise from the nearby grass. It was already night. "You know," he said, "I wish I could go with you up North. I'd like to see New York and do as I please for once."

"So why don't you?"

"Like I said, I'm afraid to leave home and the family, not that I like them all that much but . . ." His voice trailed off uncertainly.

"Well, you can come with me if you want to."

"Next year, after I graduate, I'll come."

"*If* you can find me. I don't know where I'll be by then. I'm a rolling stone."

"Don't worry. I'll find you. Anyway, we'll write."

Then they walked down to the narrow boulder-strewn beach. Bob scrambled onto a flat rock and Jim followed him. The river swirled about them as they sat side by side in the blue, deep night.

One by one, great stars appeared. Jim was perfectly contented, loneliness no longer turning in the pit of his stomach, sharp as a knife. He always thought of unhappiness as the "tar sickness." When tar roads melted in the summer, he used to chew the tar and get sick. In some obscure way he had always associated "tar sickness" with being alone. No longer.

Bob took off his shoes and socks and let the river cool his feet. Jim did the same.

"I'll miss all this," said Bob for the dozenth time, absently putting his arm around Jim's shoulders.

They were very still. Jim found the weight of Bob's arm on his shoulders almost unbearable: wonderful but unbearable. Yet he did not dare move for fear the other would take his arm away. Suddenly Bob got to his feet. "Let's make a fire."

In a burst of activity, they built a fire in front of the cabin. Then Bob brought the blankets outside and spread them on the ground.

"There," he said, looking into the yellow flames, "that's done." For a long moment both stared into the hypnotically quivering flames, each possessed by his own private daydream. Bob's dream ended first. He turned to Jim. "Come on," he said menacingly. "I'll wrestle you."

They met, grappled, fell to the ground. Pushing and pulling, they fought for position; they were evenly matched, because Jim, though stronger, would not allow Bob to lose or to win. When at last they stopped, both were panting and sweating. They lay exhausted on the blanket.

Then Bob took off his shirt and Jim did the same. That was better. Jim mopped the sweat from his face while Bob stretched out on the blanket, using his shirt for a pillow. Firelight gleamed on pale skin. Jim stretched out beside him. "Too hot," he said. "Too hot to be wrestling."

Bob laughed and suddenly grabbed him. They clung to one another. Jim was overwhelmingly conscious of Bob's body. For a moment they pretended to wrestle. Then both stopped. Yet each continued to cling to the other as though waiting for a signal to break or to begin again. For a long time neither moved. Smooth chests touching, sweat mingling, breathing fast in unison.

Abruptly, Bob pulled away. For a bold moment their eyes met. Then, deliberately, gravely, Bob shut his eyes and Jim touched him, as he had so many times in dreams, without words, without thought, without fear. When the eyes are shut, the true world begins.

As faces touched, Bob gave a shuddering sigh and gripped Jim tightly in his arms. Now they were complete, each became the other, as their bodies collided with a primal violence, like to like, metal to magnet, half to half and the whole restored.

So they met. Eyes tight shut against an irrelevant world. A wind warm and sudden shook all the trees, scattered the fire's ashes, threw shadows to the ground.

But then the wind stopped. The fire went to coals. The trees were silent. No comets marked the dark lovely sky, and the moment was gone. In the fast beat of a double heart, it died.

The eyes opened again. Two bodies faced one another where only an instant before a universe had lived; the star burst and dwindled, spiraling them both down to the meager, to the separate, to the night and the trees and the firelight; all so much less than what had been.

They separated, breathing hard. Jim could feel the fire on his feet and beneath the blanket he was now uncomfortably aware of small stones and sticks. He looked at Bob, not certain of what he would see.

Bob was staring into the fire, face expressionless. But he grinned quickly when he saw Jim watching him. "This is a hell of a mess," he said, and the moment fled.

Jim looked down at himself and said as casually as he could, "It sure is."

Bob stood up, the firelight glittering on his body. "Let's wash up."

Pale as ghosts in the dark night, they walked to the pond. Through the trees they could see the light from their fire, yellow and flickering, while frogs croaked, insects buzzed, river thundered. They dove into the still black water. Not until they had returned to the fire did Bob break the silence. He was abrupt.

"You know, that was awful kid stuff we did."

"I suppose so." Jim paused. "But I liked it." He had great courage now that he had made his secret dream reality. "Did you?"

Bob frowned into the yellow fire. "Well, it was different than with a girl. And I don't think it's right."

"Why not?"

"Well, guys aren't supposed to do that with each other. It's not natural."

"I guess not." Jim looked at Bob's fire-colored body, long-lined and muscular. With his newfound courage, he put his arm around Bob's waist. Again excited, they embraced and fell back onto the blanket.

Jim woke before dawn. The sky was gray and the stars were fading. The fire was almost out. He touched Bob's arm and watched him wake up. They looked at one another. Then Bob grinned and Jim said, "You're still going Monday?"

Bob nodded.

"You'll write me, won't you? I'd like to get on the same boat with you next year."

"Sure, I'll write you."

"I wish you weren't going . . . you know, after this."

Bob laughed and grabbed him by the neck. "Hell, we got all day Sunday." And Jim was satisfied and happy to have all day Sunday with this conscious dream.

CHAPTER

3

I

BOB WROTE ONE LETTER from New York: things had been tough but now it looked as if he'd be shipping out on the American Export Line. Meanwhile, he was having a swell time and had met a lot of girls, ha-ha. Jim replied promptly, only to have his letter returned, "Addressee unknown." There was no second letter. Jim was hurt but not entirely surprised. Bob was not much of a letter writer, particularly now that he was absorbed in that new life which they would soon share, for Jim had already made up his mind that once high school was done with, he would follow Bob to sea.

On the greenest and the warmest day of the next June, Jim graduated from high school and began a two week's battle with his father. Jim won. He would go to New York for the summer and work, with the understanding that in the fall he would return to Virginia and enter college. Natu-

rally, he would have to work his way through the university, but it was not every father who was willing to offer his son that opportunity. And so, early one bright yellow morning, Jim kissed his mother, shook his father's hand, said a casual good-bye to his brother and sister, and got on the bus to New York with seventy-five dollars in his pocket, more than enough, he reckoned, to keep him until he found Bob.

New York was hot, gray, dirty. Jim found it astonishing (where did all those people come from? Where were they all hurrying to?) and oppressive in the summer heat. But then he was not a tourist. He was on a quest. After renting a room at a YMCA he went to the Seamen's Bureau, where he learned that there was no record of a Bob Ford. For a moment he experienced panic. But then one of the old-timers explained to him that men often shipped out using other men's papers. In any case, the best thing for him to do was to apply for a berth as a cabin boy. Sooner or later, he and Bob would meet. The sea was surprisingly small; paths always crossed. Jim was put on a list. There would be a wait, perhaps a long one. While his papers cleared, he visited bars, got drunk twice (and disliked it), saw dozens of movies, and became an interested spectator of the life of the street. Then, just as his money ran out, he was signed on a freighter as cabin boy.

The sea was a startling experience. It took time to get used to the constant throb of engines beneath steel bulkheads, the slap and fall of a ship going full speed into the wind, the close confinement in the fo'c'sle with thirty strangers, foulmouthed but for the most part amiable. He ended by enjoying the life. In Panama he learned that a deckhand named Bob Ford had recently passed through the port, on his way to San Francisco. Jim's luck was improving.

He transferred to a cargo ship bound for Seattle by way of San Francisco. But the trail ended in San Francisco. He could find no trace of Bob. Disconsolately, he roamed the city and visited waterfront bars, hoping for a sudden glimpse of Bob. Once he thought he saw him at the far end of a bar, but when he approached, heart beating fast, the figure turned toward him and showed a stranger's face.

Jim signed on as cabin boy aboard the Alaska Line and spent the rest of the year at sea. Entirely absorbed in his new life, he no longer wrote to his parents. Only the absence of Bob shadowed the full days he spent aboard ship during that first snow-bright winter of his freedom.

On Christmas Day the ship was off the coast of southeastern Alaska, headed for Seattle. Jagged mountains rose from black water. The sea was heavy, the wind rising. Those passengers who were not sick were having breakfast in the dining saloon. They sat at round tables and made brave jokes about the motion of the ship and their fallen comrades, while the messboys hurried back and forth between galley and saloon, carrying heavy china plates of food.

Only one of Jim's passengers had come to breakfast. She was a plump, thick woman with bad skin. She was very jovial. "Good morning, Jim," she said brightly. "Nasty weather, isn't it? I suppose all the landlubbers are sick."

"Yes, ma'am." He began to clear away the remains of her breakfast.

"Me, I've never felt better." She inhaled the close cabin air. "This weather agrees with me." She patted herself and glanced at Jim as he picked up his tray. "When are you going to fix that porthole thing of mine, the thing that's broken and keeps rattling all the time?"

"I'll try, when I make up your cabin."

"That'll be fine," said the plump woman and she left the

table, swaying slightly as she walked, using what she called her "sea legs."

Jim took the tray back to the galley. Breakfast was over. The steward dismissed him. Whistling to himself, Jim walked down the companionway to a small cabin aft where he found Collins, a short, square young man of twenty with dark curly hair, blue eyes, and a love of himself which was surprisingly contagious. On his left arm he had an intricate vein-blue tattoo which pledged him forever to Anna, a girl belonging to the dim past, when he was sixteen and living in Oregon, not yet a seaman. Collins was sitting on an upright box, smoking.

"Hello, boy," said Collins.

Jim grunted and sat down on another box. He took a cigarette out of Collins's shirt pocket and then lit it with his own match.

"Only two more days," said Collins, "and then . . ." He rolled his eyes and made obscene designs in the air. "Can't wait to get back to Seattle. Hey, what've they got planned for today? You know it's Christmas."

"Sure, I got a calendar, too," said Jim callously.

"I wonder," said Collins more specifically, "if we'll get any liquor. This is the first time I ever been to sea at Christmas. Some ships, foreign ships mostly, serve liquor to the men."

Jim exhaled sadly. "I don't think they will," he said, watching the smoke fade. "But we ought to get some truck from the passengers."

"Hope so." Collins yawned. "By the way, how you doin' with the hog?" The messboys enjoyed kidding Jim about the plump woman at his table. Her interest in him was hardly secret.

Jim laughed. "I keep her in deep suspense."

"Wonder if she's got any money. You might pick up some

extra change there." Collins was serious, and Jim was disgusted, but he didn't show it because Collins was his best friend aboard ship. Also, Jim was never sure if Collins really did the things he said he did or not.

"I'm not that hungry," said Jim.

Collins shrugged. "I always need money. All the time I need it and now we're going to Seattle I'll need a lot more than I got. Well, maybe somebody rich'll die and leave it to me." Collins was essentially a thief, but it was good policy to appear to have illusions about shipmates. Besides, Collins was guide as well as friend. He had made Jim's life easier aboard ship by showing him different ways to avoid work, as well as places like this cabin to hide in.

Jim stretched. "I got to start making beds."

"Plenty of time. Steward won't be looking for you for a while." Collins stamped out his cigarette butt and quickly lit another. Jim finished his own cigarette. He disliked smoking. But aboard ship it was important to keep your hands busy when there was nothing to do, and in his months at sea there were days on end when there was little to do, except listen to the men talk of women and ships' officers, of good ports and bad. And once each man had said what he had to say he would promptly repeat himself, until no one listened to anyone else. There were times when Jim could conduct an entire conversation with Collins and at the end not remember a word that either had said. It was a lonely time.

Suddenly he was aware Collins was talking. The subject? He waited until he caught the word *Seattle*.

"I'll show you around. I really know that town like nobody's business. Show you these girls I know, Swedes, Norwegians . . . you know, *blonde*." His eyes shone. "You'll be real popular. I was when I was your age. Oh, they all used to make a fuss over me. They used to roll dice to see who was going to go with me. I was something, I guess. You'll be the same way because they like young guys."

Jim was going to ask more but they were interrupted by the steward, a tall lean Scot with no sense of humor. "Willard, Collins, why're you not working?"

They fled.

On deck the wind was cold and sharp and full of spray. Jim squinted in the wind as he made his way to the plump woman's cabin.

He rapped on the door. "Come in."

His admirer wore a pink silk dressing gown that made her look somewhat heavier than she actually was. She was cleaning her nails. A strong smell of salt and gardenia perfume was in the air.

"Late today, aren't you?"

He mumbled agreement as he took the broom out of the locker and began to sweep, quickly, self-consciously. She watched him.

"Have you been a sailor long?"

He kept on cleaning. "No, ma'am."

"I didn't think you had. You're not very old, are you?"

"Twenty-one," he lied.

"Well, you had me fooled. You certainly look younger than that." He wished she would stop talking. She went on. "Whereabouts are you from?"

"Virginia."

"Really? I have relatives in Washington, D.C. You know where that is, don't you?"

He was amused and irritated. She obviously thought him simple. But he played the desired role. Nodding vaguely, he opened the cabin door and swept the dirt out onto the deck. "Where did you learn such housekeeping?" She was endlessly inventive in her lust.

"Just came natural, I reckon," he said, mouth slightly ajar, idiot boy catching flies.

"Oh, really?" She was unaware that he was giving a performance. "I'll bet you never did that back home, did you?"

He said oh, yes, and began to make the bed, first brushing out the cigarette ashes. She continued to babble. "My friends in Washington say Virginia is lovely. I went to see the Blue Ridge Mountains once. You know where they are, don't you?"

This time he said no, and looked bewildered. She was informative. "I went all through those caverns underneath the mountains and they were very interesting, with all those stone things growing down and the others up. Is your mother alive? Are your family living in Virginia?"

He replied accurately.

"My, but your mother must be almost as old as I am," said the plump woman, making her first tentative move.

"I expect she is," he said evenly, taking the round on points.

"Oh." She was silent. He worked quickly; there were other cabins to be done.

"This is my first trip to Alaska," she said at last. "I have relatives in Anchorage. You've been to Anchorage, haven't you?" He nodded. "It's very civilized for Alaska, don't you think so? I mean I always thought of Alaska as being like the North Pole, all ice and snow. But Anchorage is just like a small town anywhere and they've got trees and beauty parlors, just like in the States. 'Outside,' they call the States. Isn't that a funny way to refer to the rest of the world? 'Outside'? I enjoyed myself very much visiting my relatives and so on. But you've traveled around a lot for someone so young, haven't you? I'll bet you've had some interesting experiences."

"Not so many." He finished making her bunk. When she saw he was ready to leave, she said quickly, "Oh, you're going to fix that porthole thing for me, aren't you? It keeps rattling all the time and I can't sleep at night."

He looked at the porthole cover and saw that a screw was loose. With his thumbnail he tightened it. "I don't think it'll bother you anymore," he said.

She got up, pulling her silk dressing gown tight at the throat, and joined him at the porthole.

"Aren't you clever! Why, I tried all night long last night to fix that thing and I couldn't."

He moved toward the door.

She spoke again, quickly, as though to prevent him from leaving by her talk. "My husband used to be good at fixing things. He's dead now, of course. He's been dead since 1930, but I've a son back home. He's much younger than you. He's just starting college. . . ." Jim felt as if he were being pushed to the edge of a cliff. With a son his age, she was trying to seduce him. Suddenly homesick, lost, he wanted to run away, to hide, to vanish. She was still talking as he opened the door and stepped out onto the wet, shining deck.

But he had no time to be lonely that evening. There was a party for the passengers, and it was a hard evening for the messboys.

The saloon was decorated with imitation holly and shedding branches of pine, which the steward had thoughtfully brought from Anchorage. Not until two in the morning did the last passenger leave the smoky saloon. Then the steward, red-faced and sweating, congratulated the messboys and wished them a Merry Christmas and told them that they could have their own party in the saloon.

Tired as they were, they managed to drink a good deal. Jim drank beer and Collins drank bourbon from a bottle given him by a young girl passenger. Then some of the men started to sing and soon everyone sang loudly, to show what a good time they were having. As Jim continued to drink beer, he felt a certain affection for the others. Together they would sail forever back and forth between Seattle and Anchorage until the ship sank or he died. Tears came to his eyes as he thought of this beautiful comradeship.

Collins was drunk now. "Come on, boy," he said, "stop being so gloomy."

Jim was hurt. "I feel fine," he said. "I'm not gloomy." Then he did become sad. "But I never thought that I'd be 'way up here last Christmas, be here on Christmas Day one year when a year ago I was home." He was not sure if this made sense but it had to be said.

"Well," said Collins happily, "I know I never thought I'd go to sea, back in Oregon where I lived. Old man was in the lumber business. Outside Eugene. Wanted me to go in the business, too, but I had to go places and so I went. But sometime, maybe, I'll go back. Settle down. Raise a family. . . ." His voice trailed off, bored with what he was saying. Then he stood up shakily and together they left the saloon. The night was cold and clear. The clouds were gone and across the shifting black water the peaks of Alaska were visible, defined by starlight.

Exhilarated, Jim breathed the cold air deeply.

"Some night," he said. But Collins was only interested in keeping his balance as they walked forward to the fo'c'sle.

The fo'c'sle was triangle-shaped with double-deck bunks and bare lightbulbs overhead, and heavy with the smell of too many men living in too small a place.

Jim had an upper bunk; Collins slept below him. Groaning to show how tired he was, Collins sat down on his bunk. "I'm wore out." He took off his shoes and stretched out. "I can't wait to get to Seattle. You never been there, have you?"

"Just passed through."

"Well, I'll show you 'round these dives I know. They know me at all the waterfront places. And I'll get you a girl. A real good one. What do you like?"

Jim was uncomfortable. "I don't know," he said. "Almost anything."

"Hell, you got to be *particular* or you'll catch something awful. Me, I never caught anything . . . yet." He touched the wooden side of his bunk. "Get you a blonde, they're best. Natural blondes, I mean. Swedes, that kind. You like blondes?"

"Sure."

Collins pushed himself up on his elbow and looked at Jim, suddenly alert. "Hey, I'll bet you're a virgin."

Jim flushed and couldn't think of anything to say; the pause was enough.

"I'll be damned." Collins was delighted. "I never thought I'd find a guy who was. Well, we'll be real careful about the girl. How come you waited so long? You're eighteen, aren't you?"

Jim was embarrassed. He cursed himself for not having lied as all of them did about their affairs. "Oh, I don't know," he said, trying to dismiss it. "There wasn't much chance back home."

"I know just the girl for you. Name's Myra. Professional but nice, and clean. She don't drink or smoke and because she don't drink she takes care of herself. She won't give you no dose. I'll get you and Myra together."

"I'd like to meet her," said Jim, and the beer he had drunk made him excited at the idea. He dreamed occasion-

ally of women, but most often he dreamed of Bob, which
disturbed him when he thought about it.

"I'll show you around," said Collins, undressing. "I'll
show you one good time. Yes, sir, I know my way 'round."

II

It was already evening when Collins and Jim left the ship.
Collins wore a brown suit with red checks. Jim wore a gray
suit that was already too tight in the shoulders. He was still
growing. Neither wore a tie.

They took a streetcar to the theater district. Jim wanted
to see a movie but Collins told him there was no time for
that. "First we find us a room."

"I thought we were going to stay with these girls you
been telling me about."

Collins gestured. "How do I know if they're in town, or
if they ain't already booked for tonight? We'll get us a
room; then we'll have a place to take whoever we find."

"You know a place like that?"

"I know a lot of places."

They found what they were looking for not far from the
waterfront, in a street where the buildings were red brick
and dingy and there were many bars, crowded with seamen
prowling.

A bald wrinkled man sat behind a desk at the top of a
long flight of flimsy steps. He was the proprietor of the
Regent Hotel.

"We want a room for tonight," said Collins, and he put
his lower jaw out to show that he meant what he said.

"Double room?"

Collins nodded and so did Jim.

The bald man said, "Pay in advance, two dollars apiece."

They paid in advance. "I don't want no loud noise or drinking or bringing women up here. You know the law, boys. You from a boat?"

"Yeah," said Collins, his jaw still out.

"I was a sailor myself once," said the bald man mildly. "But I don't follow the sea no more." He led them up two flights of steps, then down a dark, damp-smelling corridor to a small room. He turned on the light. The room was fairly clean, though the paint was flaking off the walls. A large iron bed was at the center of the room. A single window looked out upon the side of another brick building.

"Leave the key at the desk when you go out," said the bald man. He looked around the room a moment, pleased with what he saw. Then he left.

"Isn't this something?" Collins sat down on the bed and it creaked.

Jim was depressed. Though he had slept in worse places, he did occasionally wonder if he would ever again live in a room like his room in Virginia, a clean place with familiar walls.

"Come on," said Jim, turning to the door. "I'm hungry."

"Me too!" And Collins winked at Jim to show what he was hungry for.

They walked the dark streets, looking tough whenever they saw seamen, whistling boldly when any girls gave them the eye. It was good to be in Seattle on a clear winter night.

They stopped in front of a restaurant-bar. A neon sign announced spaghetti. "Here it is," said Collins. "This is the place."

"Where the girls are?" asked Jim.

"What else?" They went inside. The restaurant was large but only half-filled. A dark-haired waitress led them to a booth.

"So what've you got, honey?" Collins twinkled.

The waitress handed him a menu. "That's what I got," she said flatly and walked away.

"Stuck-up bitch," commented Collins, and Jim saw that his charm was not infallible. "Women shouldn't work anyway. Not with the Depression and all. They ought to stay home."

Jim looked around the restaurant. Red booths, brown walls, yellow-shaded lights: a cavern somewhere in hell.

After spaghetti, Collins belched and then announced, "We'll stay here awhile. Over there, at the bar. Then, if we don't see nothing we want, we'll go over to the Alhambra, this dance place where I know everybody."

The bar was not crowded. They ordered beer. "Swell place," said Collins, with a self-congratulatory air.

Jim agreed, adding somewhat maliciously, "Of course, they got hundreds of places like this back in New York." Collins had never been to the East Coast.

Collins frowned at his beer. "Well, I'll stick to little old Seattle." He took a drink of beer. "I'll bet," he said, making a point, "that *Hollywood* has got New York beat a mile." He knew that Jim had never been to Hollywood. "Yes," he went on, pleased at his own tactic, "I'll bet they got more pretty girls and crazy people and queers in L.A. than any other town."

"Maybe so."

Then the girl came up to the bar. Collins saw her first and nudged Jim. She was a slim girl with khaki hair, gray eyes, large features, large breasts. She sat down at the bar, smiling slightly. Red lips.

"What do you think of that?" murmured Collins.

"She's pretty."

"Real class, too," said Collins. "Probably works in an office." Apparently the bartender knew her because he said something to her in a low voice and they both laughed. He gave her a drink and she sat with it in her hand, watching the door.

"Here goes," said Collins, and went toward the men's room. On his way, he paused at the end of the bar. He looked at the girl, pretending to be puzzled by what he saw. He spoke to her. Jim couldn't hear what he said but he could see her frown, then smile. They talked a moment. She looked at Jim. She smiled again. Collins gestured for Jim to join them.

"Jim, this is Emily." They shook hands.

"It's a pleasure to meet you," said Emily, and her voice was husky and ladylike. Jim muttered a greeting.

"Don't mind him. He's real shy. We're on the same ship. We only got in today."

Emily was impressed, as she was supposed to be. "But you ought to be out on the town celebrating."

"We plan to. But the night is young, like they say."

"And so are we." Emily took a tiny sip of her drink. "Is this your first visit to Seattle?"

Collins shook his head. "I been in and out of Seattle most of my life. I know this old town backward and forward. In fact, I was thinking of showing Jim here some of the sights."

"Where are *you* from?" When Jim told her, she gave a little cry. "Oh, a Southerner! I love Southerners. They have such good manners. So you're from Virginia." She said Virginia as though it were Vur-gin-ee-ah. "But you haven't got much of an accent, have *you-all*?" Emily and Collins laughed at her mimetic skill.

Jim smiled. "No," he said, "I guess not."

"By the way"—Emily turned to Collins—"what sort of sights had you planned on seeing tonight?"

"Well, I thought maybe we'd go over to the Alhambra. . . ."

"Why, that's my very favorite place! My girl friend and I go there a lot to dance. You meet such nice people there. Not the rough gang you get in some places."

"Oh, you live with another girl?" Collins was on the scent.

Emily nodded. "We work in the same office and sometimes we go out on dates together. Tonight she was supposed to meet me here. Two boys she knows are coming into town (we think) and she was going to bring them here."

"Oh hell." Collins scowled and looked unhappy. "And here I was hoping maybe you and your friend could join Jim and me. You see the only girls I know in town happen to be away right now so I was hoping maybe . . ."

"Well," said Emily thoughtfully, "I *could* call her up and find out whether they are definitely going to come tonight or not and if they aren't . . . well, I think she would be *glad* to join us."

And so it was that Emily went to the back of the bar to telephone her roommate.

"How's that for operating?" asked Collins.

"Good." Jim was genuinely impressed. "Do you think her girl friend will really come?"

"Are you kidding?"

"She's pretty," said Jim, watching the blonde girl through the glass door of the telephone booth. He appreciated her handsomeness, but he was not moved by her in the way Collins was. He wanted very much to be excited by her. But it was no use, at least not while he was sober. It was very odd.

Emily joined them at the bar, red lips smiling. "My friend, Anne, is going to meet us in a few minutes at the Alhambra. She said that our two friends are *not* coming after all. You know, some people are so undependable that way. So, as I said to her, it's a lucky thing for us to have such a nice invitation from two boys just in town after such a long time at sea. Anne's just crazy about the sea. Once they gave an office party, a picnic out on the Sound, and Anne went sailing with one of the fellows and they could hardly get her back to shore she liked it so much."

"I guess," said Collins with a wink, "that Anne will be Jim's date. If that's all right."

Emily laughed and both of them watched her breasts shake. "Why, if it's all right with you, it is with me." And she looked at Collins, lips parted seductively. Then she turned to Jim. "I'm sure you'll like Anne. She's a lot of fun."

The Alhambra was a large dance hall on a side street, with a bright neon sign which flashed on and off above the mock-Moorish door.

Inside, the hall was crowded and dim. A small band played swing.

A gray-haired woman in a black evening dress led them to a table. Collins greeted her warmly. She looked at him blankly and left.

"Old friend of mine," said Collins. "I used to come in here a lot last year. She always remembers me."

A waiter came over and after a short discussion they ordered rye. Meanwhile, Emily made an unconscionable amount of conversation. "I expect to see Anne any minute now. She's the fastest dresser I've ever seen for a woman. And then we live just a few blocks from here."

"Yes?" Collins was alert.

"Just a few blocks," repeated Emily. Then: "Anne is really such a clever girl. Why, she even used to do modeling work."

"She must be real pretty," said Jim, forcing excitement.

Emily nodded. "Anne *is* good-looking. She's one of the

most popular girls in the office. She and I date together all the time and I'm sure that the fellow with me is always wishing he was with Anne." This was an excellent opening for Collins to protest. He protested. Emily continued. "She's younger than I am. She's twenty and I'm twenty-two. How old are you, Colly?"

"Twenty-five," lied Collins and he pulled his chair nearer hers.

Emily looked at Jim. "I'll bet you are not a day over twenty," she said with a grin.

Jim nodded solemnly. "That's right." Now that false ages had been established all around, the evening assumed direction.

Finally, Anne arrived. She was small and thin and she wore a brown dress. She looked about her uncertainly until she saw Emily. Then she hurried over, smiling, posing. Emily introduced everybody and then, as she was a little drunk, she introduced everybody a second time. This proved funny.

While Anne laughed, Jim decided that she was indeed pretty, though nearer thirty than twenty. Not that it made the slightest difference to him.

"And so you're Jim," said Anne after she had taken a drink and the excitement of her entrance was gone.

"That's right. Emily's been telling us a lot about you."

"Flattering, I hope?" At times Anne sounded like an English movie actress. Like her friend, she had a good deal of small talk.

"We work in an office in a department store. I file things and Emily types and does things like that. Are you from the South?"

He nodded and she made up a funny sentence with "you-all" in it and everybody laughed and then Emily and Collins got up from the table and announced that they were going

to dance. So Jim invited Anne and all four of them went out
onto the dance floor. Jim made an effort to dance well.
There were so many things to be proved this evening.

Anne pressed close to him, her cheek against his; he
could smell powder and soap and perfume. Once he looked
down at her and saw that her eyes were closed.

Collins came by with Emily. "Hey, Jim," he said. Anne
opened her eyes and Jim moved a few inches away from her.

"Yes?" said Jim.

"Emily here's suggested we go over to their place for a
while. They've got liquor over there and a radio and we can
dance where it won't be so crowded."

"That's a good idea, Emily," said Anne brightly.

They went back to their table, paid the check, gathered
coats, and left the Alhambra. Though the night was cold,
Jim was sweating from whiskey.

In a side street they stopped before a small apartment
house. Emily opened the door. At the top of two flights of
clean and carpeted stairs, Emily showed them into an apartment consisting of a sitting room, a small kitchen, and a
bedroom. The door to the bedroom was open and Jim
could see twin beds inside.

"Home," announced Emily, turning on the radio while
Anne disappeared into the kitchen, returning a moment
later with a bottle of rye and some glasses. "Get some ice,
will you, Emily?"

Emily went into the kitchen, followed by Collins. Anne
put the glasses down on the table and Jim stood beside her,
awkward, unsure of himself.

"Let's dance," she said, when she had arranged the glasses
on a table. He held her away from him, but she pressed
close. He was ill at ease. He wanted desperately to be carried
away by the music and the whiskey and this girl, but all he
could think of was the flecks of dandruff in her hair.

He heard a laugh from the kitchen. Then Collins and Emily came into the sitting room. Both were flushed and Collins's eyes were bright. Emily put a bowl of ice cubes on the table and Collins produced a bottle of soda water.

"Let's all have a drink," said Emily. They all had a drink. Collins proposed a toast to Emily and she graciously proposed one to him. Jim and Anne toasted each other. Jim was drunk now. His eyes refused to focus. Everything was suddenly warm and cozy and intimate. Boldly he put his arm around Anne and they sat down on a couch, side by side, and watched Collins and Emily dance.

"You really dance well," said Anne. "You must've taken lessons. I never took any lessons but I picked up a lot from the girls I knew in school. I went to a secretarial school and we used to have a lot of dances. I enjoyed them so much. And that's where I learned how to dance."

He wanted to keep her talking. "Did you always live in Seattle?"

She scowled to show that this was a question which troubled her. "Yes, I've always lived here but I don't like it. You see, I want to travel. I've *always* wanted to travel. That's why I envy you men on ships, you get to travel so much and see so many things."

"Where would you like to go?" As Jim held her, he was pleasurably astonished at his own bravery. She moved close to him.

"Everywhere," she said. "But mainly I want to see Southern California. I want to go to Hollywood. You know, I think I'd like to be in the movies." She said this in a low voice, confidingly.

"I guess a lot of people do." Jim had read a few movie magazines and he had been impressed by the difficulties movie stars encountered in becoming movie stars.

"I know," said Anne. "But I think I'm different. No,

really. I'm serious. I think I'm going to be famous. Why, even when I was younger and saw people like Jean Harlow on the silver screen I knew that would be me one day. But for now I got to work in an office and I don't know when I'll be able to get to Hollywood. But I'll get there someday. I just know it."

"You've certainly got ambition."

"Oh, I've got plenty of that! Just think what it'd be like to wear all those pretty clothes and have men with mustaches and tweed suits take me out to eat in those expensive places with palm trees." She stared into space, her mouth open with longing for this other life.

Jim muttered soothing things, aware that Collins and Emily had disappeared. The door to the bedroom was still open, and he could see Collins in his shorts approaching Emily, who lay naked on one of the beds. Emily giggled. Jim looked away, blushing.

"What's the matter?" Anne abandoned her Hollywood vision. Then she saw what was happening in the bedroom. She giggled, an echo of Emily.

"You're only young once," she said. Jim looked at her and saw that her eyes were bright, shiny, bestial. He had seen the same look in Collins's eyes, in Emily's eyes, yet not in Bob's eyes. He was repelled. But Anne, unaware of his response, put her face so close to his that he could smell the whiskey on her breath. "My, but they're having fun!" Her body was against him now and he could feel the rapid pounding of her heart.

"I'll bet they're having a good time," she repeated. "You're only young once, that's what I say." She kissed him. It was a wet and tongue-involving kiss. He pulled away. Aware of his withdrawal, she started to cry. "I used to be in love, too," she said, missing the point. Between small actress sobs, she said that she understood the way he felt and she knew that what she was doing was terribly bad but she was lonely, without anyone to care for her, and God knows they were only young once.

He made himself kiss her, his mind full of memories and half-forgotten fears. With an effort of will, he tried to melt the fear in his stomach. Gradually, desire began. He was startled but pleased. Soon he would be ready. But suddenly she stood up and said brightly, "I better take my dress off. Don't want to get it rumpled."

She went into the bedroom. He followed her to the door and stood watching Collins and Emily on the bed. Neither of them seemed to care if they were observed or not. They were involved in the intricate act of becoming one. Fascinated, Jim watched them. They made primitive noises and writhed blindly, according to the mindless ritual of the sexes. Jim was frightened, unready for this.

Anne appeared, and posed for him without her clothes. He stared, fascinated. He had never seen a naked woman before. She walked toward him. She put out her arms. Involuntarily, he backed away.

"Come on in, Jimmy," she said and her voice was high-pitched and artificial. He hated her then. He hated her passionately. This was not what he wanted.

"I got to go," he said. He went into the sitting room. She followed him and he found himself staring at her again and this time he compared her with Bob, and found her wanting. He no longer cared whether or not he was different from other people. He hated this woman and her body.

"What's the matter? What did I do wrong?"

"I got to go." He couldn't say anything else. She started to cry. Quickly he went to the door and opened it. Just as he left, he heard Collins shout to Anne, "Let the queer go! I got enough for two."

Jim walked a long time in the cold night and wondered

why he had failed so completely in what he had wanted to do. He was not what Collins had called him. He was certain of that. Yet why? At the moment when what should have happened was about to happen, the image of Bob had come between him and the girl, rendering the act obscene and impossible. What to do? He would not exorcise the ghost of Bob even if he could. Yet he realized that it would be a difficult matter to live in a world of men and women without participating in their ancient and necessary duet. Was he able to participate? Yes, he decided, under other circumstances. In any case, the word Collins had shouted after him was hardly apt. It couldn't be. It was too monstrous. Yet because it had been said, he could never see Collins again. He would jump ship and go . . . where? He looked down the dark empty street, searching for a sign. Just opposite him was a movie house. "*Yesterday's Magic,* starring Ronald Shaw," proclaimed the marquee in unlit lightbulbs. He thought of Hollywood, recalling Anne's voice droning on wistfully about the movies. That did it. At least he would get there before she did. Obscurely pleased at this small vengeance, he returned to the hotel.

The bald-headed man was still behind the desk. "You're a sailor. I can tell. Me, I was a sailor but I don't follow the sea no more. No, no more of that for me." Jim went to his room and tried to sleep, tried to forget what Collins had called him. He slept and he forgot.

CHAPTER
4

I

OTTO SCHILLING WAS HALF-AUSTRIAN and half-Polish. He
was blond with a brick-red face, much lined from weather.
He was tennis instructor at the Garden Hotel in Beverly
Hills.

"You were a sailor, yes?" Otto's accent was thick, though
he had been in America half his life.

"Yes, sir." Jim was nervous. He needed this job.

"When did you leave ship?"

"Last December."

Otto looked thoughtfully out the window at his kingdom, the eight clay courts which adjoined the hotel pool.

"That was six months ago. You have been in Los Angeles
since then?"

"Yes, sir."

"You have been what?"

"Working in a garage mostly."

"But you play tennis, yes?"

"Yes, sir. I used to play back home at school."

"How old are you?"

"Nineteen."

"You think you know enough to help around here? Roll courts, be ball boy, string rackets . . . you can do this?"

"Yes, sir. I talked to the guy who was here before and he told me what the work was and I know I can do it."

Otto Schilling nodded. "I take you on trial. That boy was here before was lazy. You better not be lazy. You get twenty-five a week, but I make you work hard for all that money. If you're any good, you help me give lessons. Maybe I let *you* give lessons, if you play good. You play good?" His wide blue eyes looked at Jim.

"I was pretty good," said Jim, trying to sound both modest and informative.

Otto nodded approvingly. He did not share the American passion for modesty. When he had been singles champion of Austria, there were those who had thought him conceited. But why not? He had been a great player. "You will live in the hotel," he said finally. "Go see Mr. Kirkland, the manager. I call him on the phone now. You start in the morning, seven-thirty o'clock. I tell you what to do. Maybe I play with you and see what you know. Go on now."

Jim murmured "Thank you" and left the tennis house. On his right was a large swimming pool edged with imported beach. Prosperous-looking men and women sat beneath umbrellas, while several young girls were photographed by a sinister-looking cameraman. Jim wondered if the girls were movie stars, and if so, who they were. But they all looked alike, with white teeth, bleached hair, slim brown bodies. He recognized no one.

Jim climbed the steps to the Garden Hotel, a large,

rambling, white stucco building set among palm trees. After six months of uncomfortable rooming houses, he was delighted at the thought of living here, if only temporarily. He was quite used by now to being transient. He took it for granted that his traveling would not end until he found Bob. Then they would work out some sort of life together, though precisely what that life would be he left deliberately vague. Meanwhile, he took what work he could find, and lived happily in the present. Except for the golden image of Bob beside the river on that sunshine day, he was without history. In memory, his father was a dim blur; his mother, too; both gray, shadowy. The sea was dark and vaguest of all. Everything forgotten except Collins and the two girls in their Seattle apartment. Only that night was vivid in his memory. With an effort, he tried not to think of it as he hurried up the steps to the Garden Hotel.

Mr. Kirkland's office was large and modern and looked much more expensive than it actually was. So did Mr. Kirkland. He was a short man whose real name was probably not Kirkland. He affected a British accent, while his clothes and manner were exquisite and discreet, except for the large diamond he wore on the little finger of his left hand, an outward and visible sign of sudden rise and of unfamiliar affluence.

"Willard?" the voice was sharp.

"Yes, sir. Mr. Schilling sent me to you."

"You're going to be ball boy, I understand." Mr. Kirkland pronounced the title as though it were an accolade. "As such, you will be paid twenty-five dollars a week. Quite a large amount for a young boy, but I trust you will work for it to the best of your ability." Jim recognized a speech that had been made before. "We here at the Garden Hotel like to think of ourselves as a family, in which each one must do his part, from myself"—he smiled tightly—"on down."

He looked at Jim. "You start work as of tomorrow morning. I suppose you gave your references to Mr. Schilling. Ask the housekeeper in the servants' wing to assign you a room." With a nod, Mr. Kirkland ended the interview and Jim departed.

The lobby of the hotel was large with square marble pillars, which pretended to hold up the lozenge-patterned ceiling. The floor was carpeted in royal red. Behind a plywood desk simulating mahogany, clerks in formal clothes received guests, simulating welcome. Bellboys in livery lounged on a bench at the front door, waiting to carry bags and run errands. The lobby was usually a busy place, for there was always someone arriving or departing. Jim found the magnificence awesome and the bored air of the bellboys infinitely sophisticated. Perhaps one day he would be as casual.

Jim crossed the lobby, conscious of his shabby suitcase. He approached one of the bellboys and asked uncertainly, "How do I get to the employees' wing?"

The young man looked at him with slow boredom. Then he yawned and stretched. "I'll take you back." They went from the lobby to the famous tropical garden, which gave the hotel its name. Dazzled by color, Jim followed his guide through the artificial jungle.

"What's your job?"

Jim told him.

"An outdoor boy! So where you from?"

Jim decided to be impressive. "Nowhere. I been to sea."

The young man was respectful but inquiring. "To sea *where?*"

Jim was offhand. "Caribbean, Pacific, Bering Sea, all over. I been around."

"I guess you have. So what're you doing here?"

Jim shrugged. "Killing time. What else?"

The young man nodded and thoughtfully scratched one of a number of pimples.

Jim was assigned a small room overlooking the parking lot. The housekeeper was pleasant and the bellboy promised to show him the ropes. The thing was done. He now had a small place in the world of others.

In Southern California September was not much different from any other month. The weather was clear and bright and there was no rain. According to the newspapers there was a war in Europe, but Jim was not quite sure what it was all about. Apparently there was a man named Hitler who was German. He had a mustache and comedians were always imitating him. At every party someone was bound to give an imitation of Hitler making a speech. Then there was an Englishman with a somewhat larger mustache and of course there was Mussolini but he didn't seem to be in the war. For a while it was very exciting, and there were daily headlines. But toward the end of September Jim lost interest in the war because there had been no battles. Also, his days were now occupied teaching tennis to rich men and women who were not very interested in the war either.

Schilling liked Jim, and, after they had played together several times, he allowed him to instruct. He also encouraged him to go into tournaments, but Jim was satisfied to continue as he was. The life was easy and healthy. He gained weight; his body thickened with muscle. He was popular with the people who used the courts, particularly the young girls who lived in the hotel. They flirted with him, and he always responded politely, if evasively, which made them think him sensitive as well as handsome.

He was now used to the sight of famous actors and actresses playing tennis and sunning themselves beside the pool. In fact, one brilliant old actress (almost forty) took lessons from him every day, swearing obscenely whenever she made a bad shot. He thought her most impressive.

Jim had also begun a social life. Several times he had gone on parties with the bellhops. Most of them wanted to be actors, which explained the somewhat detached air with which they did their various jobs around the hotel. Several took a fancy to Jim because he didn't want to become an actor; also, he seemed sincerely to admire them. Jim was not without social guile. Yet his new companions puzzled him. Their conversation was often cryptic, their eyes quick-moving, searching. Ill at ease with outsiders, they were quarrelsome with one another. The one thing they had in common was the desire to move in splendor through the lives of others, to live forever grandly, and not to die.

They had many rich friends who gave parties, consisting largely of middle-aged women, widowed or divorced, and plump men with unpleasant habits when drunk. The women particularly took a fancy to Jim and he was often told that he was a "real person" and not like the others, whatever that meant. The plump men were also nice to him but, when through ignorance he did not respond to the suggestive ritual of their conversation, they left him alone.

Otto Schilling warned Jim about the bellhops. He explained that since they were not normal young men, they would try to corrupt him. Otto was stern as he explained these matters to Jim, who managed to look so shocked and unbelieving (he *was* surprised) that Otto spared him the full explanation of what he meant.

Jim went through several stages after his discovery that there were indeed many men who liked other men. His first reaction was disgust and alarm. He scrutinized everyone carefully. Was he one? After a while, he could identify the obvious ones by their tight, self-conscious manner, particularly when they moved, neck and shoulders rigid. After a time, as the young men grew used to Jim, they would talk frankly about themselves. Finally, one tried to seduce him. Jim was quite unnerved, and violent in his refusal. Yet afterward he continued to go to their parties, if only to be able to experience again the pleasure of saying no.

Late one afternoon, a bellhop named Leaper entered the tennis house just as Jim was finishing his shower. Leaper peered into the shower room. "Hey, Jim."

Jim rubbed soap out of his eyes. "Hi!" Though Leaper was one of those he had refused, they had remained on good terms.

"You want to go to a party?"

"Where?" Jim turned off the shower, picked up his towel, and joined Leaper in the locker room. As he dried himself, he knew that he was being examined with passionate interest. He was more amused than irritated.

"At Ronald Shaw's. In Beverly."

Jim was surprised. "The movie actor?"

"The very same, and they say he is quite *sympathetic*." Leaper made a feminine gesture. "He asked a friend of mine to collect some beauties so I thought of you. Of course you may be the only straight guy there, but then you can never tell, there might be some girl with red hair hanging on to the fringes." Jim had developed a mythical reputation for liking girls with red hair. Leaper chattered happily about Ronald Shaw while Jim dressed.

"It's really something to go to one of Shaw's parties. He's an honest-to-God Movie Star, with all the girls everywhere mad for him! That's a joke, isn't it? Why, when I worked in a picture with him at Metro . . ." Like most of the bellhops, Leaper had done extra work in the movies and he spoke often of stars he had "worked with." "These Girl Scouts came around to give him some sort of prize and he said: 'Will you please take these pubescent monsters and lay them end to end on the back lot.' Of course they covered it all up, just like the time he was knocked down in a bar at Santa Monica by this Marine from Pendleton. Oh, that guy is *something*!"

"He's pretty young, isn't he?" Jim parted his wet hair in the mirror.

"Thirty, maybe. You can't tell about those guys. Anyway, you better be warned, he'll make a pass at you, which I bet you wouldn't mind one bit."

"Just let him try," growled Jim into the mirror, aware that his suntanned face made him resemble a South Sea–movie islander. "Sure I'll come," he said, ready for adventure.

II

AT THIRTY-FIVE, RONALD SHAW was disturbingly handsome, with features of such ordinariness that they were, paradoxically, unique. Dark curly hair tumbled over a classic low forehead to give him a look often described as "impish" by admirers, "Neanderthal" by detractors. With his light blue eyes, he seemed typically "black Irish," a type which occurs most often among Jews. Ronald Shaw had been born George Cohen. At one point he had thought that to be taken for George M. Cohan might be rewarding, but it was not, and so George Cohen became Ronald Shaw, a handsome, fiery young Irishman whose films made money. George Cohen of Baltimore had been very poor but now that Ronald Shaw was wealthy neither was going to be poor again. Shaw was notoriously mean, except with his mother in Baltimore. As every reader of movie magazines knew, his mother was his "best girl" and the reason that he was still a bachelor, which was exactly right, as any Freudian would agree.

Although Shaw had been a star for five years, he had never bought a house in Hollywood. He preferred to rent large impersonal houses where he could give parties for young men behind thick walls and an elaborate burglar-alarm system. In his way, he was discreet. Yet everyone in the homosexual world knew that he was one of them. Naturally there were rumors about other actors, but where in other cases there was often some vestigial doubt in the minds of even the most passionate apologists for Socratic vice, there was none in Shaw's case. He was always mentioned by the great fraternity with pride, envy, lust. Fortunately, the women of America remained in ignorance, regarding him as a satisfying love object, unattainable but useful as a companion in dreams, the boy-man of advertising come alive thirty times life-size upon the screen.

Ronald Shaw had it made, and since he was nothing if not human, he found most human relationships disappointing. His sexual partners were selected for a combination of physical beauty and hard masculinity. Each affair began as though the creation of the world was to be reenacted, and each usually ended in less time than it took the Old Testament Creator to put up the sky. No one could please Shaw for very long. If a boy came to love him (and to disregard the legend) Shaw was affronted and endangered; yet if a lover continued to be dazzled by the idea of him, he soon grew bored. Nevertheless, Shaw was a happy man, and if he had not been told about romantic love, it would never have occurred to him to take coupling seriously.

Jim was much impressed by the magnificence of Shaw's house. An interior decorator had done it for nothing; unfortunately, the affair had ended before the bedrooms were done. Nevertheless, the downstairs was a success, a riot of Spanish baroque with a huge drawing room whose windows looked down upon Los Angeles, glittering to the west. Over a cavernous fireplace hung a portrait of Ronald Shaw, half again as large as life. The original of this glamorous work of art stood at the center of the room, graciously directing the party's traffic. It was an odd group. For one thing, there were three times as many men as women. Jim recognized several character actors: Ronald Shaw needed only the flimsiest support. The women were all elegant, with high voices, large jewels, towering befeathered hats. They were not, Jim was assured by the knowing Leaper, lesbians. They had simply passed the age of being able to attract normal men and so, still craving attention, they were drawn into the world of hairdressers and couturiers. Here they could gossip and make stage love and avoid boredom, if not despair.

"Isn't this swell?" murmured Leaper, in his awe forgetting his role as sophisticate and guide.

Jim nodded. "Where's Ronald Shaw?"

Leaper pointed to the center of the room. At first, Jim was disappointed. Shaw was smaller than he had expected. But he was handsome, there was no denying that. In contrast to the others, he wore a dark suit, which gave his slim figure dignity. At the moment he was surrounded by women. The young men were more circumspect; they held to the periphery of the party, waiting.

"You better meet him," said Leaper.

They crossed to the group of women and waited until Shaw had finished telling a story. Then, during the sharp, loud laughter, Leaper said hurriedly, "You remember me, Mr. Shaw, don't you?" Shaw looked blank but Leaper kept right on talking. "It was Mr. Ridgeway who asked me to come tonight, and I brought this friend of mine with me, Jim Willard. He's real keen to meet you. . . ."

Ronald Shaw smiled at Jim. "How do you do?" His hand was cool and hard.

"I . . . like you in the movies," said Jim, to Leaper's horror. This was impossibly bad form. With movie stars, one was supposed to appear unimpressed.

But admiration never offended Ronald Shaw. He grinned, showing white teeth. "That's nice of you to say so. Come on, let's get you a drink." Gracefully, Shaw extricated himself from the women and together they crossed to the far end of the room.

Acutely embarrassed, Jim was conscious of many eyes watching him. But Shaw was serenely at ease as he stopped a waiter and took a glass from the tray. "I hope you like martinis."

"Well, I don't drink very much."

"Neither do I." Shaw's voice was low and confiding, as if the only person in the world whose company and good opinion he sought was the bedazzled Jim. And though he asked only the usual questions, his warm voice made those familiar phrases sound significant, even the inevitable "Are you an actor?"

Jim quickly told him what he was.

Shaw grinned. "An athlete! Well. . . . You look too young to be an instructor." They were standing now at one of the large windows. Out of the corner of his eye, Jim noticed that his fellow guests were preparing to close in on Shaw and recapture him. They did not have much time. Shaw sensed this, too. "What's your name again?" Jim told him. "You must," said Shaw, looking thoughtfully down at the city, "come see me someday. When are you free?"

"I'm not working Thursday afternoon," said Jim, startled at the speed of his own response.

"Then why don't you drop by here Thursday. If I'm still shooting, you can swim until I get back. I'm usually through at five."

"Sure. I'd like to." Jim felt his stomach contract with fear and expectancy.

"See you Thursday." Then Ronald Shaw, with a distant polite nod calculated to deceive his audience, allowed the young men to surround him.

Leaper joined Jim. "Well, you're in." His eyes glittered. "He fell for you like a ton of—"

"Shut up, will you?" Jim turned away angrily.

"Don't con me. You hooked him. Everybody saw you. They want to know who you are. So I've been telling them you're straight as a die, which just makes their mouths water all the more. You're a hit, boy. Look at them all staring at you." Jim looked but caught no one staring. "So what did Shaw talk to you about?"

"Nothing."

"Oh, sure! Well, you better put out this time. He can do a lot for you."

"Sorry, I got no plans to shack up with him. Or anybody else."

Leaper looked at him with genuine surprise. "So maybe you're not queer, but *this* is an exception. Why, this is something people dream about. You could make a fortune out of him."

Jim laughed and moved away. He tried to appear relaxed and at ease, but he was neither. Soon he would have to make a decision, on Thursday to be precise. What to do? Mechanically he moved through the evening, his heart pounding. When it came time to say good-bye, Shaw smiled and winked. Blushing, Jim turned away. He said not a word to Leaper as they rode home in the bus.

III

JIM WILLARD'S EROTIC LIFE took place almost entirely in dreams. Until that day with Bob beside the river, he had dreamed of women as often as of men, and there had seemed no set boundary between the two. But since that summer day, Bob was the constant dream-lover, and girls no longer intruded upon their perfect masculine idyll. He was aware that what he dreamed of was not what normal men dreamed of. But at the same time he made no connection between what he and Bob had done and what his new acquaintances did. Too many of them behaved like women. Often after he had been among them, he would study himself in a mirror to see if there was any trace of the woman in his face or manner; and he was always pleased that there was not. Finally, he decided that he was unique. He was the only one who had done what he had done and felt the way he did. Even the elegant, long-haired youths all agreed that he was probably not one of them. Nevertheless, women expected him to make love to them, and when he didn't (he could never quite explain to himself *why* he didn't) they felt that it was they who were lacking, not he. None suspected that he dreamed every night of a tall boy by a river. Yet as Jim got more and more involved in Leaper's world, he found himself fascinated by the stories they told of their affairs with one another. He could not imagine himself doing the things they said they did. Yet he wanted to know about them, if only out of a morbid desire to discover how what had been so natural and complete for him could be so perfectly corrupted by these strange womanish creatures.

In a mood of indecision, Jim went to see Ronald Shaw, and what he suspected would happen did happen. He allowed himself to be seduced, impressed by Shaw's fame and physical beauty. The act was familiar except that this time he was passive, too shy to be the aggressor. With Bob he had taken the initiative, but then that was a different occasion and a more important time.

The affair began. Shaw was in love, or at least he talked of love, and how they would spend the rest of their lives together ("like those two ancient Greeks—you know the ones, Achilles and so-and-so—who were such famous lovers"). Not that there was to be any publicity. Hollywood was a merciless place and they would have to be extremely discreet. But for those who did know about them, they would be worshiped as a dazzling couple, two perfect youths, reenacting boyhood dreams behind the stucco walls of the house on Mulholland Drive.

Although Jim was flattered by Shaw's protestations of love, the older man's body did not excite him. Jim was oddly reluctant to touch a mature man's flesh, no matter how handsome he was. Apparently only those his own age had the power to attract him. Yet when he shut his eyes, he enjoyed himself, for then he would think of Bob. And so the affair began, or the "relationship," as those who had undergone analysis would say. It was a new experience for Jim and not entirely a pleasant one.

The first skirmish with the world occurred when Jim told Otto Schilling that he was going away.

Schilling was surprised. "I don't understand," he said. "I don't understand why you want to leave here. You get more pay somewhere else?"

Jim nodded.

Schilling looked at him sharply. "Where? How?"

Jim was uncomfortable. "Well, you see, Ronald Shaw, the actor, and these other people" (he added vaguely) "want me to teach, you know, on their courts, and so I said I would."

"Where will you live?"

Jim could feel the sweat trickling down his side. "I'll stay at Shaw's place."

Schilling nodded grimly and Jim kicked himself for not having lied. Everyone knew about Shaw. Jim felt ashamed. "I didn't think you were like that," said Schilling slowly. "I am sorry for you. There is nothing wrong with seeing a person like Ronald Shaw, there is nothing so wrong with being that way, but to be a kept boy, ah, *that* is bad."

Jim wiped his forehead with the back of his hand. "Is there anything you want me to do before I go?"

"No," said Schilling wearily. "Tell Mr. Kirkland you're leaving. That's all." He turned away.

Shaken, Jim went to his room and started to pack. Leaper joined him. "Congratulations!" he exclaimed. "Beginner's luck, you can't beat it."

"What're you talking about?" Jim packed furiously.

"Come off it. It's the talk of the circuit how you're going to live with Ronald Shaw! So what's he like?"

"I don't know." Jim felt his facade of normality crumbling.

"So what're you going to be, his cook?"

"I'm going to teach him tennis." This sounded idiotic even to his own ears. Leaper brayed contempt. But Jim stuck doggedly to his story, explaining how Shaw was to pay him fifty dollars a week, which was true.

"Ask me over sometime," said Leaper as Jim finished packing. "We could play doubles."

Jim merely glared. Yet in all of this one thing surprised him: Leaper, believing that Jim was heterosexual, took it for granted that any normal boy would live with a famous actor, given the chance. In Leaper's world all men were whores and all whores were bisexual.

Shaw was sitting beside the swimming pool when Jim arrived. The swimming pool was set like a navel in a red-brick terrace flanked by two bathhouses resembling the turreted pavilions of a medieval knight. Shaw waved as Jim approached.

"Did you make a clean break?" The deep voice was mocking.

"Clean enough. I told Schilling I was going to teach you and some other people tennis."

"You mentioned me?"

"Yes. I wish I hadn't. I'm sorry. Because he knew exactly what was going on. He didn't say much but I felt like dirt."

Shaw sighed. "I don't know how the hell they know so much about me. It's the damnedest thing." Like most homosexuals, Shaw was astonished that anyone saw through his mask. "I guess it's because so many people are so bloody jealous of me." Shaw sounded both sad and proud. "Because everyone knows who I am and because I make a lot of money, they all think I must be terribly happy, which they resent and which isn't so. Funny, isn't it? I've had all the things I ever wanted and I'm not . . . well, it's an awful feeling not having anybody to be close to. Oh, I tried to get my mother to come out here but she won't leave Baltimore. So here I am, all alone, like the song says. At least until now." He gave a flashing smile. Jim smiled back, in spite of himself. He couldn't help thinking that the man did have everything, and if he hadn't found a lover by now it was doubtless his own fault.

Jim unbuttoned his shirt. The day was warm and the sun was pleasant. He sat very still, trying not to contemplate the

sadness of the life of Ronald Shaw. But Shaw was persistent.
"You know," he said, "I don't think I've ever known
anyone like you. Somebody so natural and . . . well,
unscheming. I also didn't think you could be made. You
don't seem the type." Jim was pleased to hear this, faith in
his own manhood momentarily restored. Shaw grinned.
"But I'm glad things turned out the way they did."

Jim smiled, too. "So am I."

"I hate those others, those lousy queens." Shaw lifted
one shoulder and gave a curiously feminine shake to his
body, mocking in a single gesture the entire legion.

"They're OK, some of them."

"I'm not talking about them as people," said Shaw. "I
mean for sex. If a man likes men, he wants a man, and if he
likes women, he wants a woman, so who wants a freak
who's neither? It's a mystery to me." Shaw yawned.
"Maybe I ought to be psychoanalyzed."

"Why?"

Shaw examined his biceps muscles critically: his appearance was his livelihood. "I don't know. Sometimes I . . ."
But he did not pursue the thought. The arms went slack.
"Bunch of fakes, every last one of them, telling you stuff
you already know. No, what matters is being tough. You *got*
to be tough in this world. There's no place for the weak,
like Mamma used to say. She was right, too. That's how I
got where I am, being tough and not feeling sorry for
myself."

Jim was impressed by the sternness of this speech. He was
also reminded of his own situation. "That's OK for you,"
he said, "this being tough. You had talent. You knew what
you wanted. But what about me? I'm just a better-than-
average tennis player. So what do *I* do? Toughness isn't
going to help me play any better."

Shaw looked at him, obviously making an effort to

consider the case. "Well, I don't know." The beautiful eyes went slightly out of focus. "Would you . . . uh, like to act?"

Jim shrugged. "Me? Why?"

"Well, that's not what I'd call burning ambition. No, you've got to *want* this thing so much it hurts." And Shaw resumed the monologue which pleased him most, the chronicle of his own rise in the world, aided by no one except Mamma. Within the circle of his own self-love, Shaw was content, and Jim did not in the least resent being at the periphery of that self-absorption. Jim accepted Shaw completely and uncritically. After all, their affair was but a temporary halt on a long voyage whose terminus was Bob.

When Shaw had finished his hymn to achievement, Jim said, with an admiration not entirely false, "I guess I haven't got it," he said. "I don't want anything that bad."

Shaw fondled the vertical line of dark hair on his own chest. "We could certainly get you work as an extra. Then—who knows?"

"Who knows?" Jim rose and stretched. Shaw watched him, pleased and aroused.

"Put your bathing trunks on," he said, and he led Jim into the knight's pavilion.

IV

TWO MONTHS PASSED PEACEFULLY. Jim enjoyed the large house with its rooms like movie sets. On the days when Shaw was at the studio, Jim would play tennis with various friends who wanted to meet Shaw's new lover as well as improve their backhand. Jim was agreeably surprised to find himself something of a celebrity, at least in this one world, and the interest he inspired compensated somewhat for the shame he had felt with Schilling.

Jim enjoyed Shaw's parties and he quickly made himself useful. He learned how to cope with drunks, mix drinks, and discreetly cue Shaw if there was a story he wanted to tell. Jim was much impressed by the beautifully dressed people who drank heavily and talked incessantly of their sex life. Their harsh candor both shocked and pleased him. They feared nothing, at least behind the high stucco walls of Shaw's estate.

Jim found Shaw not only an agreeable companion but, more important, informative. He showed him the secret Hollywood where, so it was said, nearly all the leading men were homosexual and those few who were not were under constant surveillance. A number of women acted as outriders to the beautiful legion, and they were often called upon to be public escorts. They were known as "beards." But they were not always reliable. One evening a drunken outrider tried to make love to Shaw and, when he pushed her away, she shouted obscenities at everyone present; then she was led away and no one ever saw her again.

For purposes of publicity, Shaw appeared regularly at nightclubs with girls, often rising actresses. He did this to satisfy the head of the studio, a nervous businessman whose nightmare was that scandal might end the career of his hottest property.

Jim liked Shaw, though he never believed him when, together at night, he would tell Jim how much he loved him. For one thing, the speeches flowed so easily that even the inexperienced Jim recognized that the actor was playacting. Nor was Jim disturbed. He was not in love with Shaw, nor did he pretend to be. For one thing, the idea of being in love with a man was both ludicrous and unnatural; at the most a man might find his twin, like Bob, but that was rare and something else again.

One day, Shaw took Jim to the studio. As a rule they

never went out in public together, but today Shaw thought it time Jim saw him work.

The studio was an immense enclosure of white sound-stages, resembling mammoth garages. As Shaw drove through the studio gate, he was saluted respectfully by the gateman, while a pack of girls gave shrieks of recognition and waved autograph books at him.

Beyond the gate was another world, peopled with costumed extras, executives, technicians, laborers. Twenty films were being made simultaneously. Nothing else on earth mattered here.

They parked in front of a bungalow framed by hibiscus.

"My dressing room." Shaw was already beginning to get businesslike. Inside, stretched on a sofa, was a small bald man.

"Baby, you're late. I got here half an hour ago, like we agreed. And so far I've read *Variety,* the *Reporter,* and even the script."

"I'm sorry, Cy." Shaw introduced Jim to the man on the sofa. "Cy's directing my picture."

"If that's what you can call what I'm doing in this miserable place." Cy moaned. "Why did I ever leave New York? Why didn't I stay with the Group Theater?"

"Because they didn't want you, baby." Shaw grinned as he shed his jacket.

"There he stands. Pound for pound, the worst actor in America." Cy turned to Jim. "All he's got is that adorable smile and those obscene pectorals . . . or pector*i*als, as they say out here."

"Jealous, baby?" Shaw stripped to his shorts and flexed his celebrated pectorals. Cy groaned with disgust and shut his eyes.

"I can't stand it!" He pointed to a door. "Get your costume on. Makeup's been waiting since seven."

Shaw stepped into the next room, leaving the door ajar. "So what's the schedule?"

"A new scene, that's what. The writers were at it all night. They wrote this wonderful new scene on a menu at the Cotton Club. You'll love it."

"Am I terribly brave?"

"What else? They've given you a stiff upper lip, a tight sphincter . . . *everything*."

"A tight what?"

"I'll say one thing, if they ever educated one of you dopes it'd be the end of the American Dream. You agree, baby?" Cy gave Jim a sharp look.

"Sure," said Jim.

"Sure," mimicked Cy. "What am I doing here?" he asked the ceiling.

"Making fifteen hundred a week" came Shaw's voice from the next room, "and that's nothing for a good director, but for you . . ."

"Is this my reward for coming here to try and help you with this crucial new scene so that when you face the Big Brownie you'll know what you're doing? Yes, this is my reward, and you'll just wing the words like always, and another moneymaking bagel will drop into the laps of the American moviegoers. I guess you want to be an actor, too?" Again the sharp eyes turned to Jim.

"Well . . ."

"Well, *of course!* Where else in the world can a guy with no brain and no talent get to be rich and famous all because . . ."

Shaw entered in full eighteenth-century costume. "All because I am a Sex Symbol," he said happily. "Look at those legs, baby. Drool at the thought." Shaw patted a muscular thigh with obvious affection. "That's what they want out there in the dark and I got it."

"Keep it, please."

Jim had never seen an actor in full makeup. He was quite awed by the transformation. This was not the man he knew but someone else, a glamorous stranger. As usual, Shaw was conscious of the effect he was making. He gave Jim a conspiratorial grin.

"What sort of picture is it?" asked Jim.

"Shit," said Cy, quietly.

"Popular entertainment," said Shaw. "Which will gross four million domestic. It's a remake of this classic French novel by Dumas *fils*," he added in a rehearsed voice, suitable for instructing interviewers in the commissary.

"Dumas *fils* was the Ronald Shaw of his day, God help him." Cy stood up. "So let's get down to the set. The Bitch Goddess is already there."

Shaw explained to Jim that the Bitch Goddess was his costar, a famous lady whose presence in a film guaranteed success. The combination of Shaw and this lady was considered especially potent.

"She hungover?" asked Shaw as they stepped from the bungalow into the main street of the studio.

"At dawn, her eyes were like two rubies," said Cy, dreamily. "And her breath was reminiscent of a wind in summer over the Jersey Flats."

Shaw grimaced. "We got a love scene?"

"Kind of." Cy handed him two pages. "That's it. Straight from the back of the menu of the Cotton Club. You'll love it."

As they walked, Shaw studied the two pages intently. Jim noticed that all the marvelously dressed people who crowded the studio street stared enviously at Shaw; and Jim took vicarious pride in this attention. Just in front of the soundstage, Shaw handed Cy the script. "I got it," he said.

"You mean you learned it, which isn't exactly getting it."

"Quickest study in the business." Shaw turned to Jim. "I've got this photographic memory. I can see the whole page in my head when I'm acting."

"And that's just about what comes across." Cy was mocking. "Shaw even gives you the typos. Remember that time you said, 'But where is your hubsand'?"

"Knock it off," said Shaw, and all badinage ended as they stepped onto the soundstage, where he was in his proper kingdom. The Bitch Goddess, looking extraordinarily beautiful, lay on an incline board in order not to crush her elaborate costume. When she saw Shaw, she shouted in her celebrated hoarse voice, "Hiya, Butch!"

"You got the new scene?" Shaw was flat.

His costar held up the pages. "It's even worse than the old scene."

"Academy Award time," said Shaw lightly.

"Academy Award? We'll be lucky not to end up in radio when this turkey hits the nabes." She threw the script down.

Then Cy came over. "Ready, folks?" Obediently, they followed him to the center of the set. He then talked to them in a low voice, rather like a boxing referee before a bout. The rules understood, Cy yelled, "Places!" The extras fell into position, some talking in groups of three or four, some ready to walk slowly from group to group when the action started. A buzzer sounded and Cy shouted, "Start moving, children! Let it roll!" There was silence on the soundstage. As the camera approached the female star, she turned, smiling, then, seeing Shaw to her left, she looked surprised.

"Why did you come?" Her voice was clear, the question vital.

"You knew I would." Shaw's voice was resonant and warm. Jim barely recognized it.

"But . . . my husband . . ."

"I've taken care of him. Get your cloak. Quickly! We must leave tonight for Calais."

"Cut!" yelled Cy. The room became noisy again. "Let's take that over again. Shaw, remember to keep your left shoulder down when you walk into range. Darling, try and remember to show surprise when you see him. After all, you think that your husband has had him locked up. OK. We'll take it again."

Jim watched them do this scene for several hours. At the end of the day he was no longer interested in acting.

V

DECEMBER CAME AND JIM found it hard to imagine that it was winter, for the sun continued warm and the trees green. And he was able to play tennis every day. He was beginning to make money, and acquire a reputation as a good teacher. When a magazine photographer came to take pictures of Shaw's house, he also took pictures of Jim. These were published in a fan magazine. As a result, Jim got many offers to give lessons, which he accepted. Offers of another sort he sternly rejected.

Although Shaw approved of his earning money, he disliked it when Jim left the house. One night when Jim did not come home until after dinner, Shaw accused him of being ungrateful and thoughtless. They shouted at one another until Jim went to his room, angry at being treated like a possession. It was even worse later, when Shaw came to his room to say that he was sorry, and to make love, and to tell Jim how great the love was he had to give but how hopeless it all was knowing that such deep feeling could never be returned. Jim could not help but think that perhaps Shaw had less to give than he suspected.

As Jim lay very still in the dark, his arm beneath Shaw's head, he wondered if he should at least speak up and say that he wanted to be free to go wherever he pleased and see people he wanted to see without giving excuses to a lover who was not in love. But Shaw divined his mood.

"I'm sorry I'm so jealous, Jimmy, but I hate to think of your being out with anybody else. I depend a lot on you when I'm tired and want to get away from all these hangers-on. You're different from all the others. You really are. And, God, I'd love to quit this whole racket one of these days. Get out of this town of fakes and go off somewhere in the country and buy a farm maybe. Then Mamma could come live there with us. Of course we'd have to be a little careful with her around, but we could manage. Yes, I'd like that, wouldn't you?"

Jim moved uneasily in the dark. His arm was beginning to go to sleep beneath Shaw's head; he clenched his fist, trying to restore circulation.

"I don't know, Ronnie. I don't know if I'd like to settle down just yet."

"Oh." Shaw's sigh was bitter and stagy. "You really don't give a damn, do you? It's the same old routine: upward and onward. Whores of the world, unite. Because of me, you can now make a living with those tennis lessons, if that's what they are. So I'm nothing to you." Shaw moved over to the other side of the bed and Jim was relieved to feel the blood circulating again in his arm.

"That isn't true, Ronnie. I like you a lot but I haven't had an awful lot of experience with this sort of thing before. I'm still pretty new at it" (he had never told Shaw about Bob) "and I don't think you're being very fair. You can't expect me to give up my whole life when I don't know but what you might find another guy you like more than me, and where'd I be then?"

"What would you do if you did leave me?" Shaw's voice was distant.

"I'd like to start a tennis school maybe. That's what I'm saving for." Jim realized that he had said too much; he had not wanted Shaw to know that he was carefully saving money, three thousand dollars so far.

"You're not really planning to leave?" Shaw was plaintive.

"Not until you want me to," said Jim simply, making up for his blunder.

After breakfast Christmas morning, Shaw telephoned his mother in Baltimore and talked to her for half an hour, regardless of the cost. Then he gave presents in front of the tree. Jim received an expensive Australian tennis racket. Next came dinner at one o'clock, the high point of the day.

Shaw had invited a dozen guests, old friends, men without families who had no place to go at Christmas. Jim knew them all except one, a sandy-haired young man who was talking intensely to Cy. Through the window, Jim caught a glimpse of a palm tree. No, it was not really Christmas, he thought as he said hello to Cy, who looked like a Persian vizier from one of his own pictures. Drunk and merry, he introduced Jim to the sandy-haired man.

"Jim Willard, this is the great Paul Sullivan." They shook hands and Jim wondered why Paul Sullivan was great. Then he excused himself and helped Shaw serve eggnog. Shaw's face was flushed; he was in a gay mood.

"Lovely party, isn't it, Jimmy?"

Jim nodded. "Who is this guy Sullivan? Should I know who he is?" Shaw was usually careful to let Jim know who people were and what they did so that he could treat them

accordingly. That was Hollywood procedure. In the hierarchy of money, each man was treated with the deference his
salary called for.

"He's a writer who writes books and he came out here to
work with Cy on a picture. He's a real highbrow, which
means he's a real pain, always bitching about Hollywood.
These guys take the industry's money, then they complain.
He's typical."

At dinner, Shaw carved the turkey. Champagne was
served. The guests were happy. And to Jim's inattentive ear,
the conversation sounded brilliant. Even though most of it
was about movies: who was being signed for what picture,
and why.

Sullivan sat beside Jim. He was a quiet man, with dark
eyes and a slightly upturned nose. His mouth was too full
and his ears were too large. But he was attractive.

"You're a writer, aren't you?" Jim spoke respectfully,
wishing to make a good impression.

Sullivan nodded. "I came out here to work on a picture
but . . ." The voice was light and boyish. Deliberately he left
the sentence unfinished.

"You don't like working for movies?"

Sullivan glanced at Cy, who was sitting across from him.
"No," he said in a low voice, "I don't like it at all. Are you
in this business?"

Jim shook his head. "You write books, don't you?"

Sullivan nodded.

"Novels?"

"Novels, poetry. I don't suppose you've read any of
them." This was said sadly, not defensively.

"I don't expect so." Jim was truthful. "I don't seem to
find time to read."

"Who does in this damned town?"

"I guess they like their work," said Jim uncertainly. "They think about pictures mostly."

"I know." Sullivan ate a stalk of celery and Jim watched him, wondering if he liked him. Most of the people who visited Shaw seemed all alike. They said what they thought about everything, including themselves, and usually they liked themselves rather more than other people did. Sexually they were obvious, unlike Sullivan, who appeared perfectly normal.

"Are you from the East?" asked Jim.

Sullivan nodded. "New Hampshire originally but I live in New York."

Then Sullivan asked Jim many questions and Jim answered most of them truthfully. It was a bit like a cross-examination. Jim had never known anyone to ask so many questions. By the time dessert was served, Jim had told Sullivan most of the facts of his life. As for Sullivan, he was twenty-eight (Jim thought that was old), married once and divorced, an impressive achievement which explained why he was not like most of the sensitive young men who visited Shaw. Obscurely Jim was glad.

Dinner over, the guests gathered in the drawing room. As usual, a group gathered about Shaw. But Sullivan was not one of them. He sat alone in a window seat, his large hands playing idly with a silver matchbox. Jim joined him.

"A beautiful place," said Sullivan.

"You mean this house or . . ."

"The whole thing. It's idyllic. Like going to Heaven before your time. Perfect climate, bright colors, fantastic houses. And beautiful people with suntans, white teeth, empty heads."

"Like me?"

"Yes. No!" Sullivan laughed. Suddenly he was a boy, and

Jim was captured. "Like our host," said Sullivan. "I'm sorry. I shouldn't have said that. You live with him, don't you?"

"Yes."

"Then he must be all right."

"He is," said Jim, realizing that he should say more but not able to.

"You give tennis lessons on the side?"

"That's how I make my living." Jim tried not to sound kept. But it was no use. The thing was plain enough.

"What would you like to do eventually?"

"Set myself up as a teacher. Buy some courts. But that takes money."

"And *otherwise,* do you know what you want?"

"No," said Jim accurately. "I don't know what I want."

"Neither do I." Sullivan smiled, reminding Jim of Bob. Then he rose to go.

"Would you like to play tennis sometime?" Jim was bold. They made a date and Sullivan left. Not until then did Jim realize that Shaw had been watching them.

CHAPTER
5

I

JIM AND SULLIVAN MET every day, unknown to Shaw, who
suspected but did not know for certain what was happening. The lovers would meet at Sullivan's hotel each noon,
the only time during the day when Sullivan was able to leave
the studio lot. Since Jim was usually the first to arrive, he
would go straight to the room and wash up after the morning's tennis. Then he would lie on the bed and wait for
Sullivan, heart beating fast, surprised to find that he was
excited not only by their lovemaking but also by Sullivan as
a person. He was intrigued because Sullivan never mentioned their affair, destroying Jim's theory that all homosexuals talked continually of love, like Shaw. Reticence was
a relief, while it lasted. But eventually words became necessary. Sullivan's contract with the studio was ending. Soon
he would leave California. That meant they needed to

understand one another before plans could be made, *if* plans were to be made.

"How many times have you done this?" Sullivan was abrupt. Jim hesitated, then he told the truth. "Three times. Three different people."

Sullivan nodded. "I thought so."

"What do you mean? Flattery or insult?"

"Just that you haven't followed the usual pattern. I could tell right off. So could Shaw. I expect that's why he wanted you to live with him." This was the first time Sullivan had mentioned Shaw.

"So what's the usual pattern?"

Sullivan lay back on the bed, his eyes on the ceiling. "It starts in school. You're just a little different from the others. Sometimes you're shy and a bit frail; or maybe too precocious, too handsome, an athlete, in love with yourself. Then you start to have erotic dreams about another boy—like yourself—and you get to know him and you try to be his friend and if he's sufficiently ambivalent and you're sufficiently aggressive you'll have a wonderful time experimenting with each other. And so it begins. Then you meet another boy and another, and as you grow older, if you have a dominant nature, you become a hunter. If you're passive, you become a wife. If you're noticeably effeminate, you may join a group of others like yourself and accept being marked and known. There are a dozen types and many different patterns but there is almost always the same beginning, not being like the others."

"I'm pretty ordinary," said Jim, almost believing himself.

"Are you? Perhaps. Anyway you started late and I don't think you're much involved with others. I don't think you could ever love a man. So I hope you find the right woman for yourself." Sullivan stopped. Jim did not answer. He had not told Sullivan about Bob, and yet Sullivan had revealed him to himself as just like the others, varying hardly at all from what must be a familiar pattern. With self-knowledge came alarm. If he was really like the others, then what sort of future could he have? Endless drifting, promiscuity, defeat? No. It was not possible. He was different, Bob was different. After all, hadn't he been able to fool everyone, even those like himself, even Sullivan? Deliberately he banished the unsought revelation to that part of his brain where he disposed of unpleasant memories and then, truth disposed of, he found that he was hurt by something Sullivan had said. Was it true that he was so unfeeling in his relationships? Perhaps with Shaw and Sullivan, but not with Bob. Certainly no one had ever felt as desperate and as lonely as he when Bob had left. Yes, he was perfectly capable of love, at least with someone who could be his brother. And though Sullivan was hardly this longed-for twin, at least he was wiser than Shaw and less demanding and Jim felt easy with him, if not candid, and even affectionate.

"I think you're the unluckiest type." Sullivan rolled over on his stomach and looked at Jim. "You'll attract everybody, yet you won't be able to do anything about it. Not really. Oh, maybe someday you'll find a woman who'll suit you, but not a man. You're not like the rest of us, who want a mirror. It's exciting in a way but it's also sad."

"I don't know what you mean," said Jim, who knew exactly but chose to maintain his secret: a memory of a cabin and a brown river. Someday he would relive all that again and the circle of his life would be completed. Meanwhile he would learn about the world and please himself and scrupulously hide his secret from those who wanted him to love.

· · ·

In February Sullivan's option was not renewed. A few days later, coincidentally, Shaw took a new boy. Jim tried to avoid the obligatory scene of parting, but Shaw had waited two months for this moment and so it was played through to the end.

Knowing what was coming, Jim packed his bags that morning and tried to leave the house, but Shaw had insisted that they have a "last supper" together, with Jim in the role of Judas. So Jim remained.

Shaw was silent during most of dinner, crown of thorns resting heavily on his brow. Not until after coffee did he speak. He started in a low voice, more in sorrow than in anger. "I suppose you and Sullivan are going to leave town?"

Jim nodded and Shaw smiled gently. "It's such a shame, Jim. I really was counting on you. I really felt that *this* was the one, the big one that would last. In a funny way, I'm kind of innocent. I thought you were different, and you weren't. Not that I'm blaming you," he said quickly, eager to seem fair. "I know it's tough living with somebody like me, and all the people around us trying to break things up. I know, God knows I know, what the temptations are. Only an awfully strong person could resist, a really strong character—or else someone in love. Which you weren't. Not that that was your fault. I don't blame you. How could I?" Not wanting to be interrupted, Shaw was careful to give both sides as he went along. "After all, love is something which few people are capable of. You were too young. And I should have realized that. You can only love yourself, and now that you've gotten the most out of our relationship, you're ready to move on to this writer, this misfit who's just as incapable of feeling as you. Yes, I've heard a lot of things about Sullivan," said Shaw darkly. "*You* wouldn't believe what I've heard, of course. You must find them out for yourself. I'm only telling you this now because I'm still very fond of you, in spite of what you've done, and to show you that I'm not bitter. As a matter of fact, I'm happy because I've found Peter, who's coming to live with me." He paused, ready for the defense. But there was none. Jim stared at him politely, wondering when he could decently go.

Disappointed, Shaw tried walking on water. "I'm sure Peter can return the affection I give. At least I hope so. My bad luck has *got* to end someday. Oh, I hate to sound as if I'm accusing you, Jim. I'm not. I know how difficult it must have been for you. You never really cared for me and at least you were honest; you never *said* you did. But then since you never said you *didn't,* I hoped and even believed sometimes that you did care a little. It's only now that I have Peter that I can regard what we had together, our affair, detachedly and with *complete* understanding. I see that you weren't mature enough and that's probably my fault for trying to attain the impossible." Jim recognized this last line from one of Shaw's recent films. Tag ends of scripts tended to work their way into his conversation.

"I hope," Shaw continued, turning the other cheek, "that you will realize these things about yourself before you hurt Sullivan, too. Yes, I admit I've been hurt, terribly hurt by you, but I don't hold it against you. Which is the one quality I have that you will never find in anyone else. I always forgive. Will Sullivan?" Jim tried to appear interested in this new question, which he knew would soon be answered. It was. "You see, Paul Sullivan is an unusual person. There's no doubt about that. They got him here for snob appeal, or so they thought. He's an *intellectual,* and I suppose in Greenwich Village the left-wingers think he's wonderful, though he's never written a real best-seller or

anything anybody has ever read. I certainly haven't. Not
that I have much time for reading, but at least I've read all
the classics—Walter Scott, Dumas, Margaret Mitchell, all
that crowd, and *they* were popular. . . ." He stopped, aware
that he was making too much of a case for the popular.
"Anyway, it's not important whether he's a good writer or
not. The important thing is whether he is capable of feeling,
whether he has the maturity to overlook your shortcom-
ings. He was quite cruel to one boy, I'm told. But I'm sure
you'll have better luck. I want you to be happy. I really
mean it. I do." Shaw's radiant smile almost disguised the
hatred in his eyes.

There was a sound in the hall and a dark-haired youth
appeared in the doorway.

Shaw rose from the dead. "Come in, Peter, and have
some coffee. Jim was just saying good-bye."

II

SULLIVAN WAS THE FIRST person Jim had ever met who
found obscure pleasure in his own pain. Obsessed by failure, professional and private, and unable to relieve himself
in scenes like Shaw, Paul's only outlet was to write. Yet even
in his work he was so studied and inhibited that all he could
ever convey was a light bitterness, a casual anger at a world
which, all in all, had done well by him. A doting family,
until he ceased to be Catholic at sixteen. There was much
argument then, but he would not budge. Even the family
priest gave him up at last, perfectly bewildered by this
unlooked-for apostasy. None suspected that he had forsaken the Church because he was homosexual. For a long
time he had tried to exorcise the unnatural spirit, demanding furiously of God that he be freed of this terrible inclina-

tion. He prayed continually. But in the end, God failed him, and he turned to Hell. He studied a book on witchcraft, celebrated a Black Mass, tried to sell his soul to the devil in order to be free of lust. But the devil had no use for him either, and so Paul Sullivan abandoned all religion.

For a time Paul was happy. If only in this one act, he had at least demonstrated that he could be free. But his happiness did not last long. At school he fell in love with a young athlete. It was months before he summoned up the nerve to speak to him. During this time he could do nothing more than sit near him in class, watch him play football, and wait. Finally, late one afternoon when everyone else had gone home, they met in front of the school. The boy spoke first. It was easy after that. Though Paul was thin and shy, he had always been accepted as one of the boys. Since he was admired because he was known to read a lot, an athlete would not lose caste by being his friend. So it began. Together they experimented with sex and Paul was as happy as he would ever be again in his life, and perfectly pleased that Heaven and Hell had forsaken him.

But the next year everything changed. The athlete liked girls and they liked him, and so Paul was abandoned and suffered accordingly. He became shyer, more aloof than before. He made no friends. His parents worried about him. His mother was certain that his unhappiness came from the denial of God and Church. He let her believe this, unable to tell her what it was that set him apart from others and made him feel obscurely superior to all the heterosexual world, if only because he had a secret that they could not guess and an insight into life that they did not have. Yet simultaneously he hated himself for needing the body of another man to be complete.

Women were attracted to him, particularly older women, and they were kind to him and, as a result, Paul learned a good deal about women at a time when his contemporaries were learning only about girls' bodies. But this knowledge had its price. Imperceptibly, these amiable companions would begin to presume that conversational intimacy might lead to something else. When that happened, flight was in order.

At seventeen Paul went to Harvard. For the first time in his life he found himself in a tolerant environment. He soon made a number of friends, all of whom were going to write books. Spurred by them, he concentrated on writing. When his father suggested that perhaps he should prepare for the Business School, he reacted so strongly that the subject never came up again.

In college Paul wrote his first novel, about a young man who wanted to be a novelist. (Thomas Wolfe was popular that year.) The novel was rejected by every publisher he sent it to. He also wrote poems; several were published in little magazines. Confident that he was a poet, he left Harvard without a degree, went to New York, broke off all communication with his family, did odd jobs, and wrote a novel about a bitter young man who did odd jobs in New York. The prose was crude, the politics Marxist, the dislike of Catholicism authentic. The book was published and he found himself with the reputation of a person of promise, living in New York with other persons of promise.

One day, in a spirit of rebellion against his nature, Paul married a girl his own age. The marriage was not consummated. He loathed the bodies of women. He liked their faces but not their bodies. As a child he remembered watching his mother undress and being horrified by her sagging body. Since then all women were associated with his mother, not only taboo but unaesthetic. His wife left him and the marriage was annulled.

Paul had many affairs. Some for physical relief, some as

the result of boredom, a few for love or what he thought
was love. These all ended badly; he never knew exactly why.
Of course the men that he liked were usually simple athletic
types, bisexual, who preferred the safety of family life to the
edgy pleasures of a homosexual affair, and so he turned to
those bars where he could always find a boy who would
spend the night with him, in cold blood as it were, through
callousness, giving him the pain he had come to expect and
secretly need. He lived alone and saw few people. He traveled a good deal and he wrote novels. He put everything
into his novels. Yet the result was disappointing. His books
were praised but not taken seriously. He made enough
money to live but he was not a best-seller. He had an honest
contempt for the bad novels that sold well and yet he
secretly envied their authors, damned by reviewers but
wealthy. Nevertheless, he continued to write. There was
nothing else to do, no other life for him but the surrogate
one of putting words on paper.

As Paul got older, he deliberately opened himself wide to
suffering, and he was not disappointed. He even gained
strength. But the bitterness never left him, and at heart he
remained the same furious boy who had performed the
Black Mass. He was secretly convinced that sooner or later
the devil would grant him complete and reciprocated love,
whether man or woman made no difference. He would
exchange his soul for that.

After a time, Paul became so used to his loveless estate
that he had to discover new and more subtle tortures for
himself. So he decided to follow in the wake of all those
legendary damned souls who had deserted their art for a
rich suffering among the orange groves of California. After
a long negotiation (it is never easy to sell out) a movie
studio agreed to give him the price his agent had demanded
and he moved to Hollywood, where he was depressed to

find that he really rather enjoyed himself. But fortunately he met Jim and found that he was still vulnerable. Their affair looked to be most promising, with endless possibilities of disaster.

After the break with Shaw, Jim and Sullivan went to New Orleans. Here they stayed in a large hotel in the modern part of the city, while they explored the French Quarter with its narrow dirty streets, low buildings, iron galleries, long shuttered windows, and of course a thousand bars and restaurants, particularly along Bourbon Street, which echoed day and night with jazz and blues music, as everyone prowled: men from ships and men from the country, looking for dark, wiry-haired girls who giggled and looked at them impudently and hinted at "the good time" to come.

In spite of the heat, night in New Orleans was stimulating. So much promise in the air, so much pleasure to be had. One by one like the stations of the Cross, Jim and Sullivan visited the bars, listening to Negro singers, observing the men and the whores. It was a pleasant way to pass time, without guilt or any sense of future.

In the mornings Sullivan would work on a novel (a story of unreciprocated love told with light bitterness) and Jim would go sightseeing. In the afternoons they would go to the YMCA to swim.

In the evenings they would visit queer bars, pretending to be innocent tourists and fooling no one.

A bar called Chenonceaux particularly intrigued them. On the edge of the Quarter, in a quiet street, it occupied all of an old stone building from whose walls most of the plaster had fallen. At one end of the room a small fire burned on a stone hearth, while candles burned and the jukebox played soft popular songs. The result was so soothing that even the wildest patrons tended to behave themselves at the bar, their cries muted, their sibilants hushed, their cruising become demure.

Jim and Sullivan always sat near the fire, where they could watch the men and women come and go, acting out their various rituals of courtship for the benefit of strangers.

As Sullivan watched the menagerie, he would talk in a low voice, saying many things that he would not say in other places, and Jim listened to him, waiting as always to learn something new about himself. But Sullivan spoke only of others.

In March Jim was twenty, and he found himself brooding on the many things he had done and seen since he left Virginia; it was almost as if he had been deliberately courting odd experiences in order to be able to tell of them when he was an old man, sitting in a Virginia store with other old men, none of whom had had so many adventures. Not of course that he would be able to tell everything. At times he wondered if Bob was leading the same sort of life. Was Bob like himself? He hoped not. Yet if they were proper twins, he would have to be the same. It was not easy to sort out. But one day he would know the answer. Now he gave himself up to experience.

Jim's birthday was celebrated at Chenonceaux's by the owner, a fat motherly man who had once been a decorator in New York but was now "reformed." Though he knew only their first names, he suspected that they were wealthy or important or both, but he was far too discreet to ask for information which was not volunteered. Besides, these two young men were much admired by the other patrons, and that was good for business.

"Paul, Jimmy, how're you tonight?" He smiled at Jim, his favorite, and Jim smiled back. He liked the owner despite the motherly ways.

"What'll it be?" They ordered beer and he brought it to them himself. Then he sat down at their table.

"What's the gossip?" asked Paul.

"Well, you'd never guess it, but that tall pale boy, you know the one who used to make such eyes at Jim . . . well, he's gone off with a *Negro* truck driver! It's the funniest thing to see those two together. They're quite wrapped up in each other and I understand the Negro beats him regularly. Really, it's the funniest thing!" They agreed that it was indeed funny, and Jim wanted to know if many Negroes were that way; he had always supposed that they were not.

The fat man rolled his eyes. "Loads of them, literally loads of them! Of course, I expect being a Negro in America is enough to make anyone neurotic. So this added bit, this extra kick, is nothing to be surprised at. Then of course many of them are truly primitive, and primitives don't seem to mind *what* they do if it's fun."

"We should all be like that," said Sullivan.

The fat man frowned; thought of any sort was an effort. "But we have to have *some* conventions, some order, or everyone would be running around wild, committing murder and everything."

"I meant only the sexual taboos, which shouldn't be the business of the law."

"Maybe they shouldn't be but they certainly are! The times I've been picked up by plainclothesmen who made *all* the advances, just awful. Sometimes it costs you a hundred dollars or more to pay off. They're such crooks, especially here."

"Which is all wrong!" Jim could see that Paul was angry. "Why should any of us hide? What we do is natural, if not 'normal,' whatever that is. In any case, what people do together of their own free will is their business and no one else's."

The fat man smiled. "But do you have the nerve to tell the world about yourself?"

Paul sighed and looked at his hands. "No," he said, "I don't."

"So what can we do, if we're all too frightened?"

"Live with dignity, I suppose. And try to learn to love one another, as they say."

"Fair enough," said the fat man. "I have to get back to the bar." He left them.

"Do you really care?" asked Jim. "Do you really care that much about the rest of the world?"

Paul shrugged. "Sometimes, yes. Sometimes I care very much."

They drank their beer and watched the people.

In many ways, the women were the most pathetic. Particularly one old woman who was known as the Major. Gray hair cut like a man's and dressed in a skirted suit with a somber tie, she made a great fuss over the pretty girls, particularly the ones who were shy and clinging.

"There," said Jim, motioning to the Major, "there's somebody honest. You want to be like that?"

"That isn't what I meant. I just want a little simple honesty, and acceptance. Why anyone is anything is a mystery, and not the business of the law."

Jim changed the subject. "How long do you want to stay in New Orleans?"

"Why? Are you bored?"

"No, but I've got to go to work one of these days . . . that tennis deal, I told you about it before."

"Relax. You've got a lot of years to do all that in. Save your money. Have a good time. Wait."

Jim was relieved that neither he nor Sullivan pretended they were going to live together forever. But it did not occur to him how much it hurt Sullivan, who was almost in love, to be so casual. Since they did not understand one another, each was able to sustain an illusion about the other, which was the usual beginning of love, if not truth.

They were joined by a handsome blonde lesbian girl who looked not unlike the Apollo Belvedere, reproduced in plaster. She was much in demand.

"Hiya, boys! Got a drink for your best girl?" They had the drink.

III

THE DAYS PASSED QUICKLY and Jim enjoyed living without purpose. He was happy to get up in the morning; he was happy to go to bed at night with the thought of a new day to look forward to. He knew his life was aimless, and he could not have been more content.

Suddenly the war in Europe occupied even the attention of the people in Chenonceaux's bar. They discussed whether or not Britain would be invaded, and it seemed that everyone had some sentimental reminiscence about Stratford or Marble Arch or Guardsmen in Knightsbridge. Rather self-consciously, people became absorbed by the bit of history through which their century was passing.

By the end of May, New Orleans had begun to bore them. Jim spoke of going to New York to work, while Paul thought they should go to South America; but he was not insistent; he merely indicated that he would like to continue with Jim for a while longer. Then, unexpectedly, their course was set for them.

One night at the Chenonceaux, while talking to the

owner, Jim saw a woman enter the bar, quite alone. She was dark, exotic, well-dressed, impossible to classify. Diffidently she ordered a drink. She attracted the owner's attention. "Oh, dear!" He looked distraught. "This one's come to the wrong bar. I can tell a mile off!" He got to his feet. "We'll lose our reputation, if civilians start coming here." He crossed to the bar, scowling. Then Sullivan recognized the woman at the same time she recognized him.

"Paul!" she exclaimed and she took her drink from the bar and joined them. Whoever she was, Paul was delighted to see her. When he introduced her to Jim, she gave him a genuine smile, showing interest but not curiosity, for which he was grateful.

Jim watched her face as she talked, thin eyebrows arched naturally, hazel eyes, dark hair. Slim with an unobtrusive figure, she moved like a dancer.

She spoke of Amelia, Sullivan's ex-wife. "Where is she now?" asked Paul.

"Still in New York, I think." Maria's accent was all her own, delicate and evocative.

"Do you think she'll get married again?"

"I doubt it. But who knows? She works for a magazine. I saw her just a week ago. She's now developed a large . . . *world*-consciousness. She's interested in nothing so small as the marriage of two human beings. She thinks only of the masses and the spirit of history. At the moment she is violently against the Russians because they are pro-Hitler. Ten months ago she was a Stalinist. I'm afraid she's abandoned all thought of a private life. She is entirely public, and most formidable."

Jim listened with interest. Sullivan seldom mentioned his brief career as a married man. "Poor Amelia," said Sullivan finally. "She hasn't had a very happy time of it. Is she making money?"

Maria nodded. "I should think so. In that world she's quite well thought of."

"What have *you* been doing, Maria?"

She laughed. "Nothing, as always. But it keeps me busy. I was in France until the autumn. Then the war started and I came back to New York, where I was very proper."

"Do you ever hear from Verlaine?"

She frowned slightly and made sketches on the table with her long fingers. "He's in the Army, I understand. No, I haven't heard anything from him. I haven't seen him in years."

"Are you painting still?"

"No," she said. "How was Hollywood?"

Paul grinned. "It was perfect, until they asked me to write something for them and then of course I had to go."

Maria laughed. "Still Don Quixote?"

"I'm afraid so." Sullivan was obviously delighted at being thought impractical yet pure of heart.

They were silent. Jim studied the smooth, well-cared-for face of Maria Verlaine, aware that the more he looked at her the more beautiful she became. Finally Sullivan asked her what she was doing in New Orleans.

"I'm en route."

"To any place, or just in general?"

"In general. But most immediately to Yucatán."

"What a curious place."

"I have a reason. My father died last winter and left me a plantation where they grow whatever it is you make rope out of. Now I have an offer to sell the place. They need me there."

"Is it civilized?"

"No, but it's near Mérida, which is a proper city."

Sullivan turned to Jim and saw that he was looking at

Maria Verlaine. He frowned, but neither noticed. "And you," Maria asked, "are you en route?"

Sullivan shrugged. "No destination that I know of. Jim and I just drift."

"I see." And it seemed that she did. Then: "Why don't you drift with me? They say Mérida's fascinating, full of ruins, and if sightseeing gets dull, you can always fly up to Mexico City. Oh, do say you'll come! It will save my life." And so it was decided that they would travel together.

In their hotel room Jim asked Sullivan about Maria. Sullivan was unusually communicative. "She was married to a Frenchman, a bit of a gigolo. They were divorced. She's had a number of affairs, usually with artists, always doomed. Of course she's the Isolde sort. Also, she's attracted to difficult men, particularly homosexuals, and they usually find her attractive, too. Don't you? I do. I even went to bed with her years ago."

Jim wondered if this was true. "She seems very nice," he said cautiously.

"You'll like her. That's a promise." They got into bed. Sullivan was enormously pleased with himself. He had now endangered his affair with Jim. He had deliberately brought him into contact with the one woman who might appeal to him. There was now an excellent chance that he would lose Jim, and the thought gave him a profound and bitter pleasure. He would suffer. He would know pain. With infinite care and patience, he set about destroying his own happiness.

CHAPTER
6

I

YUCATÁN IS A FLAT land of low scrub jungle and sisal fields. The capital city of Mérida is close to the Gulf of Mexico. Sisal plantations surround the city and, from the air, travelers can see the white pyramids of Chichén Itzá and Uxmal, the ancient Mayan cities. So much for the guidebook.

As they drove from the airport to a hotel in the center of town, the driver pointed out the cathedral, a baroque church with many cracks in its stucco walls, overlooking a great plaza filled with shade trees. Here the natives sat on stone benches, small and brown with faces more Indian than Spanish. Small ragged boys scurried about the plaza, shining shoes and playing games with tops.

Once a private house, the hotel was a large square pink building whose interior smelled like the inside of an ancient cigar box, musty and stale. A tall bandit with a thick mustache welcomed them. He was the manager and had known Maria Verlaine's father. He treated them like royalty as he showed them their rooms.

Jim and Sullivan were given a three-room suite decorated in French Provincial bordello, with a smoky glass chandelier, a tile floor, and two great beds shrouded in mosquito netting. "You will like, yes?" Yes, they would like. And they did. Jim even got used to sleeping in the middle of the day. As for Maria, she was at last removed from a world that had come to bore her; also, she enjoyed being with Jim, aware that a flirtation was now inevitable. He in turn was attracted to her but he was not sure in what way. The game was new to him. He had to learn the rules as he went along. Meanwhile, the opening moves had been made.

Sullivan knew with a curious prescience exactly what would happen. He was like God. He had arranged a set of circumstances, and now all that he needed to do was to wait for the expected climax.

After the first week of sightseeing, they did not go about much in the town. Men would come in the morning to talk business with Maria. Sullivan would read and Jim would go swimming at the mineral baths. Nothing more strenuous was possible, the heat was too enervating.

Then Sullivan began to drink heavily. Jim was shocked. Sullivan had seldom drunk before. Now he drank steadily through the day so that by dinnertime he was ready for bed. Politely, if shakily, he would excuse himself, insisting that Jim stay with Maria and keep her company.

One evening after Sullivan had gone to bed, Jim and Maria sat down together in the patio. A crescent moon shone white and clear in the black night, and a breeze rustled the fronds of the palm trees.

"I know how difficult it is." Maria guessed his mood. "Paul's a strange man, so bitter about everything. Everyone. When you praise another writer, it hurts him, even if you're praising Shakespeare. If you say you like people with dark hair, he'll be hurt because his hair isn't dark. And now he has turned completely away from people. I don't know why. In the old days he was different. He was more . . . alive. He felt that he had been given great insight, greater than anyone else's, and he regarded it as a sacred gift, which it is, though perhaps the gift was never so great as he thought."

"But he's very good, isn't he?" Jim wanted to know.

"Yes," said Maria quickly, "he's very good. But not good enough. Not as good as he wanted to be. I think that hurts him."

"Is it so important, being a great writer?"

She smiled. "It's important to those who think it's important, who've given up everything to be great."

"Has Paul given up so much?"

"Who can tell? Is he capable of love?"

The question was direct, and Jim blushed. "I . . . I don't know. I think so." But Jim was not at all certain that he knew what love was. He assumed that it must be something like what he felt for Bob, an emotion which, as he grew older, became even stronger, as though absence in some way preserved it pure. Also what he felt had the virtue of being unstated, a secret all his own. He smiled, thinking of this, and Maria said, "What amuses you?"

"I was just thinking how far I am from Virginia, from the town I was raised in. I was thinking how different my life is from all the rest of them back there."

She misunderstood. "Do you mind it very much, being different?"

It was the first time she had made direct reference to the affair with Sullivan, and he hated her for mentioning it, furious at being marked. "I'm not as different as all that."

"I'm sorry." Aware of her mistake, she touched his arm. "I was clumsy."

Jim forgave her, but not completely. Obscurely, he wanted to hurt her, to throw her on a bed and take her violently against her will, to convince himself and her and everyone that he was not like the others. A pulse beat in his throat. He was afraid, even as they talked lightly of other matters.

Sullivan was reading when Jim came upstairs. He looked a ghostly figure beneath the mosquito netting. "Have a nice time?"

"What do you mean by that?" Jim was ready for battle.

"With Maria, you know what I mean. She's attractive, isn't she?"

"Sure. Sure." Jim let his clothes drop to the floor; the night was hot; he was suddenly weary.

"Wait till you know her better. She's a marvelous lover."

"Shut up."

"Just wait. That's all. Just wait." He grinned drunkenly. Jim cursed him. Then he turned out the lights and got into his own bed. It was several hours before he could sleep.

II

MARIA VERLAINE WAS A curious woman, subtle, not easily apprehended. At forty she seemed a girl, slender, expectant, dreamy, her whole life devoted to that desire and pursuit of the whole which obsesses the romantic and confounds the rest. She moved from affair to affair, drawn to the sensitive, the delicate, the impossible. Her imagination could transform the most ordinary of men into dream-lovers, if the occasion were right and his response sufficient. But in time imagination flagged. Reality intruded, and the affair would end, usually in flight. Yet she continued like some gallant warrior committed to a losing cause; after all, her favorite legend was that of Don Quixote and the impossible quest. Believing this, she had made it her life. But as time passed, she found herself drifting more and more toward men younger than herself, to youths whose delicacy was almost feminine. Adolescents could often give gentleness for gentleness, heightened awareness for heightened awareness, and of course they too believed in love. But she usually stopped short of homosexuals. She had lived too long in Europe. Too many of her contemporaries had been captured by the league of dressmakers and decorators, and she had vowed that she would not be trapped by them, though they amused her, made her laugh, treated her as a confidante. Yet out of kindness, not malice, they tried to unsex her and make her one of them. Fortunately, she had a genius for flight. She knew when to leave without inflicting pain. So they allowed her a temporary visa in their world, and she enjoyed being a tourist.

Now she was attracted to Jim. He was exotic to her. Never before had she been attracted to an ordinary man, much less a boy. Aesthetically he pleased her. She had always been drawn to the Nordic gods. Blue eyes, blond hair, pale skin intrigued her. Did they feel anything at all, these silvery northerners? Were they quite human? But more to the point, he touched her. He was so completely locked in himself, inarticulate, without means of communication, with nothing to offer but his body, which he used almost as a sacrifice to propitiate some dangerous god. She wanted him. If there was some silver Nordic mystery, she wanted to partake of it. She hesitated only because of Paul. At a signal from him she would withdraw. But the signal never came, and she took this to mean complaisance.

One afternoon she drove with Jim in a horse-drawn carriage to a pool where they often swam. Sullivan had stayed at the hotel.

"How long do you think it'll be before your business is done?" asked Jim.

"I don't know. I really don't know. They're so slow here. In a few weeks, perhaps. You must be terribly bored."

"No, I'm not bored. Not yet, anyway. I even like hot weather. But I want to go to New York before the fall."

"And start playing tennis again?"

"Yes, I like to work."

"Will you live in New York with Paul?" The question was asked.

Jim paused. "Maybe. But I'm on my own." The question was answered.

"What did you do in Hollywood?"

"Taught tennis. Not much."

"Hollywood must be interesting. I've never been there for very long. Did you know . . ." She mentioned names and he answered "yes" or "no." Then, subtly, she asked names of homosexual figures; he answered "yes" to many of them. They talked, finally, of Shaw.

"I met him once in New York. I thought he was a vain little man."

"He's not so bad when you know him." Jim was loyal. "He isn't very happy, God knows why. He has everything."

"Except what he wants."

"I don't think he knows what he wants, like the rest of us."

Maria was amused: she had underrated Jim. "I expect you're right. Not many people know. And even when they do, it's not easy finding it."

"I think I'd like money," said Jim. "Enough to live anyway."

"Is that all?"

"Well, there's one other thing."

"And that?"

"Is my secret." He laughed.

The summer passed. Maria's business was done but they did
not leave. Sullivan drank. Jim swam with Maria and looked
at ruins. The heat was almost palpable. To cross a street left
one wet with perspiration. But they remained, and no one
spoke of leaving, not even Jim.

All three were waiting.

One day they visited the ruins of Chichén Itzá and stayed
overnight in the adjacent inn, where they were picked up by
a couple from Seattle named Johnson. The Johnsons were
young, lively, and innocent. Mrs. Johnson ("I read everything") was thrilled to meet Sullivan. Actually, she had read
only one of his books and had forgotten what it was about.
Even so, she was excited at meeting a genuine author.

That night, after dinner, they sat outside among the palm
trees and Mrs. Johnson did most of the talking. They were
all pleasantly drowsy. Maria sat with her hands folded in her
lap, looking at the ruins in the distance: pyramids and
square ornate buildings monstrous by starlight. Jim tried to
hide his yawns. He wanted to go to bed. Sullivan drank
tequila and Mrs. Johnson's praise.

"I really do envy you writers. You have such a good time
going around from place to place. You know, I used to
think I'd be a writer. You know, somebody like Fannie
Hurst. But I guess I had more important things to do." She
looked fondly at her husband.

"Yes," said Sullivan. "I'm sure you did."

"Are you married, Mr. Sullivan? If you'll excuse me being personal."

"I'm divorced."

"Oh, now that's a pity. This may surprise you, but I didn't really *live* until George and I were married. But I expect you'll be getting married again, Mr. Sullivan. I mean a distinguished man like yourself and still young . . ."

"I don't think so."

"That's what they all say!" Mrs. Johnson chattered gaily about marriage and its heady pleasures.

Jim always felt oddly superior when he was with normal people who assumed that everybody shared their tastes. If they only knew, he thought, smiling to himself in the dark. He glanced at Maria and saw that she was sitting still as the statue they had seen that day among the ruins, a goddess with a skull mask. Paul had laughed when he saw the stone figure; he found it significant that the only goddess in the Mayan hierarchy was Death.

"Are you a writer, too, Mrs. Verlaine?" The Johnsons had decided that these three people were a bit unusual, traveling together, but that they were probably *all right*. If they weren't all right, then it was even more interesting.

"No," said Maria, "I am nothing."

"Oh." Mrs. Johnson turned to Jim, but then decided not to question him; he looked too young to have done anything worth talking about.

"Don't you find the Indians here absolutely charming, Mr. Sullivan?"

"In what way?"

"Well, they're so basic and yet . . . inscrutable. I think they're probably quite happy even if they are poor. Certainly it'd be a mistake to educate them. They'd just be miserable, that's all." She talked awhile about Indians. Then, inevitably, they spoke of the movies.

Mrs. Johnson saw almost as many movies as she read books. She was happiest when she was seeing a movie made from a book that she had read. She always remembered every character and she disliked unfaithful representations. "Of course my favorite actor is Ronald Shaw. He's so *forceful*. I happened to be reading in a movie magazine—I see them at the hairdresser, they always seem to have them— and I read where he was going to marry that Spanish actress Carlotta Repollo, who is years older than he is. Such a pity, don't you think?"

Sullivan glanced at Jim, who blushed. Maria was also amused. Three people in disguise were performing a play for an audience that could never know or appreciate the quality of the performance.

"I should like to see the ruins," said Maria suddenly.

"By starlight?" Sullivan was mocking. "Well, why not? You take her, Jim."

"Well . . ." He looked at Maria.

"I think we should all go," she said.

"No. You two go. You're the romantic ones."

The Johnsons looked at the trio, aware of undertones. Then Maria left the table and Jim followed her. They walked out of the small square of electric light and into the darkness. The starlight made no shadows in the cool night. Like disembodied spirits, they walked down an avenue of cropped grass and then, at the same instant, without words, they sat down side by side on the shattered stone remains of a forgotten god.

Jim looked up at the stars, brilliant and white in the black sky. He breathed deeply. There was the scent of sage in the air as well as the dry odor of sunburned stone.

He turned to Maria and saw that she was waiting. He was surprised that he was not afraid.

"One feels dead here." Her voice was distant and remote among the ruins.

"Dead?"

"In a peaceful way. All things finished, inevitable, like one of these stones: there is to be nothing else."

"*If* death is like that."

"It must be."

They did not speak for a long while. At last Maria spoke. "We've been playacting."

"Yes."

"And dishonest."

"With Paul?"

"With Paul. Ourselves." She sighed. "I wish I knew more about people. I wish I could understand why things are as they are."

"Nobody knows." Jim was amazed to find himself playing at wisdom. "I don't know why I do what I do or even who I am."

"I don't know who you are either." They looked at one another, faces white and indistinct.

"Myself. That's all. Limited."

"Limited? Not really. Actually you're everything, man, woman, and child. You can be whatever you choose."

"What am I now?"

"Until a few moments ago a child."

"What am I now?"

"I don't know."

He began to tremble; he began to hope. Perhaps it could happen.

"Are you afraid?"

"No. Not afraid." Nor was he at that moment.

"Could you kiss me?"

"I could kiss you," he said, and he did. He kissed the Death Goddess.

. . .

Everything was different afterward; different and yet the same, for nothing finally happened. Jim failed. He could not perform the act. He was inadequate. Yet in its way, his relationship with Maria was a love affair. They were with each other as much as possible. They were confidants. Yet when it came to physical contact, except for that first kiss, Jim could not bear the softness and smoothness of a woman. Maria was baffled. Because he was both masculine and drawn to her, she found his failure all the more mysterious. There seemed nothing to be done except to continue as lovers who never touched. Sullivan, however, accepted the surface affair for an actual one, and the agony it gave him was exquisite.

November came and still they did not move from Mérida. Jim and Maria were together most of the time. Sullivan refused to join them during the day. He had begun to drink after breakfast; by early evening he was often vivacious and amusing but by the end of dinner he was inevitably heavy and bitter. Their lives stopped until December, when the United States went to war with Japan, and they were once more part of the world. Sullivan stopped drinking. Plans were made as they sat in the patio after dinner. Both Sullivan and Jim were excited, brought to life. Maria was sad. "I don't like to think about it," she said. "All my life there has been a war, just begun, just finished. There seems to be no escape."

Sullivan paused in a nervous turn about the patio. "We'll have to go back," he said to Jim.

Jim nodded, caught up in the drama of new things. "I want to enlist before I'm drafted," he said, pleased at the words if not the thought.

"It's so senseless." Maria was vehement. "If I were a man I'd run away, hide, desert, turn traitor."

Sullivan smiled. "Five years ago I would have done just that."

"Why not now?"

"Because this is . . . something to do."

She turned to Jim. "Do you feel the same?"

"It solves a lot of things."

"Perhaps." She seemed unconvinced.

"We should go back as soon as possible," said Sullivan.

"What will you do?" asked Maria.

"Be a soldier. Or a correspondent. Whatever I can get."

"It looks," said Maria, "as if our Mexican vacation is at an end. I've enjoyed it."

"So have I." Jim looked at her and felt a sudden warmth; threat of war and parting drew him closer to her.

"And so have I." Sullivan's voice mocked them. "I've enjoyed every minute of it. We've made an interesting trio, haven't we?"

"Have we?" Maria was bleak.

It was decided that they return to the States by way of Guatemala City.

They rode comfortably above clouds, mountains, dark green jungle. It was pleasant to sail over the hot steaming land as though they were no longer earth creatures but something more than human, elemental, with no difficulties that could not be overcome by rigid silver wings.

Jim had bright visions of himself in the Air Corps, flying across continents and oceans, able to move rapidly over the earth and leave no scar. He longed for flight.

Guatemala City was a relief after Yucatán. The city was cool with streets which looked as if they had been recently scrubbed. The people were cheerful, the air good. And wherever one looked, volcanoes loomed, sharp, veined blue with shadow, topped by rain clouds.

At the hotel, Sullivan sent cables to various newspaper friends who might help him to get an assignment as war correspondent. Then, communication with the real world established, Jim and Sullivan went to their room.

"It's almost over." Sullivan stood at the window, looking at mountains. Jim unpacked.

"The trip?"

"The trip, of course."

"Yes," said Jim, who knew what he meant. "I guess we'll split up when we get to New York."

Sullivan smiled. "I doubt if the Army would send us to war together."

"Everything ends. I wonder why."

"Don't you know?" Sullivan was scornful. "Don't you know?"

"Do you?"

"Certainly. When you fall in love with someone else, that automatically ends the original affair, doesn't it?"

"You mean Maria?"

"Yes, I mean Maria."

"It's . . . a very complicated business, Paul. It's not what it seems to be." But Jim failed to tell the whole truth; it was too humiliating.

Fortunately Sullivan was not interested in facts; his intuition was quite enough; whatever the details were, the result was bound to be the same. "Anyway, I knew all along that this would happen. I let it happen."

"Why?"

But Sullivan could never admit to anyone why he was driven to behave as he did. "Because," he said, and he knew he was not convincing, "I thought it would be the best thing that could happen to you. She's a wonderful woman. She can get you out of this world."

"Why should I get out?" For the first time Jim admitted what he was.

"Because you're never going to fit into this sort of relationship, and so the sooner you find your way to something else the better it'll be for you."

"Maybe." Jim looked at Paul. The dark circles had gone from beneath his eyes. He was still attractive to Jim, even now, when everything was over. They spoke kindly to one another. Yet finally, each was so perfectly dishonest that neither was able to feel the slightest regret at what was ending.

On the last night they dined in a restaurant particularly recommended for those who wanted native food without diarrhea. Walls bright with primitive scenes of volcanoes, conquistadores, flowers, lakes. Rooms loud with the noise of a small marimba band. Tourist couples danced.

All during dinner Jim felt reckless and glad, like a child let out of school.

They drank Chilean wine and even Maria was gay. But toward the end of dinner, when the music grew sad and sentimental and they had all drunk too much white wine, they became sad and sentimental, too. But it was the sort of sadness that is closely related to happiness. Each was now secure in his own failure. Doubt was gone. Boundaries had been drawn and accepted.

"It's too sad," said Maria as the band rattled "La Paloma." "We've lived such a long time together. And played so many games."

"True." Sullivan was moody. "But it's also a relief to have things end."

"Some things." Maria twirled her wineglass in her hands. "I think love is always a tragic thing, for everyone, always."

"But that's what makes life interesting. How can we value anything until it's gone?"

"No light without dark?"

"Yes. And no pain without pleasure."

"What a curious way to put it." She looked at him, almost aware of his secret.

"Even so," he said quickly, "there are other things in life than being in love. Look at Jim. He's never in love, are you?"

"Of course I am. With what I want." Jim thought of Bob.

Maria was puzzled. "What do you want?"

Sullivan answered for him. "What he cannot have, like the rest of us." He turned to Maria. "Have *you* ever found what you wanted?"

"For a time, certainly."

"But not for long."

"No, not for long. I've failed, like everyone else."

"Why?"

"I suppose I may want more than any man cares to give. And sometimes I give more than any man wants to take."

"Shaw was like that," said Jim suddenly. "I mean he *thought* he was that way."

"Shaw was an idiot," said Sullivan.

"We all are," said Maria sadly, "at the end."

They were silent. The marimba clattered in the room. They drank more wine. At last Sullivan got up and went to the men's room. For the first time since they had come to Guatemala, Jim was alone with Maria. She turned to him. "I'm leaving tomorrow."

"You're not coming with us?"

"No. I'm not strong enough. You know, sometimes I

believe that there *is* a God, a vindictive, self-righteous God who punishes happiness. I was happy with you when I thought . . ." She could not finish. "Anyway, it will be years before you can love a woman. I haven't the time to wait."

"But you know how I feel about you."

"Yes," she said, and there was no more emotion in her voice. "I know how you feel." She stood up. "I'm going back to the hotel."

He stood up too. "Will I see you before you go?"

"No."

"In New York?"

"Perhaps."

"I'll be able to see you then. I'll want to see you. I don't want to lose you, too."

"When I'm happier, we'll see each other. Good night, Jim."

"Good night, Maria." She left the restaurant quickly, the black lace of her dress rustling about her legs.

Sullivan came back. "Where's Maria?"

"She's gone to the hotel. She was tired."

"Oh? Well, let's have another drink." They drank.

Though sad, Jim was relieved to have a temporary end to emotion. He had been exhausted by these two people, taken out of his depth. Now he looked forward to freedom. Released by the fact of war, he would soon be resolved by action. He could not wait for his own life to begin.

CHAPTER
7

I

JIM AND SULLIVAN ARRIVED in New York in mid-December.
Almost immediately Sullivan obtained a job with a news
syndicate, while Jim enlisted in the Army. Neither saw
Maria Verlaine; she had disappeared.

Jim went first to a reception center in Maryland, where
he was put to work tending fires while the Army decided
what to do with him. Bad weather and petty tyranny kept
him so angry that he had no time for self-pity, as he moved
stolidly through the black days, acknowledging the existence of no one else.

Waking up late one afternoon, after an all-night vigil at
the coal furnaces, Jim wandered into the recreation room of
the company barracks. A dozen new soldiers watched the
afternoon pool game, played by two members of the
permanent company. Lonely, Jim decided to break his long

silence. He turned to the soldier next to him, a man of forty, hopelessly civilian, with a small mustache and sad eyes.

"How long you been here?" asked Jim.

The man looked at him gratefully, a little surprised. "Why, almost a month." The voice was educated, unlike the guttural barks of so many of the new soldiers, recruited from slums and deep country. "And you?"

"Two weeks. I enlisted in New York. Where are you from?"

"Ann Arbor, Michigan. I was with the university."

Jim was impressed. "A teacher?"

The man nodded. "Professor of history, associate professor."

"Then what're you doing here? I thought people like you got to be majors."

The professor laughed nervously. "So did I. But I was wrong. In the age of Demos, only yokels like our first sergeant rise to the top."

"Did you enlist?"

"Yes. I'm married, have two children, but I enlisted."

"Why?"

"I had some strange idea that I'd be useful."

For the first time since Jim had enlisted he was able to feel sorry for someone else. He was pleased at this manifestation of good character. "Rough deal," he said. "What do you think they're going to do with you?"

"Classify me as a clerk. That seems to be my fate."

"Won't you get to be an officer?"

"Perhaps. I have friends in Washington. But I seem to've lost all faith in this business. Of course things were even worse in the Army of the Potomac. The Civil War," he added apologetically.

"Worse in combat now, too." They had all heard horror

stories about the Philippines, where American troops had been badly defeated.

"Perhaps," said the professor, "but I find it hard to believe. This seems like hell, in a way, or a nightmare with no way out of it. We are governed by madmen."

Two large, red-faced country boys approached. They were clumsy and good-humored. "Hey there, Professor, you look like you shot your wad. They gettin' you down?"

"Hello, boys. No, they haven't got me down just yet. I'm simply converting from peace to war at my own slow pace."

One of the boys made a joke about the word *peace,* and the professor laughed as loudly as they did, eager to be their butt. Jim was sad to see him play the buffoon. It was important to remain oneself. Even though he could not acknowledge what he was, he refused to pretend that he was just like everyone else. It hurt him now to see another man sacrifice his pride, particularly when it was not necessary.

The professor kept the red-faced boys laughing by telling them funny stories about his trials on twenty-four-hour KP. They occasionally glanced at Jim to see if he was laughing. But he did not respond and they disapproved. Fortunately, he was larger than they.

The first sergeant, a short man of fifty, came into the room and there was silence except for the click of billiard balls. "I want two men," he said. "I want two volunteers to clean out the goddamn latrine. Some son of a bitch fouled it up and I want two men." Suddenly he swooped down on Jim and the professor. "You two," he said.

"Certainly, Sergeant," said the professor, jumping to his feet. "Always happy to volunteer!"

It took them two hours to clean the latrine, during which time Jim learned a good deal about American history and the tyranny of democratic armies.

II

In February Jim was transferred to Georgia. For the next three months he was busy with his basic training. The physical side of Army life appealed to him; he enjoyed being active, although the minor humiliations continued to annoy him.

In May he was sent to the Air Corps as a general duty man (the usual classification for the unskilled), and shipped out to an air base in Colorado, where he was assigned to the headquarters of a wing which in turn was part of a command which in turn was part of the Second Air Force, devoted largely to training pilots and bombardiers. Of the two hundred men in his unit, most were headquarters personnel. Older than the average soldier, those of noncommissioned rank usually lived off the post with their wives in Colorado Springs.

Jim and his fellow infantrymen were received by the first sergeant, a tall emaciated man who had once been a salesman of household appliances.

"You're in the Air Corps now." He tried to sound ominous. "You may have heard stories that we aren't as tough as some branches, but that's just a crock. You hear me? You hear what I say? We got discipline here, a lot of it. Because this is a pretty important headquarters and don't ever forget it. We got a tough general. So you keep on the line and do your job and you'll be OK."

But the Air Corps was by no means as tough as the infantry. Discipline was spasmodic. The clerks were just like clerks anywhere and Jim was contemptuous of them. Though the wooden tar-papered barracks were gloomy and the food was bad, the life was not unpleasant. For the first months he and the other infantrymen did not associate with the Air Corps clerks; they kept their identity proudly, but inevitably they were absorbed.

One day was very like another. In the early morning a record of reveille was played over the loudspeaker. As the men yawned and swore, the first sergeant charged through the barracks, bellowing at those still asleep. Then they ran through the icy air to the latrine twenty yards away; then came breakfast in the mess hall. Jim downed the greasy food perfunctorily, unaware of what he was eating. Afterward the first sergeant would have a number of jobs for the general-duty men to do. The work was often hard—building barracks, loading garbage trucks, repairing runways. Hard work but not much of it. Jim often had whole days to himself when he would go down to the long runways and watch the B-17s and the B-24s take off and land. The bomber crews were obviously fascinated by what they were doing, unlike the rest of the men, who were listlessly engaged in pointless tasks. Jim was particularly struck by one of the pilots, a roaring boy with blond hair who was particularly popular with the ground crews. He sang popular songs in a loud toneless voice, indulged in horseplay, and generally gave pleasure. Once Jim found himself face to face with him. Jim saluted, but the pilot only grinned and clapped him on the shoulder and said, "Hi!" One boy to another. Jim was dazzled. And that was all. Rank separated them. It was sad.

Jim made no friends. He avoided the nightly bull sessions in the barracks. Instead he saw movies and read books, among them a novel by Sullivan, which seemed to him to be the work of a perfect stranger; no doubt it was. Occasionally he visited Colorado Springs, where he was very much aware of those alert-looking soldiers, forever searching for a response. But Jim ignored them; he had no interest in sex.

Eventually Jim was reclassified. One of the personnel officers, noting that he had been a tennis instructor, put him in Special Services as a physical-training coach. His life improved. He got along well with Captain Banks, the Special Services officer, a football player who had been a pilot, grounded for reasons of health. Captain Banks moved dreamily about his office, signing necessary papers, unaware of what he was doing. Like so many base officers, he had abdicated all authority to his sergeant.

Sergeant Kervinski was a slim dark man who wore a large diamond ring on his little finger and talked quickly, blushing often. His delight when Jim was added to the section was plain even to an innocent eye. Trouble ahead, thought Jim.

The Special Services detachment consisted of those who ran the post theater and library, staged plays and radio programs, edited a newspaper. Along with these mercurial types there were a half-dozen quiet youths who were physical-training instructors. But since all efforts at group discipline were invariably sabotaged by the clerks, Jim had a very easy time of it. Hardly anyone reported for calisthenics, and the instructors had the gymnasium to themselves, which suited them well since they were all dedicated bodybuilders.

Agreeable though the life was, Jim longed to be sent overseas, even though he knew that in modern armies there is seldom much action except for line troops and combat pilots. Nevertheless, he was excited by the thought of danger. He wanted release. A few of the general-duty men longed for the same thing. They too hated routine and inactivity, but they were not in the majority. Each headquarters clerk had at least one officer friend pledged to keep him from being sent overseas or, if sent, shipped to a reasonably safe place like England. The clerks were not heroes and they were honest about it. Only Sergeant Kervinski was different. It was his dream to be sent to a languorous island of white beaches and no women. When Jim asked to be put on the first overseas shipment list, Kervinski told him of this paradise, adding, "I know what you mean, honestly I do, and I'll put you on the list. Perhaps we'll ship out together, to the South Seas. Come on, let's go to supper."

They stood in line together to collect the usual heavy food. Then they sat down at one of the long wooden mess tables. A calendar with a picture of a heavy-breasted woman hung just above Kervinski's head. He glanced at it with distaste. Then he turned to Jim and made an exploratory move. "Some woman!"

"Some woman," Jim repeated flatly.

"I guess you never had the time to get yourself a woman, a wife," said Kervinski brightly. "I mean with your traveling around so much." He knew something of Jim's story.

"No, I never had time." The approach was made even more depressing by the sergeant's unattractiveness.

"Well, they say there's nothing like a wife. But not for me. After all, it's a lot cheaper to buy milk than keep a cow! Isn't it?"

Jim grunted.

"What was Hollywood really like?" Kervinski looked at him eagerly.

"Just like anyplace else." Jim had once shown some of the clerks the movie magazine with his picture in it. They had been sufficiently impressed to dislike him afterward; he had learned his lesson, and now never mentioned the past.

"I understand," said Kervinski, blushing, "that you knew Ronald Shaw and a lot of other stars. What was *he* like?"

The entire underworld knew about Shaw. "I didn't know him well." Jim was evasive. "I just played tennis with him a few times."

"Well, I hear a lot of strange stories about him but I don't see how they could be true."

"Oh? What sort of stories?" Jim was malicious.

The sergeant turned scarlet. "Oh . . . just stories. The kind you always hear about Hollywood people. I don't see *how* they could be true."

"People always talk."

"By the way," said Kervinski, examining a piece of green, watery cabbage, "I understand that ratings will be open this month."

"That so?"

"I've recommended you to the captain for a PFC stripe." The sergeant put the cabbage in his mouth.

"Thanks a lot," said Jim, fearing the worst.

Kervinski chewed thoughtfully. "We should have dinner some evening, in town. I know a wonderful restaurant out near the Broadmoor. We bachelors should stick together," he added with a little laugh.

"That would be fine," said Jim, hoping that when he eventually said no that Kervinski would not be too upset.

"Then," said Kervinski, "there are some girls I know. They're very nice and I'm sure you'd like them. Do you know any girls in town yet?"

Jim shook his head.

"Well, you certainly haven't given these Colorado girls a break! Where's that Southern chivalry?"

Jim played Southern idiot. "Well, I just don't go out much at all, I reckon."

"Just between us, neither do I. These girls here aren't half as attractive as the ones back home." He winked and Jim was disgusted. Although it was impossible for anyone in the Army to be honest about such things, at least there were more straightforward ways of going about a seduction. At his present rate, it would take the sergeant weeks to come to the point; probably just as well. Jim promised the sergeant that he would have dinner with him soon; then he excused himself and went back to the barracks, where he found a group of men sitting on his bunk. Most were clerks and not young; a bull session was in progress. Though Jim made a friendly motion, the men moved to other bunks. Jim took off his shirt and lay down. He said nothing. The bull session continued. As always, the dominant note was one of complaint. Apparently, each was losing an extraordinary amount of money while in the Army; and of course all officers were unjust and all women unfaithful.

Jim lay back on the coarse brown blanket and looked at the dark rafters. The barracks was always dark; there never seemed to be enough light or heat. He turned toward the coal stove and saw that there was a new man in the barracks, a young corporal, who sat on the bunk nearest the stove, listening politely, obviously aware that if a man wants to be accepted by a barracks, he must listen to a great deal of talk about a very few subjects, and he must accept as a law of nature that, whenever a point is made, it will be repeated a hundred times, often in the same words, rather like part-singing.

One of the more important sergeants (secretary to the personnel officer) was telling them about the general. "He's a real Section Eight case. Why, the other day he came into our office and he said to me, 'Sergeant,' he said, 'how many men've we got at Weatherley Field?' 'None,' I said, 'we lost them all to the fighter wing yesterday.' He didn't know that one of his own bases had been transferred the day before. Well, he tried to get out of it by saying he thought the transfer hadn't taken place yet. But that gives you some idea how his mind works, if it works. He's always thinking up ideas to discipline the men. As if we didn't have enough work running his wing for him. Didn't know about Weatherley being transferred!"

The others agreed that the general was too tough and not particularly bright. Or as another sergeant, whose past was mysterious with unspecified success, put it, "I'd like to see *him* hold down a job in civilian life. I'll bet he couldn't make thirty-five a week."

The others agreed solemnly that in their world the general would be far less than they, unable to make thirty-five a week.

Then the conversation turned to women.

Some liked plump women; some liked small women; some liked blondes, others brunettes, and a few liked red-haired women. But all were agreed that they liked women and as they talked their eyes brightened as they recalled wives, lovers, dreams. Jim was amused and puzzled: were these clerks really successful with women? None was attractive physically. They were either too fat or too thin, and he wondered how any woman could care for them. Yet they talked incessantly of conquests, boasting in order to impress other men who boasted—proof of what they said must be true. Even so, the thought of clerks in love was depressing.

Then one mentioned fairies. As far as Jim knew there were none in the barracks, except possibly the soldier who had started the conversation. He was small and round, with a flat unpleasant voice. "Just the other day this queer came up to me in the can in the movie house in town and wants me to go with him. Me! Well, I told the bastard what I thought of him. I told him if he didn't get out of there quick I'd break his neck, that's what I told him, and boy, he got out of there fast!" The others nodded solemnly when they heard this story, and each told an identical story, although in some instances the outraged man had indeed slugged the fairy. Jim tried not to laugh. It was always the ugliest and most suspect of the men who was invariably propositioned.

Jim glanced across at the young corporal. He was a dark-haired boy with gray eyes and a small slim body that looked strong. Watching him through half-closed eyes, Jim felt desire. For the first time in months he wanted sex. He wanted the young corporal. Mentally, he raped him, made love to him, worshiped him; they would be brothers and never parted.

"This town is full of those damn queers," the bald soldier droned on. "A guy can't be too careful." But since another conversation had started, no one except Jim heard. The soldier looked to Jim for support. "Isn't that right?"

"That's right," said Jim, continuing to look at the corporal, who yawned sleepily.

Jim was soon a friend of the corporal, whose name was Ken Woodrow, from Cleveland, aged twenty-one, in the Army a year and a half. He was a graduate of a secretarial college, and his ambition was to work for an important industrialist. Preferably in the Midwest, "where the people are real." Ken told him everything about himself and Jim listened intently, infatuated, unable to think of anything except how to get Ken to bed. Not since Bob had anyone so excited him. But with Bob there had been a sense of identity, of twins complementing one another; with Ken what he felt was absolute lust. He must have him.

They saw each other daily. Yet Ken seemed serenly unaware of what Jim wanted. Leading questions were invariably deflected by innocent answers. It was hugely frus-trating. Meanwhile, Sergeant Kervinski observed them darkly and suspected the worst; he was particularly angry with Jim, who continued to refuse to have dinner with him in town.

At last, unable to bear the waiting another moment, Jim talked Ken into going with him to Colorado Springs. It was a sharp November night. They had an overnight pass. They would sleep at a hotel. Something would have to happen.

Colorado Springs was crowded with soldiers. They came not only from the air base but also from a neighboring infantry camp, crowding the streets, bars, movie theaters, poolrooms, bowling alleys, looking for sex and a good time.

Jim and Ken had dinner at an Italian restaurant. At the next table two pretty girls dined alone.

"See that girl staring at me?" Ken whispered, delighted. "You think we ought to ask them to join us?"

"Oh, no," said Jim as though the thought tired him. "I'm not up to it. I worked hard today. And I'm beat."

"Gosh, you never go out with girls, do you?" said Ken as though the thought had just occurred to him.

Jim had been waiting for this question for weeks. He had a lie ready. "Well, I got this one girl here in town, and I see her regularly, alone."

Ken nodded wisely. "See what you mean. Keep it to yourself. I figured you must have a setup like that, because you've been here quite a while and it wouldn't be natural not to have a chick somewhere." Ken nodded several times. They ate their spaghetti. Then Ken said, "She doesn't have any friends, does she? You know the kind I mean."

"Does who?"

"Your girl in town, does she . . . well, have friends?"

"Oh, no. At least I don't think so. That is, I'd have to ask her. She doesn't go out much."

"Well, where'd you meet her?"

Jim was irritated by the necessity to invent. "I met her at the USO, but like I told you she doesn't go out much. She works for the telephone company," he added, attempting verisimilitude.

"Oh." Ken was silent for a moment, his long fingers playing with a fork. "I met a girl last week. She was really stacked, and she had this apartment out by Pikes Peak. But I got so drunk I couldn't remember where it was when it was over, and she didn't tell me her name, so I don't know how to find her. Boy, I'd give anything to see that chick again. It's awful being in a town full of GIs and not knowing anybody."

"It's rough." Jim realized that he was getting nowhere. With each piece of new evidence, Ken's normality became more and more established. From the beginning, Jim had known that Ken was engaged to a girl in Cleveland, and that as soon as the war was over they would be married. But despite the engagement, Ken enjoyed talking about other girls and more than once he told Jim, solemnly, that he wondered if maybe he wasn't oversexed because he couldn't stop thinking about women. Since there was no evidence that Ken was interested in men, Jim's only hope was to trust in the ambivalence of a young man who liked him.

"Well," said Ken at last, eyes straying again to the two girls, "I guess we better go somewhere and get drunk, if you're sure you don't want to pick up something."

They toured the bars. Jim was careful not to get drunk. He had one drink for every two of Ken's. Wherever they went, Ken invariably struck up a conversation with a woman, but because Jim had said that he was tired Ken did not make a date for himself; he was going to be a "good buddy" and get drunk.

Shortly after midnight Ken was indeed very drunk, slurred speech, eyes glazed; he clung to the bar for support.

The moment had come. "Maybe we better stay in town tonight," said Jim.

"Sure, sure . . . good idea," mumbled Ken.

The night air was reviving. Jim helped Ken to walk without stumbling. They went to a hotel frequented by soldiers with overnight passes.

"Double bed or two singles?" asked the desk clerk.

"Which is cheapest?" asked Jim, who knew.

"Double." They registered. The room was like all other rooms in similar shabby hotels.

"Jeez, but I'm drunk." Ken stared at his own reflection in the mirror, face red, sweating, dark hair tangled over blood-shot eyes.

"So'm I." Jim watched him, wishing that he *was* drunk enough to do what he wanted to do.

"Jeez." Ken sat down on the large bed, which sagged in the middle. "I sure wish I had a date. I mean that I had a date with one of those girls we saw, and you had a date, too. That'd be something, wouldn't it? Four in a bed. I had a buddy once who liked to do that. He tried to get me to do that with him and a couple of girls, but not me, I like it private. I'd hate to have somebody watching, wouldn't you?"

"I sure would."

Ken stretched out on the bed, fully clothed, and shut his eyes. Jim shook him. He mumbled incoherently. Boldly Jim pulled off Ken's shoes, then the damp socks; Ken did not stir. But when he started to undo his belt, Ken opened his eyes and smiled; he looked like a corrupt choirboy. "Now that's what I call service," he said, wiggling his bare toes.

"I thought you'd passed out. Come on. Get your clothes off."

They both undressed down to their olive drab shorts.

Then Ken flung himself on the bed. "You sure sleep good when you're drunk," he said happily, and shut his eyes once more, and seemed to sleep.

Jim turned out the light. The darkness was complete. His heart beat rapidly. He was conscious of the warmth of Ken's body close to him. Slowly he moved his hand beneath the covers until he touched Ken's thigh; he waited, fingers resting lightly on the firm flesh.

Ken moved away. "Cut that out," he said in a clear sober voice.

A pulse beat furiously in Jim's temple. Blood rushed to his head. He turned over on his side. In the morning he would have a hangover.

III

THE WINTER WAS COLD and bitter. Snow came and went but the desert remained dry, and dust was forever in the wind. Jim was cold most of the time. During the day he spent as much time as he could in the hot sun, out of the wind. But at night he was always cold.

Neither Ken nor Jim acted as if anything untoward had happened, but Ken was plainly embarrassed, and Jim was furious. They avoided one another and now Jim found himself disliking the boy who had once filled his dreams with such intense passion. It was a lonely time. He had no friends. Even Sergeant Kervinski had proved fickle, transferring his affections to another physical-training instructor, newly arrived.

During the hard winter, Jim surrendered himself to an orgy of self-analysis. He thought continually about himself and his life and what it was that had made him the way he was. He pondered his early life.

Jim had disliked his father; he remembered that more clearly than anything else. His first memory was one of bleakness and unfair punishment. On the other hand he had liked his mother. Yet he found it strange that he could not recall her face although he could remember her voice: soft, Southern, tired. Far back in memory, he could recall a wonderful safe time when he was held in her arms while she kissed and fondled him. But all that ended when his brother was born, or so he supposed. She had never been demonstrative again.

School memories were vague. Jim had once been attracted to girls. When he was fourteen he was very interested in a heavy-breasted girl named Prudence. They exchanged valentines and the other children giggled that they were in love. He had sexual fantasies involving Prudence, but they stopped when he was fifteen and became interested in athletics and Bob. From that time on no one existed in the world except Bob.

Then came life at sea. He still shuddered when he remembered the night with Collins and the two girls in Seattle. He marveled now at how little he had understood then. Yet even now he wondered what might have happened if he had gone through with that adventure. He still half-believed that should he ever have a woman he would be normal. There was not much to base this hope on, but he believed it.

Memories of Shaw were pleasant and he smiled whenever he thought of him, despite the drama of their parting. He had learned much from Shaw; and through him he had met interesting people who might still be useful to him. Also, he found himself pitying Shaw, always a gratifying emotion, since it diminishes pleasurably the object.

Sullivan and Maria Verlaine were still too close to him for analysis. But he was aware that each had been important to him. Of the two he cared more for Maria, even though he now realized that he would never be able to make love to her, if only because they had talked too much about it. Words had taken the place of the act. Sullivan, too, had tended to vanish behind a screen of words, of emotions overstated yet undefined.

As for Bob, he had vanished. No one knew where he was, according to Mrs. Willard, who wrote Jim irregularly, giving him news of his father's illness, Carrie's marriage, John's admission to the State University. Yet Jim was positive that one day Bob would appear and they would continue what was begun that day beside the river. Until then, his life was in suspension, waiting.

Unable to bear the winter cold any longer, Jim went to Kervinski. He was at his desk, surrounded by the theatrical sergeants, soft young men who knew a thousand unpleasant stories about famous people.

"Well, Jim, what can I do for you?" Kervinski smiled brightly.

"I was wondering, Sergeant, if there's any chance of my going overseas."

Kervinski sighed. "Really, Jim, you don't know when you're well off. As it is, according to current orders, you'll be shipped out in April. But who knows? Anyway, there isn't a thing I or anybody can do. It's up to Washington."

"I was wondering if maybe I could get assigned to one of the bomber outfits they're forming here."

"Possibly. But they're not going overseas until spring. Anyway, why do you want to leave?"

"It's too goddamn cold. I'm freezing to death."

The sergeant laughed. "I'm afraid you'll just have to rough it with the rest of us. You Southern boys are so . . . sultry," he added, amusing the sergeants. That was that.

• • •

Christmas came and with it a blizzard. For two days wind
and snow raged about the base. It was impossible to see
more than a few feet in any direction. Men were lost going
from building to building. Day was like night. When the
blizzard stopped, the base had become a white lunar land
with snowdrifts higher than buildings and craters that glittered in the sun.

In the club for enlisted men, a Christmas tree had been
set up and the men gathered around it to drink beer and
speak bitterly of past Christmases. Jim, bored, wandered
over to the piano, where a corporal was picking out a tune
with one finger. Not until Jim was at the piano did he realize that the corporal was Ken.

"Hello," said Jim. The moment was awkward.

"Hi." Ken was flat. "Kind of dull."

Jim nodded. "And I don't like beer."

"I remember. You been busy?" Ken continued his one-
finger piano playing.

"Just trying to keep warm."

"I thought you were in Alaska once."

"But since then I was in the tropics too long. I hate cold
weather."

"Why don't you transfer to Louisiana? We got a new base
there."

"How?"

Ken was now playing the Marine Corps Hymn. "Well, if
you want me to, I can fix it up with the sergeant in personnel. He's a good buddy of mine."

"I wish you would."

"I'll ask him tomorrow."

"Thanks." Jim was grateful, also suspicious. Why was
Ken so willing to help? Did he want him to leave Colorado?

The next day, by accident, Jim met Sergeant Kervinski in the post library. The sergeant was reading a movie magazine.

"Hello, Jim." Kervinski blushed. "I expect we're both goldbricks today. By the way, Ken told me he spoke to you about Louisiana."

"That's right." Jim was startled. "I didn't know you knew him."

"Oh, yes!" Kervinski beamed. "As a matter of fact, we're going into the Springs for dinner tonight. Why don't you join us?" The invitation was put in such a way that it was perfectly clear that the last thing in the world Kervinski wanted was for Jim to join them.

"No, thanks. Not tonight. He's a good guy, Ken."

"I think so. I first noticed him when you and he used to go around together when he first arrived, remember? Such a sincere person."

"Yes." Jim was suddenly angry. "Yes, he's OK." He paused, searching for a way to wound his successor. The best he could do was "I guess Ken's going to be married soon."

Kervinski was serene. "Oh, I don't think there's any *immediate* danger. He's having too good a time. Besides, it's a lot cheaper to buy milk than keep a cow."

Jim looked at Kervinski with perfect loathing. But the sergeant gave no sign that he was aware of Jim's dislike. "You know that we'll be shipping quite a few men down to Louisiana."

Jim got the point at last. "Yes, Ken's going to see if I can be one of them. Do you think it'll be all right with Captain Banks?"

"Of course it'll be all right. We'd hate to lose you, naturally." Jim was baffled. He had failed with Ken. Kervinski had been successful. It seemed impossible, yet obviously something had happened and both were now eager for Jim to be shipped out.

"Thanks," said Jim, and left the library, contemplating murder.

But Jim was not transferred to Louisiana. On New Year's Day he caught a chill. He went to the hospital and was put to bed, with a streptococcic infection of the throat. For several days he was delirious, tortured by memory, by certain words and phrases which repeated themselves until he swore aloud and twisted in his bed. He dreamed of Bob, of a menacing, subtly distorted Bob who retreated when he tried to touch him. Sometimes the river was between them, and when he tried to swim across, he would be dashed against sharp rocks, Bob's derisive laughter ringing in his ears.

Then he would hear the voice of Shaw talking and talking and talking of love, saying the same things in the same way, until Jim knew how each sentence would end by its first word; yet there was no way of silencing the voice; it was literally maddening.

Then there were memories of his mother, holding him in her arms, the face no longer gray and lined but young, the way she had been when he was a child and secure. Then his father would approach and he would slip from her arms and his father would beat him, while the river roared in his ears.

The pain in his throat was sharp, like a knife blade probing, underscoring his nightmares. He remained in this dream-haunted state for what seemed years. But on the third day, chronologically, the fever broke and the dreams ended, and he woke up one morning, tired and weak; the worst was over.

Jim was in a small room in the base hospital. Through the window he could see snowy mountains. He was conscious of being quite alone and for a moment he wondered if he might not be the only person left in the world, but then the muffled sound of voices reassured him and the nurse entered the room.

"I see we're better today." She took his pulse and put a thermometer in his mouth. "You know, you were quite sick for a while there." Her tone was accusing, as she removed the thermometer from his mouth. "Normal at last. Well, we stuffed enough sulfa into you."

"How long've I been here?" Jim's voice was weak; it hurt him to talk.

"This is your third day, and don't talk. The doctor will be around soon." She put a glass of water beside his bed and left.

The doctor was cheerful. He examined Jim's throat and nodded with satisfaction. "Good. Good. You'll be out of here in a few weeks."

Apparently Jim had nearly died. This did not surprise him. There had been times in his delirium when he would have been glad to depart. "Anyway, it's over now. But it may be weeks before you can go back to active duty."

The days passed quickly and pleasantly. It was the most comfortable period of Jim's Army career. He read magazines and listened to the radio. In time he was transferred to a ward with twenty other convalescents. He was perfectly content with life, until the pains began, first in his left knee, then in his left shoulder, a constant aching, like a bad tooth. After a number of tests, the doctor sat on Jim's bed and talked to him in a low voice while the others in the ward tried to hear.

"Are you absolutely certain that you've never had these pains before?"

"No, sir, never." Jim had been asked this particular question a dozen times.

"Well, I'm afraid that you've got what we call rheumatoid arthritis." He sighed. "Contracted while in the Army."

The ward boy had already given Jim the same diagnosis and so he was prepared for the verdict. Even so, he managed to look alarmed. "Is that bad, sir?"

"Not in this stage, no. It'll be painful, of course. Not that we know much about arthritis, though I'm willing to bet your throat infection had something to do with it. Meanwhile, you'll be sent to a warm, dry climate. Does no good, of course, but it'll make you feel better. Then they'll probably discharge you with a pension, because the calcium deposits show up in the X rays, and it all happened to you while serving your country in time of war, and you've got a swell racket from here on out."

"Where will I be sent, sir?"

"California desert, maybe Arkansas, Arizona. We'll let you know." The doctor stood up slowly. "I've got the same thing as you." He chuckled. "Maybe they'll discharge me, too." He left, and Jim wondered if there was anyone in the world he liked so much as this particular doctor.

"You going to be shipped out?" asked the Negro soldier in the bunk next to his.

Jim nodded, hiding his great happiness.

"Man, you're lucky. I'd sure like to be shipped out of here, to anywhere."

"It's tough."

The Negro then talked about intolerance and discrimination. He was certain that even if he were dying the white officers would not take proper care of him. To cite an example, he told a long rambling story about a Negro soldier who had gone to an Army doctor a number of times for backache and the doctor had told him that there was nothing wrong with him. One day when the soldier was sitting in the waiting room and the nurse went in to tell the doctor that he was there, he heard the doctor say distinctly, "Well, send the nigger in." White doctors were racially intolerant. Everyone knew it. But someday . . .

As the Negro talked about the miseries of his race, Jim thought only of his own happiness. He had long since given up all idea of going overseas. From the stories he had heard it was hardly more exciting than duty in the States. He was now eager to leave the Army. He had been no use at all to the war. Soon he would be free. Meanwhile the thought of his pending release made him want to resume relations with those who had been important to him. He borrowed writing paper from the Negro soldier and slowly, laboriously, in his awkward, childish handwriting, he began to write letters, using them as a net in order to recapture his own past.

CHAPTER
8

RONALD SHAW WAS TIRED and there was an uncomfortable pain in his duodenum which he was convinced was an ulcer, if not cancer. His death took place before his eyes, beautifully lit and photographed, with Brahms playing on the sound track. Then there was a slow dissolve to the funeral cortege as it moved through Beverly Hills, escorted by weeping girls carrying autograph books.

Tears in his eyes, Shaw turned into the green oasis of Bel Air. It had been a bad day at the studio. He disliked his new director and he hated the part he was playing. For the first time he was supporting a woman star. He wished now that he had turned down the part, or at least had it rewritten, or retired from the screen before he died of overwork and cancer. The bright cheerful sun made things worse; his head ached; perhaps he was going to have sunstroke.

But the house was cool and he gave a weak sigh of relief as the butler held the door open for him.

"A bad day, sir?" The butler was sympathetic.

"Terrible." Shaw picked up his mail and went out to the swimming pool, where George was taking a sunbath. George was a sailor from Wisconsin with hair so blond that it was white. He had been with Shaw for a week. In another week he would go back to sea. Then what? Shaw asked himself bitterly.

"Hi, Ronnie." The boy pulled himself up on one elbow. "How's the salt mine?"

"Rotten." Shaw sat down beside the pool. "The director's an untalented, lousy, professional kike." Shaw had begun lately to make anti-Semitic remarks, which amused rather than distressed those who knew him.

"I guess they're pretty lousy, some of them out here." George was a happy youth who believed everything that he was told. Shaw tousled the blond hair idly. They had met in a bar in Hollywood. Shaw had started to frequent bars, a dangerous pastime, but he was bored and restless, and morbidly aware of time passing, and of the fact that his hair was quite gray beneath the dye and that his stomach was bad, and life was ending even though he was hardly forty. Why? Too much had happened to him, he decided; his career had burned him up and of course he had been unfortunate in love, cheated and betrayed.

George stretched out again beside the pool while Shaw read his mail. He opened Jim's letter. The handwriting was unfamiliar and at first he thought it was a fan letter. Then he saw that it was signed quite formally, "Jim Willard." Shaw was pleased, flattered, suspicious: if Jim wanted money, he would not get it. That would be Shaw's revenge as well as a good lesson for Jim, who had deserted a truly genuine human being for a self-centered writer. Shaw was slightly disappointed to find that the letter was friendly and nothing more.

Jim wrote that he was in the Army hospital but no longer
sick. He expected to be discharged soon and he would like
to see Shaw again. It was puzzling and yet in character. Jim
had always been direct. Shaw experienced a sudden ache of
sexual memory. Then he saw that George was watching
him. "What you got?" asked George. "A fan letter?"

Shaw smiled dreamily. "No, it's from a kid I used to
know, Jim Willard. I showed you his picture once."

"What happened to him?"

"He went into the Army," Shaw lied glibly. "He writes
me often. I suppose he's still in love with me, at least that's
what he says. But I don't feel anything anymore. Funny,
isn't it?"

George nodded, impressed. Then Shaw sent him into the
pavilion for a drink. As the late afternoon sun shone in
Shaw's face and a soft flower-scented wind cooled him, his
unhappiness turned to a detachment that was not at all
unpleasant. He was utterly alone in the world. This knowledge thrilled him. Of course there was his mother in Baltimore and a few friends at the studio, as well as the millions
who knew of him and would doubtless be honored to be his
friend; yet having conquered all the world, he was still very
much alone and it struck him that there was something
magnificent in being a prisoner of fame. He allowed a
brooding look to come into his eyes. What a waste, he
thought, contemplating the inability of others to recipro-
cate the love he had to give. None could equal his intensity.
A tragic figure, he sat with the western sun in his eyes,
perfectly content.

George approached with two glasses. "Here you go." He
gave Shaw his drink.

Shaw thanked him very gently.

"You feeling OK, Ronnie?"

"Oh, yes, thank you." The gin was cold. Suddenly a

spasm went through his stomach. For an instant he was panicky. But then he belched and the pain went away: it was only gas.

Mr. Willard was dying and Mrs. Willard wished that he would die soon. Apparently years of bad temper had damaged his liver and weakened his heart. The doctors were able to keep him from pain with great doses of morphine.

Mrs. Willard grimaced as she entered the sickroom; the odor of medicines and dying was overpowering. Mr. Willard lay on his back, breathing noisily. His face was yellow and sagging and the once-commanding mouth hung loose. His eyes were like gray glass from the morphine.

"That you, Bess?" His voice was hoarse.

"Yes, dear. How're you feeling?" She arranged the pillows.

"Better. The doctor said I was better." The evening before, the doctor had told Mrs. Willard that her husband would not live another week.

"I know, he told me the same."

"I'll be up and around soon." Mr. Willard would not admit to himself that he was going to die. He asked his wife about the courthouse.

"They're doing fine, dear. Mr. Perkins is doing your job until you're ready to go back to work."

"Perkins is an ass," said Mr. Willard.

"I'm sure he's doing his best. After all, he's only filling in."

Mr. Willard grunted and shut his eyes. Dispassionately his wife looked at the sunken yellow face, and wondered where the insurance policy was. She had not been able to find it anywhere in the house, but of course the will would tell, and the will was at the lawyer's office. Mr. Willard's eyes shut, and he seemed to sleep. She left the room.

On the floor in the hall were several letters. As she leaned over to pick them up, she groaned. The older she got, the more she disliked bending over. But then she forgot her pains: one of the letters was from Jim.

She read it slowly. He was in the hospital and that alarmed her, but he reassured her that he was now well and would soon be getting out of the Army. He promised to come home and visit her as soon as he was free. Her heart beat more quickly as she read this.

She thought of her older son, and wondered what she felt about him after such a long separation, much of it without communication of any sort.

She had not wanted him to leave home. She had wept the night he left even though she realized that he could never live in the same house with his father. In her quiet way, Mrs. Willard had hated her husband from the first day of their marriage. During family quarrels, she had sympathized with Jim and longed to tell him that she felt as he did but that they both had to bear those things which could not be changed. Unfortunately, she had never spoken frankly, and because she had not, Jim left home. Now, of course, it was too late. Jim would never belong to her again. She wanted to cry but she could not.

Mrs. Willard sat erect, the letter in her hands, wondering what had happened to her life. Soon she would be alone, without even a husband to hate in the last years of her life. Where had all the time and all the promise gone to? She pitied herself, but only for a moment. After all, Carrie and her husband lived nearby and so would John once he was a lawyer.

The thought of Jim's return cheered her considerably. She wondered how he looked now that he was a man. She had no clue except the photograph in the movie magazine which she had shown to everyone, creating an impression that Jim was a movie star, an impression she had never entirely corrected.

Mrs. Willard daydreamed pleasantly of the future. There were several nice girls who would make Jim the kind of wife who would be glad to share him with his mother. As for a job, Jim could take over the physical-training post at the high school. She knew enough politicians to make this possible. Yes, the future could be good, she decided, putting the letter away and returning to the sickroom to find that her husband's eyes were open. He was staring at the ceiling.

"I've a letter from Jim."

"What does he say?"

"He's been in the hospital—it's not serious—and he thinks he'll be discharged from the Army soon. Then he'll come home."

"Probably broke." Mr. Willard scowled briefly; his features were too weak to hold even a scowl for long. "Wonder what he'll do when he gets out? Can't go on playing games forever."

"I thought perhaps he could get a job at the high school. I . . . we could get him something, don't you think? I'm sure Judge Claypoole would be glad to arrange it."

Mr. Willard's skeleton hands fumbled with the white sheet. "How old's the boy now?"

Mrs. Willard thought a moment. "Twenty-two come April."

"He's grown." Mr. Willard was gloomy.

"Yes," said Mrs. Willard happily. Jim would take care of her. "He's grown."

"Don't know why he wants to wander all over."

"But the experience is good for him and anyway you know what they say about wild oats."

Mr. Willard shut his eyes. Conversation tired him. Mrs. Willard went to the kitchen, where she found Carrie. "How is he, Mother?"

"It's almost over. A few more days at the most. Thank the Lord he feels no pain."

"That's something to be grateful for." Of them all, Carrie was the only one truly sorry about her father's approaching death. They had been fond of one another. But her sorrow was somewhat assuaged by the fact of pregnancy. Inclined to plumpness, Carrie was now round and contented and looked to be exactly what she was, a comfortable housewife fond of her husband. Mrs. Willard gave Carrie Jim's letter.

Carrie was delighted. "I do hope he comes back and lives here!"

"So do I."

"I wonder what he's like now."

"We'll know when we see him. Now I expect you better go in and see Father."

Carrie left the kitchen and Mrs. Willard began to fix broth for her husband. It would be a great relief to her when he died. She wondered idly if he might not have left the insurance policy with his friend Judge Claypoole. But of course the will would tell them everything.

London was chilly and damp and Sullivan was depressed as he walked past St. James's Palace on the way to his hotel in Mount Street.

He had been to dinner with H. G. Wells, whom he admired as a figure if not as a writer. The evening had gone well; Mr. Wells had been in good form. Yet Sullivan was obscurely irritated by the perfectly plain fact that not only had the great man never read one of Sullivan's books, he had never heard of him either. Naturally Wells was an old man but even so it was disquieting and Sullivan was again reminded of his literary failure.

The night was dark and the blackout made it even darker. A cold wind blew through the streets. Shivering, he fastened his trench coat at the neck. He would have a strong drink when he got back to the hotel bar, even if it meant running into Amelia, who was now in London. Aggressive, bustling, eager for bygones to be bygones, his ex-wife was unbearably cheery.

And of course there she was, thin and untidy, enthroned in the hotel bar, surrounded by correspondents (she herself was covering the war for a left-wing magazine).

"Paul dear, come on over!" He did.

The other correspondents greeted Sullivan respectfully. At least they knew he was an author. They were impressed by novelists, though they did not take his journalism very seriously, for which he could hardly blame them.

Sullivan shook hands all around. He knew most of them by reputation. Those who were not Stalinists were crypto-Trotskyites. Sullivan was apolitical. But Amelia was totally engaged. She talked rapidly, maintaining herself as group leader. "Paul's such a dear. Really, I always think one should be nice to one's ex-husbands, don't you?" The question was asked at large and no one answered. "I believe if we're to be really civilized we should have no bitterness when we fail at marriage or anything else, except perhaps politics." She was a little drunk. "Does that sound like that lovable old cynic La Rochefoucauld? Everything else does!" She laughed gaily, then turned to Sullivan. "Where've you been this evening?"

"I had dinner with H. G. Wells." Sullivan won that round. Immediately everyone asked him about Wells and for a moment Amelia ceased to be the center; even when she loudly demanded a drink for her ex-husband, he still retained his lead. "He was very pleasant. We talked about writing mostly. He'd read one of my books and so I was quite flattered by that. Not that I supposed he liked it, but even so . . ."

"Here's your drink, Paul." Amelia thrust the whiskey at him. He took a swallow and Amelia filled the brief silence. "I think," she said to the table at large, "that it will be years before there is a Labour government in England. The Churchill-Cliveden set are too well entrenched and, just between us, I shouldn't be in the least surprised if they created some sort of dictatorship that could *never* be thrown off without a revolution, and you know how slow these English are at revolting against anything! A nation of masochists."

Paul was surprised to find that people took Amelia seriously. He could hardly be critical; he had married her. But when they first met she was different. A quiet, thoughtful girl, she had worshiped him until it was plain that a physical relationship was impossible. Then, defensively, she had grown masculine and aggressive. It was all his fault, he decided, or at least the fault of the way he was, and this racketing woman was the result. Did nothing turn out well?

Sullivan finished his drink and stood up. "If you'll excuse me, Amelia, I must cut class." Though he said this amiably enough, he was pleased to see that he still had the power to hurt her. She stopped in midsentence: the needle had been lifted from the record. He said good night to the correspondents and left the bar. As he entered the lobby, he could hear Amelia beginning again.

At the desk Sullivan got his mail and took the lift to his room, hoping there would be no air-raid warning to break his sleep. He was weary. Not until he was in bed did he notice Jim's letter on the night table. He read the letter twice and was both disappointed and pleased. Jim was going to be discharged from the Army and he would like to see him again. Nothing more. No mention of Maria. Did that mean their affair would continue, if it was an affair? During the months Sullivan had been in England, he had thought of Jim often, dreamed of him, wanted him. Could they resume? That was the question.

It was morning before Sullivan fell asleep. During the long night he thought mostly of the books he had written, and he was filled with gloom. He had succeeded at nothing. He had no lover, no family, and H. G. Wells had never heard of him. But then as he grew sleepy, he comforted himself. After all, he was young and there was still time left in which to write a masterpiece, as well as to recapture Jim. Meanwhile, first thing in the morning, he would send Mr. Wells one of his novels, autographed.

Jim's letter made Maria Verlaine sad and somewhat embarrassed. She had been a fool to love a child incapable of response. She had deserved to suffer, and she had, for a time. Now she wanted only normal men and uncomplicated attachments.

In New York, despite the austerities of wartime, she dined out often, met strangers, made love. In constant motion, she ceased to think of herself as a tragic figure. Now this unexpected letter reminded her of that strangely lowering season she had spent in Yucatán with a boy and his lover. Did she want to see him again? She thought not. She was at an age when she did not care to be reminded of old defeats. Yet at the same time she was sorry for Jim. More to the point, was it not a proof of her own power that he had again turned to her? and of her own maturity that she could receive him as a friend? Yes, she would write to him. They would meet when he came to New York. After all, she had nothing to fear, nothing to gain. The worst had happened.

Everyone agreed that Bob Ford looked remarkably handsome in his Merchant Marine uniform. First mate aboard a Liberty ship, of all the hometown youths at war, he was considered the most successful. Of course, the Merchant Marine was not exactly the Army or Navy, but still it was quite an achievement to be a first mate and not yet twenty-five. His homecoming was something of a triumph, although, properly speaking, he had no home since his father had been committed to the insane asylum the year before, and the family home was now a boardinghouse. The new owner, however, was willing to rent him his old room at half price, and here he stayed during the two weeks of his leave, while he wooed Sally Mergendahl, the reason for his return. They had written one another for five years. During that time, Sally had grown into a quiet pretty woman, no longer "wild." As a child, she had made up her mind that she was going to marry Bob, and nothing had ever caused her to change her mind. Now her patience was rewarded. One evening, while walking her home from the movies, Bob spoke of marriage.

"Are you sure that you really *want* to be married? Could you be married and still be a sailor?"

Bob looked at her. They were standing beneath a tall elm tree; his face was in darkness, hers in the light from a nearby streetlamp.

"I'm sure I want to marry you. But I love the sea. It's the only thing I know."

"I talked to Daddy," said Sally slowly, "and he thought you would do very well in the insurance business, in his business, and he thought it was a shame that someone with your personality was away at sea all the time when you could be in business with him, selling insurance, as a partner."

"You think he'd give me a job after the war?"

Sally nodded. She had already won that battle.

"Then if it's all right with you, let's get married right away."

"I think," said Sally Mergendahl, "that that would be a very good idea."

The morning of the wedding was a Sunday. Church bells rang, and most people slept an hour late. But Bob was up early. He shaved carefully, put on his newest uniform, and went downstairs for breakfast. His landlady was ecstatic.

"What a lovely day for a wedding! Though any day's a good day to get married. I made pancakes. There's nothing like a full stomach to start you off with. Oh, by the way, here's a letter for you. It came Friday, but in the excitement I forgot all about giving it to you. I'm sorry. It was addressed to you in care of old Mr. Ford here, which means it's from somebody out of town. Well, enjoy your breakfast. I'll see you at the church. I wouldn't miss this for anything!"

Bob opened Jim's letter. He was surprised to hear from him after so many years; he also felt a bit guilty for not having answered those early letters Jim had written him. Sally occupied what little talent he had for correspondence.

The letter was simple enough. Jim was getting out of the

service and he hoped to see Bob soon, perhaps in New York. That was all. Something disturbed Bob as he crumpled the letter. He frowned and tried to remember what it was. But his mind was a blank. As he tossed the letter neatly into a wastebasket, he made a vow that he would answer Jim's letter the moment he got back to ship.

CHAPTER
9

I

JIM WAS NOT DISCHARGED immediately. Instead he was sent
to a hospital in the San Fernando Valley of California,
where he was treated and observed. In the hot sun his
arthritic condition improved but, because he was now eager
to get out of the Army, he said nothing of this to the
doctors. He continued to limp in a most distinguished way.

Jim visited Hollywood often, but he did not go to see
Shaw since he had received no answer to his letter; he
assumed that Shaw was still living with Peter and not interested in a reconciliation. But he did meet the director
named Cy, in a bar, sitting too close to a sailor, drunk.
When Cy saw Jim he shouted, "Well, if it isn't the tennis
boy!" He was exuberant. "So what's new? In that butch
uniform yet! Been to see America's Sweetheart?"

"No. Not yet."

"Where you stationed?"

Jim told him.

"A hospital? What's wrong? A rosy chancre? The dread disease that dare not tell its name?"

"No, arthritis."

"Serious?"

"Not very."

"Well, let's have a drink."

Jim shook his head. "I'm not drinking."

"Then I'll have one." Cy ordered himself gin. "So why haven't you been to see Shaw?"

"Because I don't think he wants to see me, do you?"

Cy took a swallow of his new drink and wiped his mouth with a hairy paw. "Oh, you know Shaw. He's such a ham. Who was the one who came after you? I've forgotten."

"Peter, an actor."

"That one!" Cy beamed with malice. "Well, I'm responsible for that breakup. In a way. I put the kid in a picture and, believe it or not, he was good. So the studio offers him a term contract, he takes it, and walks out on Shaw, who, by the way, got me to put him in the picture in the first place. Isn't that a hoot? But hell, I don't blame the kid. After all, he wasn't even queer. He's shacked up with a broad at this very moment, at Malibu. Saw them myself this afternoon, on the beach."

"Who's with Shaw now?" The story of Peter was not entirely surprising.

"Everybody. Nobody. He hunts the bars and the studio is worried as all hell. And . . . oh, by the way, he's going in the Navy. Now that's a *real* hoot!"

"But I thought he was supposed to be too valuable or something to go."

Cy chuckled. "You got to go to war if you want to make

pictures. He'll be commissioned and sent overseas to maybe Honolulu and we'll take a lot of pictures of him being one of the boys and then, if the Navy doesn't lock him up for raping their personnel, he'll come home with a couple of ribbons and a new contract from the studio. Last few months they've been working him hard, so there'll be plenty of Shaw pictures while he's gone. The idiots won't be allowed to forget him."

"When's he going in?"

"As soon as the Navy gets the go-ahead from *Life*."

"Nice deal," said Jim. The bartender began to move ominously toward him: nondrinkers were unpopular. "Well, I'll see you around."

"Why don't you come on up to my place tonight . . ." Cy began.

"No, thanks."

"Suit yourself."

The routine of the hospital was a relief after Colorado, and Jim enjoyed himself. He played tennis for the first time in two years. He gained weight and soon his illness was a barely remembered nightmare, like the cold white mornings on the Colorado desert.

In April his mother wrote to tell him that his father had died. Jim felt no regret. Almost the contrary: a weight was lifted in his mind, a hatred ended. Jim sat in the sun and looked across the green lawn, where patients in maroon Army dressing gowns were wandering back and forth.

Death seemed impossible in the sunlight. Yet Jim wondered what it was like. He himself had been close to death but he could recall nothing. Now, in the sunlight, he pondered death and his father. He did not believe in heaven or hell. He thought it most unlikely that there was a special place where good people went, particularly when no one was certain just what a good person was, much less what the final repository was like. What *did* happen? The idea of nothing frightened him, and death was probably nothing: no earth, no people, no light, no time, no *thing*. Jim looked at his hand. It was tanned and square, and covered with fine gold hairs. He imagined the hand as it would be when he was dead: limp, pale, turning to earth. He stared for a long time at the hand which was certain to be earth one day. Decay and nothing, yes, that was the future. He was chilled by a cold animal fear. There must be some way to cheat the earth, which like an inexorable magnet drew men back to it. But despite the struggle of ten thousand generations, the magnet was triumphant, and sooner or later his own particular memories would be spilled upon the ground. Of course his dust would be absorbed in other living things and to that degree at least he would exist again, though it was plain enough that the specific combination which was he would never exist again.

The hot sun warmed him. The blood moved fast in his veins. He was conscious of the fullness of life. He existed in the present. That was enough. And perhaps in the years ahead he would have a new vision, one which would help him, somehow, to circumvent the fact of nothing.

In May Jim went before the medical board. Since X rays showed a mineral deposit in his left knee joint, it was the decision of the board that James Willard be medically discharged from the Army of the United States, with a pension for disability. To his delight, all this came to pass. Papers at last in order, he was given a railroad ticket to New York. On the train he read in a newspaper that Ronald Shaw, the actor, had enlisted in the Navy.

· · ·

In New York Jim rented a room on Charles Street in Greenwich Village and looked for work. After some time he found what he wanted. Near the East River there was a vacant lot which had been converted to tennis courts. Here Jim met Wilbur Gray, who, with his partner Isaac Globe, owned the courts. Eventually a new building would go up on the lot but, according to Mr. Globe, that was at least five years away, and in the meantime, business was excellent.

Jim visited the courts every day. He became friends with both Gray and Globe. Finally, he offered to buy part of their business and to be an instructor as well. After many conferences and much examining of books, the men, who knew nothing about tennis, agreed to allow Jim, who knew nothing about business, to become their partner.

Jim worked for the rest of the year, giving lessons on good days, and since there were an unusual number of good days that summer and fall, he made money. Outside of work, he saw very little of his partners. They were both devoted family men and had no interest in the outside world. Neither did he while he was working. He saw no one. He did call Maria Verlaine's hotel once, but she was not registered.

One winter afternoon, on Fifth Avenue, Jim saw Lieutenant Shaw, looking rather wistfully at a display of Christmas toys in the window of F.A.O. Schwarz's.

"Ronnie!"

"Jim!" They shook hands warmly. Shaw had been at sea in the Atlantic. He was now on leave, living at the Harding Hotel. Would Jim like a drink? Yes.

The suite in the Harding was vast, with rococo mirrors and spindly gold-encrusted furniture. Shaw ordered a bottle of Scotch and then they stared at one another, each wondering how to begin. At last Shaw remarked that a lot of water had gone under the bridge since they last met. Jim agreed. Then the conversation stopped for a long time until Shaw said, "Are you living alone?"

Jim nodded. "I worked pretty hard all summer; I don't really know anybody yet."

"You're better off playing the field. I know I am. Ideally, of course, a relationship is best, but then how many people are capable of deep feeling? Practically none."

Jim put an end to that familiar dirge. "How's the Navy?"

Shaw shrugged. "I've had to be careful. But then I've always had to be careful. By the way, what're you doing tonight? I've been invited to a faggot party, very chichi. I'll take you. It can be your coming-out party in New York. They'll all be there."

Jim was surprised at how little Shaw seemed to care for appearances. In the old days he would never have gone to such a party. But now he was indifferent, even defiant.

The party was given by Nicholas J. Rolloson, heir to a notorious American fortune. Rolly, as he was known, had two passions, modern art and the military. Both were well represented in his apartment overlooking Central Park. Paintings by Chagall and Dufy hung on stark white walls. Mobiles tinkled from the ceiling. A huge Henry Moore nude dominated one end of a long drawing room in which at least one chair resembled a wrecked armadillo. Through these startling rooms a full company of soldiers, sailors, and marines wandered, awed by their surroundings if not by Rolly and his friends, who were perfectly familiar to them.

There was a hush when Shaw entered. Although there were other famous men at the party—painters, writers, composers, athletes, even a member of Congress—Shaw was most glamorous of all. Eyes watched his every move. He was a legend here, and that made him entirely happy.

Rolly welcomed them enthusiastically; he wore a scarlet blazer with a crest. As he moved, breasts jiggled beneath a pale yellow silk shirt. The handshake was predictably damp. "My dears, how lovely of you to come! I was so afraid you wouldn't, Ronnie, and I would have died of disappointment, but now my evening is made, but absolutely *made*! Now come with me. Everybody's just about out of their minds to meet you." Shaw was borne away, and Jim was left on his own. A waiter gave him a martini. Cocktail in hand, Jim went exploring, somewhat excited by the servicemen, conscripts in Rolloson's army.

In a corner of the dining room, Jim was hailed by an effeminate man with a hairpiece. "Come on over, baby. Join the party." Without alternative, Jim sat down on the couch between the hairpiece and a set of bifocals. Opposite sat a gray-haired man and a bald young man. They had been talking earnestly and both the gray-haired man and the bifocals were irritated at being interrupted.

"You came with Shaw, didn't you?" asked the hairpiece.

Jim nodded.

"Are you an actor?"

"A tennis player." Jim ground out the phrase in his deepest voice.

"Oh, how thrilling! An athlete! I adore body men," said the bifocals. "Teutonic and primitive, not like those of us who are simply frustrated and inhibited by a society grown too complex to understand. This young man is the true archetype, the original pattern of which we are neurotic distortions." The bifocals examined Jim as if he were some sort of moderately interesting experiment.

The gray-haired man objected. "Why are the rest of us necessarily the result of a distortion? In any case, you are being taken in by an appearance. We don't know his reality. He could be most neurotic of all. By the way"—he turned to Jim with a smile—"we speak of you not as yourself but as a symbol. We're not being impertinent."

"But there is something," said the bald man, "in this Teutonic theory. In Germany, isn't it the army, the athletes, the most virile men, who are homosexual, or at least bisexual? And God knows Germany is primitive enough. On the other hand, in America and in England we find that effeminacy is one of the signs of the homosexual, and of course neurosis."

"Five years ago we might have thought that true," said bifocals. "But I'm not so sure now. Of course there have always been normal-appearing men who were homosexual but never or seldom practiced, while the other type (what you call Teutonic) was not so much in evidence and we knew very little about them and thought they were just trade, you know, the truck driver who enjoyed being had but pretended that he was really interested in women and money. But I think the war has caused a great change. Inhibitions have broken down. All sorts of young men are trying out all sorts of new things, away from home and familiar taboos."

"Everyone is by nature bisexual," said the gray-haired man. "Society, early conditioning, good or bad luck—depending on how you were told to look at it—determine the result. Nothing is 'right.' Only denial of instinct is wrong."

Across the room, Shaw motioned for Jim to join him. Jim excused himself.

Shaw and Rolly were surrounded by sailors, who regarded Jim jealously as he joined them.

"I thought you looked bored with those intellectuals," said Shaw.

"Who were they?" asked Jim.

"Well, the gray-haired one is a professor at City College

and the one with glasses is a journalist—you'd know his name if I could remember it—and the other one is a perfect bitch," said Rolly, patting his thick lustrous hair. "They were probably talking politics. So dreary! I say, why worry? Let them eat cake and all that sort of thing. I mean, after all, really, isn't live and let live the best policy?"

Jim agreed that indeed it was and Rolly pinched his thigh. Shaw was suddenly carried off by the sailors and Jim was left with Rolly, trapped.

"I understand from Ronnie that you're a tennis player. Now I think that's terribly exciting . . . I mean to be an athlete and work out of doors. I've always thought that if I had my life to live over, which fortunately I haven't, I would have spent more time alfresco, doing things. As it is, I do nothing. You know I do nothing, don't you? I hope you don't hate me. Everyone's so snobbish about working these days. It's the Communists, they're everywhere, saying people must *produce.* Well, I say that there must be some-body who knows how to appreciate *what's* produced. Which is why I'm really quite a *useful* member of society. After all I keep money in circulation and other people get it and I do so believe in everyone having a good time. . . . Oh, there's that butch Marine, isn't he something? He was had five times last Sunday and still went to Mass, so he told me." Jim looked at this celebrity, who turned out to be a rather tired-looking young man in uniform.

"You know, I loathe these screaming pansies," said Rolly, twisting an emerald and ruby ring. "I have a perfect weak-ness for men who are butch. I mean, after all, why be a queen if you like other queens, if you follow me? Luckily, nowadays everybody's *gay,* if you know what I mean . . . *literally* everybody! So different when I was a girl. Why, just a few days ago a friend of mine . . . well, I wouldn't go so far as to say a *friend,* actually I think he's rather *sinister,* but anyway this acquaintance was actually keeping Will Jepson, the *boxer*! Now, I mean, really, when things get that far, things have really gone far!"

Jim agreed that things had indeed gone far. Rolly rather revolted him, but he recognized that he meant to be kind and that was a good deal.

"My, isn't it crowded in here? I love for people to enjoy themselves! I mean the right kind of people who appreciate this sort of thing. You see, I've become a Catholic."

Jim took this information in stride.

"It started with Monsignor Sheen, those *blue eyes*! But of course I needed Faith. I had to know just where I'm going when I shuffle off this mortal thing, and the Catholic Church is *so* lovely, with that *cozy* grandeur that I adore. One feels so *safe* with the rituals and everything and those robes! Well, there just isn't *anything* to compare with them. They have *really* the most beautiful ceremonies in the world. I was in St. Peter's once for Easter—I think it was Easter—anyway, the Holy Father came riding in on a golden throne wearing the triple tiara and the most beautiful white robes you've ever seen and the cardinals all in red and the incense and the beautiful marble and gold statues . . . absolutely *yummy*! Anyway, then and there I became a Catholic. I remember turning to Dario Alarimo (he was a dear friend of mine of an extremely old Neapolitan family, his father was a duke and he would have been a duke, too, but I believe he was killed in the war because he was a Fascist, though all the best people were Fascists in those days, even though we all realized that Mussolini was hardly chic). What was I talking about? I was about to make a point. Oh, yes, about becoming a Catholic. So I turned to Dario and I said, 'This is the most splendid thing I've ever seen,' and he turned to me and said, 'Isn't it, Rolly?' All my friends call me Rolly. I hope *you* will, too. So, right after that

I took instruction. Oh, my poor head! It was so difficult.
There was so much to memorize and I've a perfectly
wretched memory, but I did it. I don't like to seem carping
or to be finding fault with the Church but if they would
only cut out all that memory work, things would be a lot
simpler and they might pick up all sorts of really nice
people, not that I'm implying they don't already have the
best people. Good evening, Jimmy, Jack, Allen. Enjoying
yourselves? But as I was saying, except for that awful
memory work at the start, it's been thrilling. I go to confes-
sional once a month and I even get to the Sunday-morning
Mass, the one at ten, and *really* I think I'm something of a
model convert.

"Of course it will probably be years before I die; I
certainly *hope* it will be years. But when I go, I want to be
prepared. I've picked out the nicest crypt at the Church of
St. Agnes in Detroit. That's where my family makes those
awful motorcars. And I shall be buried there. I expect the
cardinal will officiate at the funeral. He better, considering
the money I'm leaving them in my will. Going so soon,
Rudy? Thank you, good night. I understand that the Pope
is thinking quite seriously of giving me a decoration for the
good deeds I've done. I've given them rather a bit of cash,
you know. It's the only way to defeat Communism.

"I do hope I'll go to Heaven after doing so many good
works on earth. I think sin is *terribly* fearsome, don't you?
It's practically impossible not to sin a little, but I think it's
the *big* sins that are the ones that can't be forgiven, like
murdering people. A few lies, white lies, and an occasional
infidelity, that's really the extent of my personal falls from
Grace. I have such hopes for the afterlife. I see it as a riot of
color! And all the angels will look like Marines. Too gay!
The party is going well, don't you think?"

Jim agreed, weary of the flood of talk.

"If you'll excuse me I must make my rounds. The work of a hostess is never done. You wouldn't like to spend the night, would you?"

As Jim started to say no, Rolly giggled. "So few people do anymore, that's one of the horrors of age. Well, I've enjoyed this little chat with you *immensely,* and I hope you'll come by some evening when we can have a *quiet* dinner together." Rolloson patted Jim on the buttocks and plunged into his menagerie.

Jim found Shaw drunk and surrounded by sailors.

"I'm going home."

"But it's early. Come on, what you need is a drink."

"I'll call you up in a day or so." Jim departed. It was a relief for him to breathe the fresh air of the street.

Winter passed swiftly. Jim saw Shaw occasionally and Shaw was friendly and amusing and introduced him to a number of people who had money and nothing to do. There were many different homosexual worlds in New York, and each usually had some knowledge of the others. There was also the half-world where hetero- and homosexual mingled with a certain degree of frankness; this was particularly true of theatrical and literary groups. But in the highest society, the homosexual wore a stylized mask in order to move gracefully, and often convincingly, among admiring women who were attracted to him because his understanding was as great as his demands were few. Occasionally two homosexuals might meet in the great world. When they did, by a quick glance they acknowledged one another and, like amused conspirators, observed the effect each was having. It was a form of freemasonry.

From all over the country homosexuals had converged on New York. Here, among the indifferent millions, they could be as unnoticed by the enemy as they were known to one another. Yet for every one who lived openly with men, there were ten who married, had children, lived a discreet, ordinary life, only occasionally straying into bars or Turkish baths, particularly at five o'clock, that hour between office and home when the need for relief is particularly urgent. These masculine, rather tense men appealed to Jim, who disliked the other sort he met through Shaw. Yet he learned a great deal from the bold homosexuals. Like jazz musicians and dope addicts, they spoke in code. The words *fairy* and *pansy* were considered to be in bad taste. They preferred to say that a man was *gay*, while someone quite effeminate was a *queen*. As for those manly youths who offered themselves for seduction while proclaiming their heterosexuality, they were known as *trade*, since they usually wanted money. Trade was regarded with great suspicion; in fact, it was a part of the homosexual credo that this year's trade is next year's competition. Jim was thought to be trade by most of Shaw's friends, and inaccessible trade at that.

All during the winter Jim saw a good deal of the Rolloson world. Though he was repelled by the queens, he had no other society. Furtive encounters with young married men seldom led to anything. For a time, he hoped that if he saw enough of the queens, he might begin to like their society and be happy in it. But this was not possible, and so when Shaw went back on active duty, Jim dropped out of the gay world, preferring to haunt those bars where he could find young men like himself.

On an impulse one afternoon, Jim telephoned Maria Verlaine's hotel and to his surprise he found her in. She invited him to come to see her. Maria embraced him at the door. "You look so well!" She led him into the sitting room. Her eyes were luminous; she was vivacious; she laughed often. Then Jim noticed that her hands shook as she smoked her cigarette, and that she was ill at ease. He wondered why, but she gave him no clue. "Where have I been? Well, let me see. Everywhere. Nowhere. The summer in Maine. Then Jamaica. But New York is the center where I touch base between excursions."

"You haven't been happy, have you?" Jim was direct.

"What a question!" She laughed, eyes not meeting his. "It's hard to say *what* being happy is. Absence of pain? In that case, I have been happy. I suffer no pain. Feel nothing." But she mocked herself as she spoke.

"Then you still haven't got what you want?"

"No, I haven't. I live entirely on the surface, from day to day." She was suddenly grave.

"Will you ever find him?"

"I don't know. Perhaps not. I'm not young. I won't live forever. I simply go on. And wait."

"I wonder if any man wants the complete thing that you do. I don't think men are capable of so much feeling, that's why so many prefer one another to women." He was immediately sorry that he had said this. Yet he was convinced that it was the truth.

Maria laughed. "You don't leave us much hope, do you? One must be what one is. Besides, at times I have been very happy."

"Maybe we'd all be better off just having friends and forget about lovers."

Maria smiled. "That seems like such a waste, doesn't it?"

They talked then of other things until it was twilight and Jim got up to leave. Maria had told him that she was expecting a friend at five.

"I'll see you again. Soon," she said.

"Soon," said Jim. They did not embrace when he left.

Jim went straight to a Times Square bar frequented by soldiers and sailors. He studied the room carefully, like a general surveying the terrain of battle. Then he selected his objective: a tall Army lieutenant with broad shoulders, dark hair, blue eyes. Jim squeezed in beside him and ordered a drink. Jim's leg touched the lieutenant's leg, a hard muscular leg which returned the pressure.

"You in the service?" asked the lieutenant. His voice was slow, deep Far Western.

"Yeah, I was in the Army, too."

"What outfit?"

They exchanged information. The lieutenant had served with the infantry during the invasion of North Africa. He was now stationed in the South as an instructor.

"You live around here?"

Jim nodded. "I got a room downtown."

"I sure wish I had a place. I got to stay on a sofa with this married cousin."

"That sounds pretty uncomfortable."

"It sure is."

"You could," said Jim, as though he were thinking it over, "stay at my place. There's plenty of room."

The lieutenant said no, he couldn't do that; they had another drink together and then went home to bed.

II

IN THE SPRING, JIM returned to the courts. According to his partners, it might be ten years before the lot was built on; meanwhile, it was a gold mine and Jim worked hard, and he made money.

New York was full of servicemen, coming and going. Jim moved to a larger apartment, though still in the Village. He now knew a number of people but none well. It was easier to have sex with a man than to acquire a friend.

Jim saw Maria Verlaine once or twice, but, since it was obviously painful for her to be with him, he stopped telephoning her.

That summer Sullivan returned and Jim went to meet him at his club. They greeted each other in a gruff, offhand manner. Sullivan was thinner than Jim remembered and his sand-colored hair was beginning to go gray. He wore civilian clothes. "Yes, I'm through with being a correspondent." He grinned. "I quit before they fired me. I just don't have the vulgar touch, unlike my angel wife."

"Amelia?"

Sullivan nodded. "She's a great success. She started out by telling the *Ladies' Home Journal* what it was like to be a British housewife during the Blitz, and now she's graduated to the higher politics. Everyone quotes her. The Dark Ages continue." Sullivan ordered another drink for himself. "Have you seen Maria?"

"A few times. Not much. She's out of town."

"Too bad. I wanted to see her. You know she's almost the only woman I've ever really liked as a person. She's so un . . . pressing."

"I think she's all right now." Jim was tentative.

Sullivan waited.

"Interested in some man or other. I don't know who," Jim continued doggedly, not certain why he was lying except that he did not want to hurt Sullivan again.

"Well, that's nice for her. She deserves good luck." He changed the subject. "What about your business?"

Jim was proud to be able to tell him how well he was doing. Boasting to a friend is one of life's few certain pleasures.

"That's good news." Sullivan paused. "Are you alone; are you living alone?"

Jim nodded. "I just play the bars. I like strangers, I guess."

"It's better to have one person . . . isn't it?"

"Maybe for some people. But not for me," he lied. "Sometimes I never even know their names. Sometimes we never say more than a few words. It all happens so natural, so easy."

"Sounds lonely."

"Isn't everything?"

Sullivan sat back in his chair and looked about the old-fashioned bar with its dark heavy wood. Several club members sat drinking quietly at a corner table. "You've changed." Sullivan was casual.

"I know." Jim was as casual. "When you almost die, you change. When you've been a soldier, you change. When you get older, you change."

"You seem a little more . . . *definite*, now."

"About some things. But I still don't know how to get what I want."

Sullivan laughed. "Who does? Change is the nature of life."

"But that's not true," Jim continued, intent on his own thought.

"What?"

"There's someone I knew in Virginia. Someone I grew up with." It was the first time Jim had ever mentioned Bob to anyone. He stopped immediately.

"Who was he?"

"It was a long time ago." Jim said no more. But it gave him a sense of power to realize that he could one day recapture his past simply by going home. He made a vow. As soon as the work of the summer was done, he would go back to Virginia and find Bob, and complete what was begun that day by the river.

Jim was conscious that Sullivan had asked a question and was waiting for an answer. "What? I'm sorry."

"I said"—Sullivan was awkward—"that I was alone, too, and if you wanted to, we might . . . again."

Jim was flattered but not greatly moved. He responded amiably. Their affair was resumed. And since it was no longer of much importance to either of them, their life together was rather more pleasant than it had been the first time around.

In June, Paul's new novel was published and his publishers gave a cocktail party for him. The day was hot. Jim was bored and ill at ease, but Sullivan, immaculate in a new gabardine suit, was almost happy.

In the stifling room, the talk was loud as the flower of New York publishing got drunk together. Jim drifted from group to group, eyes smarting from cigarette smoke, puzzled by what conversation he did hear. "Henry James revival? It won't last. It's the British, you know. They're responsible. During air raids, people need to be comforted, so they read James and Trollope. Return to a safe golden self-contained world, with no bombs in it."

"I suppose there will be war novels. The real horror of war is the novels which are written about it. But don't expect anything good for at least a decade. I wouldn't publish a war book for the world. Harry Brown of course is an exception. John Hersey, too."

"Carson McCullers? Yes. And of course Faulkner. The Agrarians, yes. A lot of Southerners seem to be writing. Perhaps it was the Civil War. One must have a tragedy to have a literature. Also, Southerners are not forced so quickly into business. That makes a difference. And then they talk so awfully much."

"Is the *Partisan Review* really, truly Trotskyite?"

"The Jews can't write novels. No, I'm not anti-Semitic.

And Jews do make excellent critics. But they are not creative. It has something to do with Talmudic training. Of course Proust was a genius but he was half-French and all social climber."

"Henry Miller is almost as boring as Walt Whitman, and a good deal less talented."

"I adored *For Whom the Bell Tolls.* I read it twice. Obscenity of an obscenity but it was beautiful and good and true."

"Scott Fitzgerald? I don't think I know the name. Is he here? Does he write?"

A lean young man in need of a shave asked Jim if he was a writer and when Jim said no, the young man was relieved. "Too many writers," he mumbled. He was drunk.

"What do you think of Paul Sullivan?" Jim was curious to know. But he found the answer unfathomable. "I don't like Aldous Huxley either."

Across the room Sullivan was signing a book. Jim departed.

It was a busy summer. The war continued. Jim's work was hard but rewarding. He particularly liked Mr. Globe, who knew nothing about tennis. "I'm in this for the money, Jim," he said one day. "I used to have this secondhand shop and that closed in the Depression. And then I was a clerk until I got into this for the money. I say you can make money easy if you're in things for the money but you need a little help sometimes. You know why we let you buy in the business?"

Jim shook his head, though he knew.

"Because you're not in this just for the money. You like what you do and there's always got to be a few people who know something to help the ones who're in it for the money to make money."

That summer they made money, and Jim was happy.

When Maria Verlaine returned to New York that autumn, Jim and Sullivan visited her at the Harding. She was in good form, Jim thought, and told her so.

"I've been in Argentina."

"Is that an answer?" Sullivan laughed.

"I thought you were in Canada," said Jim.

"Yes, to both of you. I'll get you a drink. I thought we'd have dinner here in the room." Her movements were swift and graceful. "It's a very simple, a very familiar story. I met an Argentine in Canada. He invited me to visit him in Buenos Aires. I did."

"Was that wise?" Paul was oddly conventional.

"Dear Paul! He's a rich poet and quite indifferent to what people say. As a matter of fact, he told everyone I was a famous literary figure from Mexico and I was worshiped. It was delightful."

"And now?"

"I'm back, as you see, and we'll be here for the winter."

"We?" asked Jim.

"Yes, Carlos is here with me. But in a different suite. We must be hypocrites in New York. We don't want to corrupt the Anglo-Saxons."

"Is he published in America?" asked Paul.

She shook her head. "I don't think he's ever really written anything."

"But you said he was a poet."

"That doesn't mean he has to write poems, does it? Actually, he does nothing at all and that's his poetry, to do nothing, with imagination of course."

"Are we going to meet him?" asked Paul.

Maria was evasive. "Of course. But not today. Perhaps later. Now tell me about your new book."

Jim listened and wondered why he felt betrayed instead

of pleased for Maria, who seemed to have found what she had been searching for. But he was not pleased. He was furious with her and with himself for being unable to give her anything except a friendship and a candor she could get as easily from others quite as understanding as he. Yet he was hurt; it was as if she had indeed been a lover who had deserted him.

Dinner was brought them in the room, and Jim drank prewar Burgundy, hoping to get drunk, but his mind was too sharply focused in its outrage.

During dinner Paul described his London meeting with Amelia. Maria was not surprised. "I was afraid she would become an Amazon."

"Now don't blame it on me."

"Never! It was not your fault, not hers. It's just this terrible country."

"Terrible?" Jim was startled from his self-pity. He had never heard anyone be quite so vehement about God's country.

"Maria's a Nazi." Paul chuckled. "Or a Communist."

"The Russians are our allies." Maria was light. "But I'm not political. Just a woman. A rather hard thing to be in your country. Either I meet men who have been . . . wounded, or I meet those who think only of women as a kind of relief, rather like aspirin."

"Latents are lousy lovers." Paul grinned. He had never been impressed by Maria's hymns to Aphrodite.

"You are perfectly right." Maria chose to take him seriously. "Everything in this country is calculated to destroy both sexes. Men are told that their desires are dirty and unwanted. Women are told that they are goddesses and that men are fortunate to be able just to worship them at a distance. . . ."

"It's the fault of advertising," said Paul. "Since women buy the most things, the advertisers flatter them the most, tell them they have more taste than men, more sensitivity, more intelligence, even more physical strength because they live longer. The advertisers of course are men."

"Well, they have a lot to answer for." Maria was uncharacteristically grim.

"Are Europeans so much better?" asked Jim.

Maria shrugged. "At least the men know who and what they are, and that is the beginning of sanity."

Paul agreed. "Americans tend to play different roles, hoping that somehow they'll stumble on the right one."

Jim turned to Maria. "When the war is over, will you go back to Europe?"

"Yes. Forever!"

"With the Argentine?" Paul was amused.

"Who knows?" She smiled. She had never seemed quite so lovely to Jim. "I live in the present." She looked at Jim and because he saw affection in her eyes, he looked away, pondering the betrayal, cursing its cause.

III

SULLIVAN'S NEW BOOK WAS not a success. He wrote articles for magazines and wondered if he should try his luck in the theater. Jim found him easy to get along with. From time to time one or the other would bring home a stranger and neither was in the least jealous or envious. From Jim's standpoint it was an ideal relationship; only the intense experience with Bob could be more satisfactory than his life with Sullivan.

Jim saw Maria Verlaine occasionally; the Argentine was

never present. Their old intimacy continued, but he was aware, now more than ever, that it was not enough. He found it unbearable that she should be happy and that he was not the cause.

At New Year's Rolloson invited Jim and Sullivan to a party: "a congenial group, my dears, just a little gathering" of what turned out to be the same group that had been there at the time of Jim's first visit. Rolloson wore a light gray suit pulled in tightly at the waist, a mauve shirt gorgeously monogrammed, and a sea green crepe de chine ascot at his rosy throat. He greeted them at the door, smelling of violets.

"How lovely of you to come, Mr. Sullivan. May I call you Paul? Paul, there are loads of people here *dying* to meet you and I'm sure you'll find a lot of old friends, too. I think literally *everybody* is here, and I did so intend to have an *intimate* party. Ah, well." He thrust Sullivan at a group of literary-looking men, among whom was the gray-haired professor from City College. With Sullivan safely put aside, Rolly took Jim about the room, introducing him to various people, all the while chattering. "First Shaw and now Sullivan. Aren't you the one, though! How do you do it? Or should I say, *what* do you have?" He gave Jim a lightning grope. Jim shied away, irritated.

"It just happens that they're the only people I know."

"But *where* did you know them?"

"In Hollywood. Did you get your Papal thing, that decoration?"

Rolly frowned. "My dear, the Church is riddled with politics, literally riddled. As a matter of fact—don't repeat a word of this to *anyone*—I think I shall take up Vedanta. I've met the most wonderful swami. At least I think he's a swami. He's here tonight unless I forgot . . . no, I remem-

ber I saw him at the Van Vechtens' and I invited him . . . or
was that the prince? I've got the most wonderful Hindu
prince here, too. You'll just love him. He looks like Theda
Bara. *He's* here, I know, because I remember compliment-
ing him on his handsome turban. But I'm not so sure about
the swami. You know, he's got millions of dollars in rubies
and emeralds right here with him in New York—the prince,
I mean, not the swami. I don't think *he* has anything but
he's terribly high-*minded*. Read Gerald Heard if you don't
believe me. Where's Shaw now?"

"Who? Oh, Shaw. Well, I think he's back in Hollywood
by now. He's been discharged from the Navy, or so it said in
the papers."

"Papers? Don't you ever hear from him?"

"No, we don't write."

"What a pity! You know, he broke so many hearts when
he was here. Good evening Jack, Jimmy, Allen. Lovely of
you to come. I think he's terribly handsome—Shaw, I mean.
He has such an *air* about him." Rolly looked about the
room at his guests. Jim noticed that he was wearing makeup.
"It's very gay, don't you think so? Oh, here comes Sir Roger
Beaston, the perfect *camp*! Do excuse me." Rolly darted
across the room to meet a pale little man with yellow hair.

Jim found Sullivan at the center of a group of people, not
all literary. They were drinking champagne and talking
animatedly about a certain European king who had taken a
new boy who was supposed to be extraordinarily handsome
and charming, even if he *had* begun his career hustling in
Miami. Jim listened, no longer surprised at hearing revela-
tions about people he had never suspected before. At first
he had disbelieved all the stories on principle, but too often
they had proved to be true. Obviously the world was not
what it seemed. Anything might be true of anybody.

Jim ambled away. In the hall he found a telephone, cradled in a piece of driftwood. Without thinking he picked it up and telephoned Maria. She answered. He could hear music behind her voice and the sound of voices.

"Jim! Where are you?"

"At a dull party."

"Then come here!"

Maria wore an evening dress of silver and a red flower in her hair. Her eyes sparkled and she seemed drunk, although she never drank. She simply became charged with energy and enthusiasm when she was with those she liked. They embraced and she led him into her apartment. Maria introduced him to a dozen handsome couples, mostly European émigrés. Then she gave him champagne and they sat in front of the mock fireplace.

"Whose party did you desert for me?"

"A man named Rolloson."

She made a face. "I've known Rolly for twenty years. He's harmless, I suppose, but he alarms me. It's like seeing oneself in a distorted mirror."

"We only went . . . well, because we were asked to come." He felt awkward because she had not invited him originally to her party. Sensing this, she said, "You know why I didn't ask you?"

"Carlos?"

She nodded.

"Is he here now, in this room?"

"No, he's gone downstairs to order more champagne. It won't hurt you to see him, to meet him?"

"No, of course not. I'd like to."

Then the bells began to ring and over the radio came the noise from Times Square and everyone exclaimed, "Happy

New Year!" and Carlos returned and kissed Maria. "I was almost too late," he said. She turned to Jim. "This is Carlos, Jim."

They shook hands. "Happy New Year," said Carlos.

"Happy New Year," said Jim. In a few minutes he went home.

CHAPTER
10

I

IN THE SPRING SULLIVAN received an advance from a publisher to write a book about Africa. "And that means six months of traveling, all expenses paid. If I don't take it, you'll have to support me."

"Not if I can help it." Jim was guiltily pleased at the thought of living alone again.

"Funny thing about travel, once you start, it's hard to stop. Like being an alcoholic. I really want to go."

"So do I. But I've got work to do."

"And someone else to find." This was flat.

"I'm not exactly looking." Jim was sharp.

"I know." Contrition. "I'm sorry. Anyway, there is something wrong with two men living together, a man and a woman, too, for that matter. Unless they have children, it's pointless."

"We're too selfish, I suppose."

"And separate. Perhaps a good thing. I don't agree with Maria's high romantic view of love. We affect one another quite enough merely by existing. Whenever the stars cross, or is it comets? fragments pass briefly from one orbit to another. On rare occasions there is total collision, but most often the two simply continue without incident, neither losing more than a particle to the other, in passing."

So they separated, with a metaphor involving stars.

The next day, as if by further celestial design, there was a letter from Mrs. Willard, full of news.

"You remember Bob Ford, don't you?" she wrote. "He was such a friend of yours in school. Well, he's in the Merchant Marine now and he was home on leave for a few days last week. He asked after you and so did his wife. I don't know if I ever wrote you that he married Sally Mergendahl last year, and they have a baby. You know that job with the school is still open and if you want to come back . . ."

There it was. Bob had returned. But he was married. Not once had it occurred to Jim that Bob could ever in any way be different from the way he had been that day beside the river. Yet he must have changed. He had married Sally. Jim experienced a sudden panic. Was it possible that he had waited years for a reunion with a man who cared only for women? No. He rejected the thought. Bob was obviously bisexual, if only because no one could have been so perfect a lover on that unique occasion and then change entirely. Jim reassured himself, and because he wanted to believe that nothing had changed, nothing changed, in his mind. Meanwhile, he made plans to go back to Virginia as soon as summer ended and take up his life at the precise point where it had left off that green summer evening seven years before.

. . .

During the summer Shaw came to town for the premiere of someone else's picture and Jim met him in a restaurant where the food and service were bad but where many people who were famous came to look not only at one another but also at themselves in the mirrors which lined the dining room.

Jim was startled to find that Shaw was gray at the temples; he was moving with unusual dispatch into middle age.

"You're looking handsome, Jimmy," said Shaw, "really handsome, I must say. Of all my graduates, you're easily the best-looking."

"That's like winning the Davis Cup. Thanks." Jim smiled. "Who're you living with now?"

"Nobody. I was with a perfect son of a bitch, from Detroit, a diver, of all things—you know, Olympic Games stuff. He had a wonderful build but stupid! My God, I don't think I've ever known anybody so stupid. All he wanted to do was drink beer and sit up late in gay bars. I kicked him out. Anyway, he had a wife and two children so I really think I did the right thing, don't you? Nobody wants to break up a home. What have you been doing?"

"Working."

"Sullivan?"

"Gone to Africa."

"Hope they eat him." Shaw was sour. "He's such a pretentious bastard. I saw where his new book got bad notices. Not that critics mean a thing. When they pan my pictures I make money, and when they praise them we lose it. After all, entertainment is entertainment."

Jim noticed that everyone in the room was aware of Shaw, but for once Jim disliked the attention; particularly when he noticed several men he had met at Rolloson's party: each accompanied by a woman, for this was enemy territory.

"Are you making a picture?"

"No. It's hard to get the right roles nowadays. I'm sitting it out. The studio thinks the war is going to be over and they'll get the old stars back and to hell with us who've been selling the tickets for them. Well, they'll find out. Gable means nothing now."

Jim wondered if Shaw was finished. It was a harsh business, as everyone liked to say.

"They'll come back to me in time. But it'll be too late."

"Why?"

Shaw looked about him; then he whispered, "I'm quitting the movies, retiring."

"And do nothing?"

"Not quite. I'm going on the stage. I start rehearsing in September."

"That's wonderful."

"But tough. I've never been on a stage, but I've got to do it."

"How's your mother?"

"Still in Baltimore. It's a funny thing, she brags about me, of course, but sometimes I think she resents my success. Imagine a mother being competitive! I guess people are people, first. Anyway, she's happy about me being married."

"Married?"

Shaw nodded. "It's the studio's idea. They think too many people are catching on. Maybe they're right."

"Who's the girl?"

"Calla Petra. Hungarian actress. Kept by the head of the studio, lost a hundred thousand dollars one night gambling at Vegas. A real tramp. But I won't give her a penny. He'll have to. We've signed a prenuptial agreement, ironclad. No money from me. She's a dyke, anyway, and she needs the publicity as much as I do."

"Sounds real cozy."

"Sounds awful." Shaw groaned.

They saw each other often during the summer. The day Shaw's play opened, he announced that he was retiring from the screen; a week later the play closed, and Shaw went back to Hollywood. His wedding to Calla Petra was the most glittering of the season.

After Shaw left New York, Jim returned to the bar life. He particularly liked one Eighth Avenue bar where both men and women gathered and some of the men were available and some were not, which gave a certain excitement to negotiations. He most liked the innocents who would say the next morning, "Gee, I was sure drunk last night!" and pretend not to remember what had happened.

One heavy summer night, Jim stood at the bar nursing a beer, examining the inmates. He had almost settled on a young Marine with blue eyes and buck teeth when a voice behind him said, "Ain't you Willard?"

Jim looked around and saw a fat bald young sailor. "That's right, and you're . . . ?" He couldn't recall.

"Collins, Alaska. Remember?"

"Sure. Come on. Have a drink."

Collins squeezed in beside him at the bar. "I'm Navy now. I was a petty officer but I got busted."

"What happened?"

"I got pissed and told a commander off. My usual trouble. Were you in the service?"

"Army. I been out a year."

"What're you doing now?"

Jim told him.

"Coining money."

"Fair. You in town long?"

"No, we're sailing soon. This is my last liberty. Boy, you got a good deal, living here, with your own business. I wish I was in your shoes."

"What're you going to do when you get out?"

"Me? I'm a sailor. What else? I don't know anything else. Once I tried to work in this machine shop, but I couldn't stand being in one place so long, so I quit, left my wife, went back to sea."

"You're married?"

"Divorced. I knew her since I was a kid in school and she always wanted to marry me but I wouldn't until I got drunk one night and knocked her up and she said I'd *have* to marry her and so I did. We got a kid who lives with her, that's in Eugene, Oregon."

"Too bad." Jim tried to sound sympathetic.

"I guess some guys just aren't meant to be family men and I'm one of them. I got this chick in Seattle now who's panting to be married but I told her, I been stung once and I'm not going to get stung again. You married yet?"

"No," said Jim. "Not yet."

"You're smarter than me. But I'll bet you got a girl in New York?"

"Kind of." Jim was noncommittal.

Collins took a long swallow of his drink and said, "You know any girls around town?"

Jim shook his head. "Just one. You see, I've been working pretty hard and . . ."

"I know how it is. Say, where did you go after you skipped ship?"

"L.A."

"Man, that's *my* town! Wide open. Where all the chicks

want a good time, like us, and no talk about marrying or any of that shit. You ever see any movie stars?"

"Some."

"Like who?"

"Calla Petra."

"No kidding! She must be something the way she's stacked. You get to talk to her?"

"Oh, lots of times."

"No kidding! You bang her?"

"No, I just played tennis with her."

"I'd sure like to play tennis with her." Collins leered. "And that ain't all I'd like to play with her."

Jim ordered another beer. Usually he could keep the same beer going for an hour, but Collins made him nervous and he found himself actually drinking the beer, an unusual gesture.

"You like the Navy?"

Collins shrugged. "They don't know nothing about the sea, that's for sure. Wished I was back in the Merchant Marine."

"Why aren't you?"

"I was on land with my wife and I was going to be drafted. So to get out of the draft, I joined the Navy, because I didn't want to be in no Army where I had to walk."

As they drank together, Jim looked about the bar. The Marine had gone. There was no one else who appealed to him. At the opposite end of the bar an old man was trying to make a sailor who in turn was trying to make a soldier. It was very funny. Collins, perfectly unaware of the comedy, suddenly asked, "Hey, why did you leave the ship in such a hurry?"

It was a question Jim had been waiting for. He spoke slowly, simulating ease. "I wanted to see California and I didn't want to have to argue with the steward, so I just skipped out."

"I figured it was something like that." Collins finished his drink. "How come you left those girls in that apartment? That was one thing I never been able to figure out."

Jim shrugged. "I didn't like the one I had, that's all."

"Well, she was madder than hell, but you was smart to leave when you did."

"Why?"

"They both had clap. And I caught it and had a hell of a time getting cured." They both laughed and Collins told Jim about the man who had had clap twenty times and been cured every time except the first. At last they parted and Jim was relieved that Collins's liberty was almost over and they would not meet again.

II

ONE COLD DAY WHEN the winter sky was bitter orange and gray and a chill haze hung over the city, Jim went home for Christmas.

Mrs. Willard stood on the porch as her son came up the path to the house. He was startled at her appearance. White hair, untidy as always, face pale and lined; she had grown old while he was away. They embraced and she clung to him, holding him tight, saying nothing, only holding him. Then they went into the house, where, at least, nothing had changed. The parlor was as depressing as ever, despite a Christmas tree, glittering with small buzzing lights. Jim felt oddly displaced in time. He turned to his mother and they looked at one another without speaking, two strangers with a common memory.

"You've grown up, Jim," his mother said at last. "You've changed."

"We all do, I guess." He was inadequate.

"You look more like my side of the family. You don't look like your father anymore. You used to."

Jim saw in his mother's face his own features grown old and he was frightened at the thought of age and death.

"You haven't changed much," he lied.

She chuckled. "Oh, yes, I have. I'm an old woman now. But I don't mind. If you haven't got beauty in the first place, age makes you better-looking, they say, gives you character."

He looked at her face in the light of the Christmas tree and he agreed with her. She had improved with time. She had achieved a face of her own, something she had lacked before.

"Are you going to get married, son?" It was strange to be called *son* again.

"Someday."

"The older I get the more I think people should be married early. I sometimes think that the reason your father and I never got along as well as we should was because we married so late. You're just the right age to settle down."

"Perhaps."

"There're some nice girls growing up here. They'd make fine wives. You'll meet them while you're home. You should marry a nice girl here rather than one of those New York girls, not that it's any of my business." Jim smiled: New York people were not very well thought of in the South.

She asked him about his work and he told her about it. She was pleased. "I'm glad you're making money. Nobody in this family ever has before and it's about time somebody did. But money's not everything, is it? I mean sometimes marriage and settling down and enjoying life are more important, don't you think so?" Sooner or later she would suggest that he stay home for good.

"I don't know, Mother. I really haven't thought much about settling down yet. I've got a good business in New York and as long as it's good I better stay with it."

Sensing resistance, she changed the subject. "Your brother is a second lieutenant now. He's in the Air Force and he's going overseas any day. Why, I don't know, since the war's almost over, or so the papers say."

"Will he be here for Christmas?"

She nodded. "He's got a few days' leave. He's a very bright young man." Jim wondered if perhaps she disliked her younger son. His mother was definitely changed. Anything was possible.

"You're taking in boarders now?"

She had written him this news. "Just a couple, a man and wife. You'll meet them at dinner. Carrie and her husband are coming to dinner, too."

"How's my nephew?"

"Nice and fat." She paused. "I can't get over how you've changed," she said finally. They were silent. Jim idly kicked his suitcase and his mother said, "You'd better take your things up to your room."

"Which one?"

"Your old room."

"Does John stay there when he's on leave?"

"Yes. Nothing's changed. I try not to change anything if I can help it. I know that's maybe living too much in the past but I think the past was pretty nice, in some ways. I think maybe the future can be even nicer."

"You mean since Father died." Jim was blunt.

She nodded placidly. "Yes, since your father died. I always

believed if you make a bad bargain, you just have to keep it. But when it's over, there's no use pretending that it was the best thing that ever happened."

"Why did you marry him?"

"Lord, son, why does anyone marry anybody? If I ever knew why I married him, I've forgotten. Probably because he asked me. I wasn't in much demand. Now take your bag up and get ready for dinner."

Everyone was at table when Jim came into the dining room. His mother introduced him to the boarders; then he shook hands with his brother-in-law and kissed his sister. Carrie had grown stout. Her breasts and hips seemed ready to burst her clothes. Without makeup, she looked tired but good-humored, and obviously she was pleased with her husband, an amiable sort who did whatever she asked him to.

"Well, Mother, he's as beautiful as ever." Carrie looked at her brother admiringly. "He sure got all the looks in this family." Her laugh was like an explosion and only stopped when her husband told her what she wanted to hear: that she was beautiful, too.

During dinner, they spoke of Jim's work and whether or not it was profitable, and if he came home, as they all desired, could he do as well as he had done in New York? And of course Carrie asked the inevitable: "When are you going to get married, Jim?"

He shrugged. "When some girl asks me." Everyone laughed at that.

"You were always shy with the girls," said his sister, her mouth full. "You really ought to settle down. There's nothing like it, is there, dear?" Her husband agreed that there was nothing like it. Jim found the masquerade depressing. He tried to change the subject and failed.

"Jim will marry when he's ready to settle down," said his

mother tranquilly. "I think he's been wise not to have gotten married while he was traipsing around the world."

They talked of marriage, secure people whose lives followed a familiar pattern, the experience of one very much like that of the other. But when they tried to advise Jim, none suspected that their collective wisdom was of no use to him, that the pattern of his life was different from theirs. This fact made him sad, as well as annoyed at the never-ending masquerade. He was bored by his own necessary lies. How he longed to tell them exactly what he was! He wondered suddenly what would happen if every man like himself were to be natural and honest. Life would certainly be better for everyone in a world where sex was thought of as something natural and not fearsome, and men could love men naturally, in the way they were meant to, as well as to love women naturally, in the way they were meant to. But even as he sat at the table, pondering freedom, he knew that it was a dangerous thing to be an honest man; finally, he lacked the courage.

"By the way," said Carrie, "you knew Bob Ford married Sally Mergendahl, didn't you?"

"Mother wrote me. Where is he . . . where are they now?"

"She's living here with her family, and he's at sea, but I think he's due back in a few days. He'll be here for the Christmas party the Mergendahls are giving. You're invited. And they have the cutest baby girl, with dark red hair just like Bob's."

"Why, Jim, I would never have recognized you, so grown up and everything! Isn't he, dear?" Mrs. Mergendahl turned to Mr. Mergendahl and got his agreement. She continued, secure in her audience. "Well, he's a grown man now. They all are. Seems like only yesterday when you played in all those tennis tournaments at school. Now look at you! And all the other boys in the Army, married, and our own little girl a mother!"

Mr. Mergendahl winked at Jim. "You better let him go, Mother, so he can meet the young girls who are dying to meet him. Got a whole new crop of 'em, too." Jim excused himself and went into the crowded, old-fashioned living room. Carrie took him by the arm. "I'll introduce you around."

Many of the people he recognized; some he had known in school, others from the town. Everyone remembered him and they seemed genuinely glad he was back, recalling events that he had forgotten. As in a dream, he moved from group to group, toward a central point where he knew Bob must be.

Then he saw Sally Mergendahl—now Sally Ford—and he broke away from Carrie to talk to her. Sally was now a tall graceful woman with dark hair braided about her head. They shook hands warmly, each scrutinizing the other, looking for signs of change.

"Congratulations!" said Jim.

"On the baby? Or marrying Bob?"

"Both." Jim sounded blithe; yet she was his rival.

"That's sweet of you, Jim. Here, let's sit down. There's so much we have to catch up on." They sat on a horsehair sofa, their conversation broken regularly by newcomers who wanted to say hello to Jim.

"See how popular you are? Oh, you really ought to settle down here with the rest of us."

"You heard I wasn't going to?"

"Well, not exactly, but you know how everybody knows everybody else's business around here. We spend all our time prying, even though there's never anything very interesting going on. We all know each other too well."

"Where's Bob?"

She frowned. "Newport News, with his ship. He won't be in until tomorrow. When he does get here, why don't you have dinner with us, just the three of us?"

"I'd like to. Bob's a first mate now, isn't he?"

"Yes. But he's quitting when the war's over."

"How come? He loves the sea."

"But Daddy needs him in the insurance business, and everybody thinks Bob will make a wonderful salesman, and Daddy says that when he retires Bob can have the company."

"That'll be nice for him." Jim saw the kindly noose being dropped over Bob's unwilling shoulders. But were they unwilling? Could he have changed? It was possible.

"He's roamed around long enough. After all, there's just so much world to see and then where are you? Anyway, all his friends are here and he can have a good job. I think everything will be just grand for us. I can't wait for you to see the baby."

"Is Bob a good . . . father?"

"Well, he hasn't had much practice. At the moment he thinks a baby is something to play with until it starts to cry, when he wants to wring its neck. Then he says that I care more about the baby than I do about him, so I tell him that, after all, the baby *is* him, which it is."

"Does he understand that?"

"Well . . . yes, at times. You know how he is."

"I don't know if I do anymore."

"It *has* been a long time, hasn't it? And he is different. Of course he looks about the same. But he laughs a lot more than he used to. He was rather grim when he was a boy. And of course he was girl crazy then. He still gets letters from girls all over the world. He lets me read them and they're really pathetic. But I'm not jealous. I don't know why. I guess it's because he came back to me, when he didn't have to."

As she talked, Jim wondered if Bob had ever been attracted to men. From what she said—and what he suspected—it seemed unlikely, which meant that their experience had been unique. And that meant Bob had made love with him not out of a lust for the male but from affection. The fact that he now preferred women to men could only make their relationship all the more unusual and binding.

Jim did not deceive himself that his return would mean an end to Bob's marriage. Their boyhood dream of going to sea together was no longer practical. Too much had happened. Each was now part of the world. Yet there was no reason why the affair could not continue, particularly if he returned to Virginia and took the job at the high school. Proximity would do the rest. He wondered about the old slave cabin by the river. Was it still there?

Sally was still talking. "I don't like to be old-fashioned. And I really don't think I am. I believe a man should have lots of affairs with women before he settles down with one. I told my mother that and I thought she would explode. She says she never *will* be able to understand the younger generation."

"When do you think Bob will be out of the Merchant Marine?"

"When the war with Germany's over. So they say. Daddy has a friend in Washington who can fix it if there's any problem. Jim, would you get me some punch? I'm parched."

Jim crossed the crowded living room, smiling at all the people who wanted to talk to him. He was surprised that he was popular. If only they knew. At the punch bowl he found himself face to face with his brother.

John was tall and dark and he looked trim in his uniform. Jim disliked him as much as ever. He was astonishingly self-confident and everyone said that he was going "to make his mark" and he believed it, too. Politics was to be his career.

"What's up, Jim? It's been a long time." John's voice was rich and deep; he had been drinking too much, Jim noticed. They exchanged greetings and perfunctory compliments. Then John indicated Sally. "She's very nice, isn't she?"

"Yes. I like her."

"Shame Bob missed the party. You must be looking forward to seeing him again."

Jim wondered if John knew about him. His brother was shrewd and he obviously remembered how much Jim had seen of Bob when they were boys. But was that enough to make him suspicious? Or did it take one to know one? Jim smiled to himself at the thought. It often ran in families, they said. He gave his brother a speculative look.

"What's the matter?"

"Oh . . . nothing. I was just thinking. Well, I better get Sally her punch."

"Don't get caught under any mistletoe," said John in his deep mocking voice.

"What took you so long?" Sally was pleasant. "I was afraid you'd deserted me."

"No, I was just talking to my brother."

"It must be wonderful to be back," said Sally Ford.

The day of the dinner came and Jim was nervous. He snapped at his mother when she told him that he should wear an overcoat, and he lost his temper with his brother, whose fountain pen in a bureau drawer had leaked all over his last white shirt. After a satisfactory row with John, Jim left the house.

With pounding heart, Jim knocked on the door of the Mergendahl house. Bob opened it.

In a daze, Jim shook hands, hardly able to speak.

"How the hell are you?" Bob was saying. "Come on in and have a drink." He led Jim into the living room. "The old folks are out for dinner and Sally's upstairs doing something or other to the baby. Gosh, but it's good to see you. You look the same. How've you been?"

Jim's voice was hoarse when he finally spoke. "Fine. I've been just fine. You look good, too." And Bob did.

Jim was surprised that he had forgotten what Bob looked like. He had always thought his mental picture of him as accurate, but apparently his memory was emotional, not literal. He had forgotten how dark Bob's red hair was, and that he had freckles and that his mouth curved up at the corners and that his eyes were as blue as the Arctic Sea. Only the body was as he recalled it, long and slim and heavy in the chest. He looked good in uniform.

They sat in front of the fireplace and Bob forgot to get the drinks. He too was taking inventory. Did he remember everything?

"You just disappeared," said Bob at last.

"Me? You! I wrote you and wrote you but you were never where I sent the letters."

"Well, I was on the move a lot, like you."

"We both were."

"Hey, you met Sally yet? Since you been back?"

"At the Christmas party."

"That's right. I forgot. She invited you for tonight."

"She's a wonderful girl." Jim wanted to establish that at the beginning.

"I'll say! I'm glad you like each other. You didn't really know her back at school, did you?"

"No. But I remember you used to go around with her even then."

"So when are *you* getting married?" That question again.

"Not for a while."

"You think you might come back here to live?"

Jim nodded. "I think I might. You'll be living here, won't you?"

"So they tell me. It looks like I'm going into the insurance business, with Sally's father. Everybody thinks I'll be good at it."

"But you'd rather be at sea?"

Bob moved uneasily in his chair, crossing and uncrossing his long legs. "Well, I've been at sea almost ten years now and I've made a place for myself. It won't be easy changing to land. But if Sally wants it . . ."

"She wants it. But you don't?"

"Yes, I do." Bob was defiant, even petulant. Then he shifted. "Well, maybe not."

"I don't see what's wrong with being a sailor, especially since you're making good money. Why wouldn't Sally like that?"

"You know women. They want you where they can look at you all the time. She says she doesn't feel she's married when I'm gone."

"So you'll settle here."

Bob nodded gloomily. "I'll settle here. Oh, I'll get used to it, all right. And I like the idea of being a family man."

"So I guess I'll be moving back, maybe."

"That'd be swell, just like it used to be. Funny, I knew all kinds of girls here but I never did know any of the guys very well, except you. It'd be nice having at least one buddy in town. To play tennis with."

"Yes."

"But you're too good for me. You're a pro and I haven't

played for years. But it sure would be nice to play again."
He was nostalgic and Jim felt an instant of triumph. Bob
would return to him, as easily, as naturally as he had gone
with him the first time.

"We had some good times when we were kids," said Bob
dreamily, looking into the fire. Jim looked, too. Yes, this
was the way it had been: fire and the mood of firelight. It
was going to happen again. He was certain of that.

"We had a good time." Jim vowed he would not mention
the cabin first.

"I wish sometimes that we had gone to the university
together. The sea was probably a mistake, though fun. You
only went because I did, didn't you?"

"That was one of the reasons."

"Do you think I . . . we made a mistake?"

Jim studied the fire. "No," he said finally. "We did what
we were meant to do. I think it was natural for you to be a
sailor and me to be a tennis player. We were never like the
other people around here. We weren't housebroken. We
got away. They hate that. Only now we're coming back."

Bob smiled. "You're the only person who understands
why I had to go to sea. Yes, we did do the right thing. But
now is it right to come back? *Can* you come back to living
in the same house, with the same people day after day? Is it
possible?"

"I don't know. I just don't know. Of course it's easier for
me. I can teach tennis here but you certainly can't be a
seaman on land. I guess you ought to do what you feel you
have to do." Jim spoke with something else in mind.

Bob sighed. "I can't make up my mind."

Jim wanted to help but he could not. "Wait," he said.
"Wait until something happens. Something always does."

They were silent before the fire. Jim could hear the
muffled sound of a baby crying upstairs, Bob's baby.

"How's your father?" asked Jim finally.

"Dead. Last month."

"Did you see him before he died?"

"No."

"Didn't he want to see you?"

"He was crazy, they say. He'd been crazy for the last five years. It wouldn't have done any good. Besides, I didn't want to see him. I didn't care if he died or not." Bob was matter of fact, all bitterness gone. "You got a girl, Jim?" he asked suddenly.

"No."

"That sounds like you. Still shy with women. But you ought to find yourself one. Changing around wears a guy out."

"Maybe I'll find somebody when I come back here."

"And then we'll be two married men. Gosh, we never thought of ourselves being that old, did we?"

"No, never."

"And in a few years we'll be middle-aged and then old and then dead."

"Morbid, isn't it?" They both laughed. Then Sally came into the room.

"Hello, Jim."

"How's the baby?" asked Bob.

"Asleep. Thank God! Bob! you haven't given Jim a drink."

"Sorry. What do you want?"

"Nothing, thanks."

"Then we'll go in to dinner," said Sally.

The dinner was good and they talked of the townspeople and their families and about the war in Germany. In the intimacy of the family dining room, Jim was completely at peace. He would not have to make a move. The thing was happening of its own accord. Soon Bob would be with him.

And, sure enough, it was Bob who maneuvered their lives into conjunction. "I think I'll be up in New York during May. Let's get together then and have one last fling before the old prison doors shut!"

Sally smiled indulgently.

Jim said, "That'd be wonderful. I'll give you my address and you call me as soon as you get to town."

III

THAT SPRING JIM TRIED to exhaust himself in work so that he would not think of Bob. But it was difficult. Nor did matters improve when May came and went and there was no word from Bob. Finally he wrote Sally, who told him that Bob was still at sea and wasn't it just awful? But at least the war was finally over and the Merchant Marine could not keep him much longer.

A year late Bob appeared at Jim's apartment. They shook hands as though they had seen each other only the day before.

"Swell place you got." Bob looked approvingly at the apartment. "Won't you hate to give this up for Virginia?"

"I haven't given it up yet." Jim smiled.

Bob sat in a chair and stretched his long legs. He still wore a uniform. "Swell place," he murmured again.

"When are you getting out?"

Bob frowned. "Damned if I know. I have a chance now to get master's papers. That's something at my age, and I hate turning it down."

"But Sally?"

"That's just it . . . but Sally. I don't know what I'm going to do. She wants me home."

"And you don't want to go?"

"No."

"Well, don't. It's your life. If you're happy at sea, stay there. Sally isn't the first woman to marry a sailor."

Bob nodded. "That's what I said to her but she's so damned set on my staying put. Her family, too. Sometimes I think it's her family more than her. She seems happy enough with the baby. I don't think she'd miss *me* all that much."

"You'll have to make up your own mind," said Jim, who preferred Bob to be at sea. They would be separated for long periods, but then he would be separated from Sally too. "How about dinner?"

They went to an Italian restaurant and drank a flask of Chianti between them. Soon the circle would close.

"Where do you want to go?" asked Jim when they had finished.

"I don't care. Anyplace I can get drunk."

"There's a bar I know."

They walked through the warm night air to a bar where men hunted men. Jim was curious to see how Bob would react. They took a table and ordered whiskey. There were enough women present to disguise to the casual observer the nature of the place.

Bob looked about him. "Not too many women here," he said at last.

"No, not so many. Do you want one?"

Bob laughed. "Hey, I'm a married man. Remember?"

"That's why I brought you here. No temptation."

They drank and talked. Their old intimacy was resumed, which meant that Bob did most of the talking, while Jim listened and waited. Bob talked of life at sea, and Jim watched the comedy at the bar. An Air Force pilot would squeeze in beside a sailor. They would talk, legs pressed together. Then they would leave, faces flushed, eyes bright.

Youth drawn to youth, unlike the sad old men, eager but
unattractive, who tried first one boy, then another; inured
to rebuff, they searched always for that exceptional type
which liked old men, or money.

"That's sort of a queer-looking crowd," said Bob
suddenly, motioning to the bar.

"Just New York." Jim was a little frightened. Suppose
Bob panicked? Had he overplayed his hand?

"I guess that *is* New York. Full of queers. They seem to
be everywhere now. Even onboard ship. Once I had a skip-
per who was, but he never bothered me. He liked niggers. I
guess it takes all kinds. Want another drink?" Bob ordered
another round.

Jim was relieved at Bob's display of tolerance.

"You know any women?" asked Bob finally. "I mean just
to talk to. Sally'd kill me if I ever did anything else. That's
why, believe it or not, I've only shacked up with one other
woman since I married, which is a pretty good record. No,
I just mean girls for company."

"Yes. But they'd be all tied up this late."

"I guess it's pretty short notice. Of course I know a few
numbers. Maybe I ought to call them."

Jim thought it wise to make no protest.

"Let's go over to my hotel." Bob stood up. "I'll call from
there." They paid for their drinks and left the bar. Envious
eyes watched them depart.

They crossed Times Square. Hot windless night. Lights
flashing. People everywhere. The mood jubilant, postwar.
Bob's hotel was on a side street. They went straight to his
room. As Jim stepped inside, he was suddenly overwhelmed
by Bob's physical reality. Clothes were strewn about the
floor, a damp towel hung from the bathroom door, the bed
was a tangle of sheets, and over the harsh odor of disinfec-

tant and dust, Jim was aware of Bob's own smell, to him erotic.

"Kind of a mess," said Bob mechanically. "I'm not very neat. Sally always gets mad at the way I throw things around." He went to the telephone and placed several calls. No one was home. Finally, he put the receiver down and grinned. "I guess I was meant to be good tonight. So let's get drunk. Might as well be drunk as the way we are." He took a bottle from his suitcase and poured two drinks. "Here's how." He drank his shot at a gulp. Jim merely tasted the whiskey. He had to keep clearheaded.

As they drank beneath the harsh unshaded light of a single electric bulb, the room became stifling with summer heat. They took off their shirts. Bob's body was still muscular and strong, the skin smooth and white, not freckled, unlike most redheads.

The duet began pianissimo.

"You remember the old slave cabin?" asked Jim.

"Down by the river? Sure."

"We had a lot of fun there."

"I'll say. There was a pond, too, wasn't there? Where we swam?"

Jim nodded. "Remember the last time we were there?"

"No, I don't think I do."

Could he have forgotten? Impossible. "Sure you remember. The weekend before you went North. Right after you graduated."

Bob nodded. "Yeah, I kind of remember." He frowned. "We . . . we fooled around quite a bit, didn't we?"

Yes, he remembered. Now it would happen. "Yes. Kind of fun, wasn't it?"

Bob chuckled.

"I guess we were just a couple of little queers at heart."

"Did you ever . . . well, do *that* again, with anybody
else?"

"Any other guy? Hell, no. Did you?"

"No."

"Let's have another drink."

Soon they were both drunk and Bob said that he was
sleepy. Jim said that he was, too, and that he had better go
home, but Bob insisted that he spend the night with him.
They threw their clothes on the floor. Wearing only shorts,
they tumbled onto the unmade bed. Bob lay sprawled on
his back, arm across his face, apparently unconscious. Jim
stared at him: was he really asleep? Boldly, Jim put his hand
on Bob's chest. The skin was as smooth as he remembered.
Lightly he touched the stray coppery hairs which grew
below the deep-set navel. Then, carefully, like a surgeon
performing a delicate operation, he unbuttoned Bob's
shorts. Bob stirred, but did not wake, as Jim opened wide
the shorts to reveal thick blond pubic hair from which
sprouted the pale quarry. Slowly his hand closed around
Bob's sex. He held him for what seemed a long time. Held
him, until he looked up to find that the other was awake
and watching him. Jim's heart stopped for a full beat.

"What the fuck are you doing?" The voice was hard. Jim
could not speak. Obviously the world was ending. His hand
remained frozen where it was. Bob pushed him. But he
could not move.

"Let go of me, you queer."

Plainly a nightmare, Jim decided. None of this could be
happening. But when Bob struck him hard in the face, the
pain recalled him. Jim drew back. Bob leapt to his feet and
stood, swaying drunkenly, fumbling with buttons. "Now
will you get the hell out of here?"

Jim touched his face where he had been struck. His head
still rang from the blow. Was he bleeding?

"Get out, you hear me?" Bob moved toward him, menacingly, fist ready. Suddenly, overwhelmed equally by rage and desire, Jim threw himself at Bob. They grappled. They fell across the bed. Bob was strong but Jim was stronger. Grunting and grasping, they twisted and turned, struck out with arms, legs, but Bob was no match for Jim and, at the end, he lay facedown on the bed, arm bent behind him, sweating and groaning. Jim looked down at the helpless body, wanting to do murder. Deliberately he twisted the arm he held. Bob cried out. Jim was excited at the other's pain. What to do? Jim frowned. Drink made concentration difficult. He looked at the heaving body beneath him, the broad back, ripped shorts, long muscled legs. One final humiliation: with his free hand, Jim pulled down the shorts, revealing white, hard, hairless buttocks. "Jesus," Bob whispered. "Don't. Don't."

Finished, Jim lay on the still body, breathing hard, drained of emotion, conscious that the thing was done, the circle completed, and finished.

At last Jim sat up. Bob did not stir. He remained face-down, clutching the pillow to his face while Jim dressed. Then Jim crossed to the bed and looked down at the body he had loved with such single-mindedness for so many years. Was this all? He put his hand on Bob's sweaty shoulder. Bob shied away from him: fear? disgust? It made no difference now. Jim touched the pillow. It was wet. Tears? Good. Without a word, Jim went to the door and opened it. He looked back once more at Bob, then he turned out the light and shut the door behind him. He left the hotel, not caring where he went. For a long time he walked aimlessly, until at last he came to one of the many bars where men looked for men. He entered, prepared to drink until the dream was completely over.

CHAPTER

11

IT WAS LATE, VERY late. He had begun to forget again. Only by great effort had he been able to remember what had happened to him. Now he felt no sorrow. Nothing. Bob was finished and that was the end of that.

He called to the bartender. The man came over. "Another one?"

Jim nodded. His head felt strangely heavy. If he nodded too hard it might fall off. "Another one."

Then a little man with a dark mustache and quick-moving eyes came up. "May I sit down? Could I buy you a drink?"

"If you want to."

"It's certainly been warm weather, hasn't it? I'm from Detroit myself. Where are you from?"

"I forgot."

"Oh, I'm sorry if I'm intruding. I didn't mean to pry."

"All right." Jim was glad to have someone sitting opposite him. Someone who liked to talk. The sound of words was peaceful if one didn't attend to their meaning.

"Isn't this a big town, though? I've been here maybe two weeks and still don't feel I've seen a thing. It's much bigger than Detroit and there seems to be everything here. I've never seen so much of *everything*. Do you work here, if I'm not being too personal?"

"Yes." Jim wondered how long it would take the waiter to bring him his drink. He could make no contact with reality or even unreality until he had another drink. Suddenly there was a glass in front of him. Jim took a swallow: cold, hot, cold, hot. That's the way it should be. He looked at the small man. He had a feeling that a question had been asked, for the little man sat looking at him. He wondered if he had heard the question and forgotten it or whether he had never heard it at all. "You say something?"

"I only asked if you lived here in town."

"Yes." Now the next question. The catechism never changed.

"Do you live with your family?"

"No."

"Then you're not married?"

"No." Jim decided that he would play for a while. Lead the man on and then pretend anger and frighten him. It would be amusing.

"Well, neither am I. You know, I've always said it's a lot cheaper to buy milk than keep a cow." He paused as though expecting either laughter or agreement. He got neither. "I'll bet they've got some good-looking girls around here." The little man winked at Jim. "I'll bet you have a girl here."

"I don't have a girl." Jim offered hope.

"Now that's strange, a young fellow like you. Were you in the Army?"

"Yes," said Jim, and he took another swallow. Everything was pleasant and warm inside his stomach. But his knees felt odd, disconnected. Then the little man put his foot next to his. Deliberately Jim picked up his own foot and, after a long thoughtful minute, brought it down hard on the little man's foot.

"Ouch!"

"Sorry." Jim was happy that he had caused pain.

"You've certainly had a lot to drink."

"How can you tell?"

"I mean . . . well, you seem to have had a lot to drink." The little man paused uneasily. "By the way," he said, "I've got a bottle of real Scotch up in my room at the hotel. If you'd care to . . ."

"I like it here."

"I just thought maybe you might like to come up for a little while, that's all. We could have a friendly chat and it's certainly much nicer there than it is here."

Jim glared at him. "You think I'm trade maybe? You think maybe I'll go home with a little fag like you, maybe? Or do you want to get me drunk in case I'm straight, and screw me?"

His brief acquaintance stood up. "Now, really, I think you've gone far enough. If you weren't drunk you wouldn't say such things to me. Such a thought never entered my mind. If you'll excuse me . . ." The man went away and Jim started to laugh. He laughed loudly for several moments and then he stopped, wanting to cry or sob or shout. But the bartender put an end to that. He came over and told him that the bar was closing and it was time to go.

Unsteadily, Jim walked out into the damp air of early

morning. It was very dark. There were no stars; no moon; only streetlamps shining in the blackness.

Then he was sober.

The edges of the buildings became sharp and clear. He knew exactly where he was and who he was and there was nothing left to do but continue, as though nothing had happened. But even as he made this vow, he recalled fire-light and heard again the river's roar. No vision ended except in something vivid and new, and there was nothing new for him. The lover and brother was gone, replaced by a memory of bruised flesh, tangled sheets, violence. Panicky, he contemplated flight. He would return to sea. Change his name, memories, life. He turned west toward the water-front. Yes, he would ship out again and travel in strange countries and meet new people. Begin again.

Then suddenly he was on the docks, with silent ships all about him. The air was cool. The morning near. At his feet the waters rose and fell slowly, gently, like the breathing of some vast monster. Once more he stood beside a river, aware at last that the purpose of rivers is to flow into the sea. Nothing that ever was changes. Yet nothing that is can ever be the same as what went before. Fascinated, he watched the water shifting dark and cold against the stony island. Soon he would move on.

SEVEN
EARLY STORIES

▼

For Howard Austen

From too much liberty, my Lucio, liberty:
As surfeit is the father of much fast,
So every scope by the immoderate use
Turns to restraint. Our natures do pursue,
Like rats that ravin down their proper bane,
A thirsty evil, and when we drink we die.

Measure for Measure
WILLIAM SHAKESPEARE

THREE STRATAGEMS

▼

I

I arrived in Key West a few days ago with enough money to last me a week. I seldom need more than a week although this time I have gone more slowly than usual, with a greater attention to detail, ignoring the young, concentrating my attention on the older men, the ones with loose dimpled figures and bad teeth. Watching these men, talking to them, I find it hard to believe that in other days they have made fortunes, created families, and often as not done noble deeds, for with us they have neither shame nor virtue. Naturally it has occurred to me that they might be wise and still not care and then again there's the possibility that they enjoy their own degradation; if that's true, I pity them, and the game's more sinister than one might at first suppose.

The beach at Key West begins at the south end of the main street and continues for a hundred yards or so, edged

by palm trees and beach houses and ending, finally, in a pink
cement building, a restaurant with an outdoor terrace. On
the beach, near this terrace, I met Mr. Royal my first day.

The sky was a startling, unclouded blue and a warm
south wind rattled the fronds of the palm trees. The day was
brilliant and for a moment I was sad and wanted to go and
hide from the sun, from the white-framed images of the sea
. . . associations all of childhood, of that contented season
of sand forts and seaweed and pink shells. Every summer of
my childhood was spent upon a similar beach with my
family; a family which has since broken up: some dead,
some married, and others, myself among them, gone into
exile in the foreign cities. . . .

"I see you haven't been here long." His voice was pleasant yet with a suggestion, oh, just the faintest suggestion, of
something else. I was immediately alert. I told him I'd only
just arrived and he introduced himself. He told me he was
George Royal and he insisted too quickly that I call him
George; so far I haven't. I told him my name was Michael.

"Could tell you haven't been here very long," he continued and we talked about the whiteness of my skin until at
last he asked me if I'd ever been an athlete (that traditional
question both wistful and vicious) and of course I said, yes.
I told him I'd played football at Princeton, which was not
true; I went to Princeton for one year but I played no games.
The lie impressed him, however. "Let's have a drink," he
said.

Together we crossed the hot white beach, picking our
way between gaudily striped umbrellas, crumpled towels,
bottles of lotion, and empty beer cans, all reminiscent once
again of my childhood. Reminiscent and yet, in one particular, different: the people have changed; they have become
hostile or at best they are dangerously impersonal. I realize,
certainly, that perhaps *I* am so changed that I see them now

as they really are, as they were all along . . . though of course it's always possible that what I first saw as a child was the reality and what I see now a private distortion, but one way or the other I see what I see: hostility and danger. I know that my attitude is extreme, and that there are some innocuous people in the world and, more important, there are many fools and for *that* happy abundance at least I give thanks.

The fools were in possession of the beach today. They sat watchfully beneath umbrellas, admiring the cold and radiant angels who could, they believed, exorcise the graceless shadow of the years and with firm flesh re-create youth and the sense of permanency, or its illusion. I suppose by now I know the hearts of the fools almost as well as I know my own and sometimes I am frightened when I watch their sad courtship of the treacherous angels for I see in them my own eventual fall from beloved angel to deluded monster. I too shall be old. I shuddered as I stepped over the ruined towers of a sand castle: yes, the beach was changed; I wonder, will it change again one day?

In a mood of odd unreality, I followed the wide, sundarkened figure of Mr. Royal to the cement terrace, where, at tables, beneath umbrellas, men and women in bathing suits sat in the vivid light and drank rum. In the bar, a jukebox played loudly and I am sure that no one heard what I could hear behind the music, the soft noise of the tide going out.

These people were well-to-do. Most of them were middle-aged and I thought that the men and women, except for the one obvious difference, looked exactly alike: wide-hipped, sagging breasts, thin arms and legs, blue-veined and weak. But the women wore paint and moved with more assurance. They laughed, drank heavily, told dirty jokes, gambled, and all in all endured the bright days gallantly. The men did not. They were quieter, more watchful; they were waiting.

Mr. Royal was looking at me expectantly. We had stopped walking and he had asked me a question which I'd not heard. Since we were standing beside an empty table, I made a guess, nodded, and smiled and, having guessed correctly, we sat down. He ordered rum for both of us.

"I come down here every year," said Mr. Royal, rubbing his small brown hands together: a yellow diamond glittered, a spray of bright sparks, of sunlight shattered. I looked away. He folded his hands and continued talking, looking over my shoulder at a party of sailors who had just arrived on the beach and were pulling off their clothes with shouts and giggles, like schoolgirls on an outing. I don't like sailors very much . . . not because they are, in a sense, competitors . . . but because their lack of direction, of a considered plan, their fundamental irresponsibility, tend to make them unsatisfactory playmates and, if taken seriously, they are often downright dangerous . . . in other words, they waste their beauty and their advantages.

I have often thought half-seriously that when I am old and hors de combat I should like to start some sort of school for young men, a school where I would teach them how to make the most of certain situations which otherwise, due to inexperience and vanity, they badly mismanage. They are usually too truculent, too unbending. But then I suppose that if one of them had sense enough to come to me for lessons he'd be quite clever enough to conduct his own affairs without advice.

"The main business is in Newton but I have another store in Belmont," said Mr. Royal, his eyes coming to focus on me again as he made this point.

"That sounds pretty interesting," I said. At first one shouldn't talk too much for talk reveals character and unless one is simple and artless and appealingly boyish, it's best not to talk at all, to remain silent and smiling, enigmatic, waiting for the proper moment to assume the character of the other's dream. It takes a good deal of experience and intuition to do this, for to be successful one must have some native power of divination to begin with, an ability to identify oneself correctly without engagement; it's not easy.

As Mr. Royal talked, I kept my eyes on the sea beyond him; I watched the solemn variations of gulls against blue and, as I did, I remembered that I'd seen no birds on this island and I wondered why there were none. Had they all been blown away by some hurricane? Or had there never been birds here? I watched the gulls and listened carefully, awaiting some sign, some omen. I have been cheated several times at the last minute, undergoing a singular martyrdom which, unlike the classic ones, persists without hope of relief and has, on more than one occasion, wrecked my plans. I have a feeling, however, that this time everything will go well; I've proceeded slowly and I am sure of Mr. Royal, if not of myself, for I suffer from the disease of visionaries without, sad to say, the compensating vision.

"I used to have a cottage here when Mrs. Royal was alive but when she died I sold it and now I just take a few rooms at the Casa Rosada. You know it, don't you? Nice place. I like the manager, an old friend of mine."

Three points: Mrs. Royal, her death, the rooms at the Casa Rosada . . . no, four points: the friendly manager. The fourth point gave meaning to the other three.

I looked at Mr. Royal. His eyes I noticed were dark and oriental-looking with black, shiny irises set in yellow whites and, about the irises, pale circles like rings of smoke indicated age.

"I walked by there this morning, on my way to the beach," I said.

"But you haven't been inside?"

"No, like I said I only got here today."

"That's right. You've only just arrived."

"I haven't looked about yet." I took a swallow of the rum. The sun was hot and there was no wind. I was uncomfortable and I wished I was in the green water swimming, or back in my room. Mr. Royal asked me where I was staying. He nodded when I told him.

"A nice place," he said, implying he knew a thing or two about nice places. "But you really ought to stay at the Casa Rosada; that's the only place to stay in this town, the only place."

I gestured and grinned, demonstrating without words that I could not afford an expensive hotel but that, even so, it made little difference to me, to one well-born. He was most tactful; he smiled shyly, showing a set of pretty white teeth with well-defined gums, pink and translucent; a fleck of tobacco on an incisor gave a certain authenticity to this cunning but rather formal craftsmanship.

Before we could speak further, more frankly, a man with long blond-silver hair came over to our table. "Hello, George," he said. His body was thin; through sunburned skin the rib cage showed, like an emaciated Christus carved with morbid detail in some Bavarian forest while, beneath the taut skin of his chest, pulled drum-tight over the bones, I could see the regular twitchings of his heart.

"Sit down, sit down," said Mr. Royal. "Haven't seen you anywhere today. How'd you make out last night? Here, meet my friend. He's a Princeton boy, just down from college, on vacation. He's a football player, too." And so I was introduced to Joe.

"I did pretty well," said Joe, glancing at me curiously. "I'm tired today." His face was so tanned I could not tell if he were young or not, sick or well.

"Joe here is a painter," said Mr. Royal, drawing us together with a puppeteer's authority.

"I'm tired," repeated Joe, blinking in the light. I noticed that his lips were trembling. "Could I have a drink?" More rum was brought. I had now begun to sweat and I felt better. I'd had no breakfast and the rum was having a familiar, a pleasant effect.

"I wanted to paint this morning," said Joe.

"Why didn't you?" asked Mr. Royal, looking at the beach, his attention wandering: two boys were wrestling nearby. He blinked several times and then, before Joe could answer, he stood up vaguely and said, "I'll be right back, got to make a phone call."

"How long've you known him?" asked Joe, watching Mr. Royal's distracted progress across the terrace.

"I only got in town today. I met him today."

White upon dark brown, his eyebrows curved. "Good work," said Joe, grinning. His face gleamed with sweat and his lips no longer trembled.

"What do you mean?"

"How do you like him?"

"I just met him. He seems all right."

"What did he tell you?"

"One store is in Belmont and the other is in Newton."

"Then you know everything. Have you met Hilda yet? No? Well, she is the other one. I got to get another drink. Be right back."

"Yes, I know."

Joe had been gone only a moment when Mr. Royal returned.

"Pleasant fellow, Joe, I like him . . . but then I like everybody. I never saw a man I didn't like," said Mr. Royal.

"That's a good way to be." I suppose during the last few years I've learned every neutral, every noncommittal remark there is.

"I think so. Life's too short, you know, and then there is a really swell group down here. You'll meet them all . . . kind of free-living, of course . . . if you get what I mean. Anything goes . . . that sort of thing. I hope you don't mind . . . that sort of thing, I mean."

"I don't mind anything," I said, unfurling suddenly like a Jolly Roger, declaring bravely my own intended piracy in these rich waters. He was noticeably pleased, ready to be boarded and scuttled.

"You're so wise," he exclaimed admiringly. "Life's too short not to enjoy every minute of it." He paused. "By the way, why don't you drop by the Casa Rosada this evening and have dinner with me? Might be fun and . . ." His voice became an incoherent blur of cozy, ingenuous goodfellowship.

"I think I can," I said slowly. I looked up and saw Joe approaching us.

"Ah," said Joe, sitting down. "Wrestlers!" We all looked at the two young sailors wrestling on the beach, their white bodies streaked with red where the sand had burned them. "Do you like to wrestle?" asked Joe, turning to me. I said no, and Mr. Royal, impervious to malice, repeated that I was a football player. "I can see that," said Joe, playing with two straws. He was going to say more when I asked Mr. Royal why there were no birds on this island, except for a few pelicans and the gulls out to sea.

II

I have always preferred the Casa Rosada to the other hotels in Florida, or anywhere, for that matter, simply because it's the best hotel in Key West and Key West remains my favorite place in all the world. I came here for the first time the winter before I was married. Until then I had always gone to Daytona Beach but, on the advice of a close friend, I came on down and I must say it was worth it. Fortunately, my wife liked it too and until she died we spent every winter here. The island of course was much different in those days. There were fewer Cubans, for one thing, and the palm trees, as I remember, were straighter, unbent by hurricanes.

Shortly after the war Mrs. Royal died in our house. I sold it immediately afterward. I can't think, offhand, of a better place to die: a clear day with a south wind and the sun shining . . . what could be better? But of course she was in pain and that's always terrible. It must be a frightful sensation to know that one will not recover, that the pain will go on worsening until at last, like falling from some great height, one dies. I should live twenty more years, at least, barring accidents: touch wood. In any case if the fear should become unbearable I can always take up Christian Science or something like that. The worst thing of all, of course, is the realization that one will never be young again, like Michael. I can no longer remember what it was like to wake up in the morning without a burning sensation below my heart, without aching joints; although having all my teeth pulled did help the arthritis. I am sure he noticed them on the beach today. He looked rather closely at me once but then I imagine that everyone sees they are false. I suppose I'll get used to them in time.

. . .

While I dressed that first night I wondered if he would be on time, if he would come at all. My hands trembled as I tied my tie, a dark red one, very discreet, not loud at all for I knew, instinctively, that he was special, not like the rest of the trade around here. I also made up my mind not to be too hearty. With him I would be subdued but responsive, moving slowly and with careful gestures, rather as though I were dealing with a strange dog, the kind that doesn't bark. We all have, I suppose, a certain ideal, a ghost we've dreamed of but never met. From the beginning Michael corresponded to that inner dream of mine.

As I went down in the elevator at five-thirty, half an hour early (there was just a chance he might already have arrived and gone to the bar), I reminded myself that I was, after all, a man of the world and that there was no reason to be too impressed by this young man. But I was. I could not help it.

I have always enjoyed the terrace of the Casa Rosada. The view of the sea beyond the palms is first-rate in the early evening. Behind me the lights of the hotel were being turned on and white-coated waiters moved up and down the brick terrace, attending to the guests who sat about, drinking quietly. And there it was above the palms like a bead of silver: star bright star light first star I've seen tonight . . . oh, the same thing, the same wish, always the same thing.

"Shall I bring you something, sir?"

"Yes, a martini. I'll have it here." I sat down at a table. Michael had not arrived yet: I could see the bar through an open French window and there was no one there. Everyone was outside in the cool air. I was wondering if perhaps he'd left a message for me at the desk when I was diverted by the arrival of Joe and Hilda.

"Hi, George, I'm dog-tired. Do you mind if we sit down?

I've been all over town with Joe, pub-crawling. We can't do things like that at our age, can we?"

Hilda is sixty-five. At thirty-five she became a widow and at thirty-seven she made a fortune on Wall Street; as far as I know she still has every penny she ever made for she seldom picks up a check except of course when she is with one of her court of extremely sissy young men; they are transients for the most part and so much alike they seem interchangeable. Joe has been a figure at court for some time now.

While Hilda talked of her day I gave orders to the waiter, smiled at Joe, and looked at my watch: it was five-forty-five. Fifteen minutes to go. I concentrated on Hilda. She wore bright colors tonight, yellow and green, and her hard dark face glowed. She looked like one of the more bitter of the Old Testament prophets. I have known her for twenty years, and, until my wife died, we were most discreet with one another; since then, however, we've let our hair down, as the saying goes, and the hairpins flew in all directions when we did. As I suspected, she had known everything for some time and I, certainly, had always known of her own activities for, by a not unusual though sad coincidence, our interests often overlapped and we were, and are, more rivals than friends, more enemies than allies. Nevertheless, I feel a kind of affection for her. We have survived the same wars and we have known the same years and when we look at one another we alone can see the true face behind the wrinkles, the firm line of the jaw beneath loose skin.

"And Joe thinks he's terribly attractive. What's his name?"

Whose name? Five minutes to six. "Michael. He's from Princeton."

"Watch out! There's always something wrong when they pull that college business. It means they're out for big game."

"And you think that I'm in season?"

"Yes, and I see you mounted right now." They roared with laughter while I smiled, not bothering to defend him. Why should I? Hilda always suspects the worse of everyone and though she's seldom disappointed, I must say I think she's wrong about *him*: he is different . . . whether for good or bad, however, I'm not able to determine, even now. I look for the best in everyone, myself, and on the surface he is dignified, apparently well-educated, and he has been around. He has no money, which is always fortunate for me: it's no worse to be loved for one's money than to be loved for something as spurious and impermanent as beauty. One must be practical and the thing to bear in mind, I've found, is not *why* one receives certain attentions but the attentions themselves. There are of course times when it is a most desperate business to realize one's only attraction is solvency, never to experience that tenuous response, that identification which, if all goes well, becomes love, or so they say. I wouldn't know although for a minute or two at a time in my youth I knew what it must be like. Ah, Michael. It was six o'clock.

"Are you waiting for someone, George? You keep looking at your watch."

I nodded and Joe smirked unpleasantly; fortunately I was not asked to elaborate, for Hilda had begun a familiar chant. "All morning I walked along the beach among the beauties," she intoned in her resonant strong voice, a voice more suited for denunciation than for idle talk. "And I found I loved them all. Isn't that tragic? It gives me such a pang when I remember that I am over fifty and that there's no time for them all!" She chuckled darkly, Jeremiah among the cacti. "But I get along, don't I, Joe? I do my best."

"I'll say," said Joe admiringly and I wondered, as I often have before, why they are always drawn to this sort of woman: did just such a woman take the shears to them in their youth?

"Today I watched one dressing on the highway, behind some rocks. Joe and I were bicycling and we'd stopped for a second where the road bends, just beyond where the boats are. I've never seen such beauty, never! I wanted to weep."

"Or do something else?" I suggested mildly. Hilda is always too vehement and her stories embarrass me for they are all like this one, voyeur stories. She shook her head, however: the goddess with the shears triumphant . . . or, perhaps, a sickle would be more in keeping, more Greek.

"No, not that," said Hilda rather sharply. "I didn't feel like that at all."

" 'There was a boy: ye know him well, ye cliffs and islands of Winander?' "

"Is that a poem?" asked Hilda.

"Yes, that's a poem," said Joe. "Look, George, there he is, the boy himself."

"Is he like the boy in the poem?" asked Hilda, squinting nearsightedly.

"No, dear, the boy in the poem died at twelve. Come, let's go. Maybe we'll see you later."

I nodded. "Yes, of course, later." Joe led the reluctant Hilda away before Michael arrived.

"I hope I'm not late."

"No, you're right on time. Would you like a little something?" A little something was brought us.

"You look flushed tonight."

"I was burned a bit: too much sun for the first day."

We talked about the beach, the day, the latitude, the weather, and the cause of storms. I noticed again how well-bred he looked. He wore a tweed jacket and slacks and a dark knit tie; I was glad I hadn't worn an open shirt . . . so far all my intuitions had been correct and, finally, when I told him that dinner had been set up in my suite, he was not surprised; he remarked it was nice to dine quietly.

My living room is quite large, on a corner, with tall windows and a view of the hotel gardens and the sea.

"It's lovely on a moonlit night," I said, indicating the dark gardens and the darker sea, vague by starlight.

Then I lit the candles on the table and turned out the overhead light. One gets rather like a vain woman as one grows older: morbidly aware of lighting, of the clash of colors, of shadows and unbecoming angles. A great actress once told me that the best light for an aging woman was a full direct one which made no shadow. To benefit from that sort of lighting, however, the bone structure must be very good; if it's not, too much light is disastrous. I'm afraid *I* must do with candlelight. And "bone structure" always makes me think of a grinning skull.

During dinner we discussed, among other things, that what the Floridians call lobsters aren't lobsters at all.

"I remember taking a trip in a sailboat up to Maine, to a place called Camden, where we lived on lobster mostly. We used to broil them on the beach, with seaweed and drift-wood." He talked freely, his first wariness gone. In some detail he told me about his life. And as I listened I was, as usual, perplexed, for my first impulse is to believe every-thing I am told and my first reaction is to believe nothing; consequently, I am doomed forever to dangle between belief and doubt.

His father was a lawyer in Washington. His father is dead. Graduating from Princeton four years ago, Michael went to

Europe and took a job with American Express. He quit his job and came home; he has no job now. He wants to travel. He is engaged to be married. As I listened, I drank wine and, after a while, I became a little confused and I was forced, now and then, to ask him to repeat himself, to clarify certain obscurities. Yet all the time while he was telling me he was to be married, I recognized response and, bold with wine, I discussed his love with him, hovering closer and closer to that revelation which, with an inner trembling, I hardly dared anticipate. "She's only nineteen but when she finishes college next year we're going to be married. Naturally there's the problem of money but I'm sure something will turn up by then; I mean it always does. Her father's one of the biggest attorneys in Washington so I'm pretty sure he can fix me up. I think I might like to go into the Foreign Service one day."

"I'm sure you'd be very good at it." As he talked, I noticed his face was scarlet and his eyes were brilliant in the uneven light of the candles; then, suddenly watching him, I realized that here before me was the beloved figure materialized, no longer a figure to haunt the night or an elusive expression remarked for a moment in a stranger's face, a similarity which, upon examination, would vanish, like a gold doubloon found on a beach in a dream and gone upon awakening, the sensation of it clutched tightly in one's palm, lingering to mock the day. I knew, as I watched him, that all of the others had been, at best, facsimiles: although, of course, I received them for I am realistic, I think, and I had never actually hoped to encounter my ghost except in that feverish period between waking and sleeping when degrading and marvelous visions compensated me for the days of nothing, for the days of approximation. Fascinated, I watched him across the table.

III

Now since that night with Michael I have learned a lot about epilepsy. It seems that Julius Caesar and Mohammed, among other celebrities, were epileptics, and until quite recently there wasn't much to be done about their malady. According to a medical encyclopedia I found in the manager's office, it has something to do with an overcharge of nervous electricity in the body, a bit like a short circuit, I suppose. Each case varies of course although there are only two main types: the "grand sickness" and the "little sickness." The "little" isn't particularly bothersome: one drifts off for a second or two and that's that. The "grand," however, is more serious and very frightening to watch, as I found out.

At first I thought he'd had a stroke. A great many of my contemporaries are dying of strokes these days and whenever anyone faints or is sick my impulse is to call a doctor who will, if it's not too late, inject adrenaline. But then I realized that he was too young to have a stroke and for one insane moment I thought that he was putting on a show for me. I stood over him, helpless, wondering what to do but then, when he began to choke, I called the house physician for the boy sounded as if he were strangling to death, which, by the way, could very easily have happened for epileptics have been known to swallow their tongues and die.

The doctor, thank heavens, was very calm and he gave me a spoon to hold Michael's tongue in place while he administered a shot of some sort. In a moment the convulsions stopped and he lay quietly on the floor among the broken dishes (the table had turned over in the confusion). After a minute or two, the doctor got him to his feet. "I'll put him up for the night downstairs," he said. "I expect he'll be all right now." I helped the doctor with him as far as the elevator. Michael was conscious by now but too exhausted to speak intelligibly.

So, for the time at least, the ghost is vanished, obscured and distorted by that figure among the shattered dishes upon the floor. I haven't talked to him since although I did see him earlier today on the beach. We did not speak. He was with an old friend of mine, a man named Jim Howard. Jim is a grand fellow about my age or, perhaps, a little older. At one time he was very wealthy, but he hasn't got a dime now. They seem to be getting on very well, however, and it will be interesting to see what happens.

1950

THE ROBIN

▼

At nine I was very much tougher than I am now. I enjoyed all sorts of unpleasant things: other people's fights (I was early an audience), automobile accidents, stories of suicides, and one particular peep show at an amusement park near Washington where, through holes in a tall imitation stockade, one could observe an immense plaster elephant goring a plaster Hindu. But best of all I liked the magazines sold in drugstores, magazines with pictures of young women entangled in giant spiderwebs on their covers and, inside, pictures of the most exciting scenes of torture. I used to sit for hours on the tile floor of a certain drugstore and carefully examine all the magazines. Sometimes I even read the stories. I liked very much the directness, the naturalness of the style. I had long since become bored with the colorless fourth-grade reader and I hadn't yet discovered the Oz books, which, at ten, helped bring to an end my tough period.

In the fourth grade I had one close friend: a thin pale-haired, pale-eyed, pale-skinned boy whose name was Oliver. I suppose he has since grown up to become a lawyer or a realtor. Most boys from our group in Washington become either one or the other. To my knowledge none has become anything interesting like a movie star or an artist though a number have been divorced once or twice and several show signs of alcoholism.

Oliver loved violence and torture as much as I did and he was almost as tough as I was, and that was very tough indeed. Our conversation was a mixture of gangster and nursery talk. We organized secret societies, encouraged gang warfare at school, and sometimes we even went to grocery stores and stole.

All of us had elaborate dreamworlds. I can guess now what Oliver's was probably like; as for my own, I can remember it vividly: the climate, the scenery, and even various plots of my imaginary life when I was nine and depraved. I know that I had great physical strength and lived in a castle, wore a cloak and very often a crown. I was not only stronger than the other nine-year-olds, I was stronger than grown men too: that deep-voiced, rough-faced alien race. And in my world I invented all sorts of tortures for my enemies. The most constant and satisfactory victim was the fourth-grade teacher, a shapeless woman with bobbed hair, gray and untidy, and a dreadful nose that was thin with a pink, translucent membrane. She almost always had a cold and a fever blister on her upper lip. She was stern, malicious, and, in moments of anger, an arm-twister. She received her reward in *my* world.

About the middle of October, shortly after my ninth birthday, on a clear bright afternoon, Oliver and I saw the robin.

First, let me say that our school was what they call a

country day school, several miles from the city. The school had broad, well-kept lawns where less imaginative boys resolved their violence in football and fighting. Oliver and I seldom joined them; we were contemptuous of such simplicity. Sometimes of course we were forced to play and when that happened I'd pick a part of the field where nothing much was going to disturb me and here I would stand and daydream. In these dreams I was the actor, never the audience.

The school occupied a large country home in Virginia some ten minutes by bus from Washington. The house was what we, in that part of the South, call Georgian, though actually it was a gracious late-nineteenth-century muddle of styles: red-brick, with tall windows on the ground floor and, inside, a curving staircase. There were high ceilings, cracks in the walls, and everywhere the sense of many generations of Southern feudal life . . . actually, the house was the relic of a rich Northerner who, having come South with a Republican administration, built this house, fancied himself a squire, willed it to his children, died, and they, true heirs, promptly sold it.

But to us, to the sixty pupils, the grounds were far more interesting than the house: smooth lawns curved from the house to the line of woods where between thin dark trees bright in autumn with the colors of the fool, one could just make out the brown slow Potomac River, which roared continuously, sealike and far away, a sad lonely sound.

The day of the robin was like any other day of autumn. I caught the school bus in front of my house and talked to Oliver as we drove to school. I haven't the faintest idea what our conversations were like when we were nine.

I suppose that Oliver and I discussed our teachers, the other boys, and the peculiarities of our parents. I do remember once turning to him and saying solemnly (this was a year later, after my mother's divorce), "We've gone through hell and high water together, my mother and I." By the time I was ten I do recall that I talked almost entirely in sonorous clichés and I had begun to demonstrate an alarming talent for didactic poetry. But at nine on this sharp October day, I was more colorful, more desperate, and certainly more original than I've ever been since.

We arrived at the school, entered the classroom, and here recollection ceases. I suppose something must have happened in those classes but I cannot remember what. During the twelve years I spent in schools, I remember almost nothing that happened in the classrooms. I have only one clear memory of my first six years in school. For some reason we built a model of the Appian Way on a card table. And since, among my numerous talents, I had a gift for modeling, I was invited to make the human figures for the Appian Way. They were beautiful, splendid Romans, happily proportioned, clothed in togas of the whitest tissue paper. Everyone was impressed. But unfortunately they would not stand up and the teacher, that thin-lipped terrible woman, squashed all the legs down to fat columns, completely ruining their classic symmetry. When I discovered this, I gave such a demonstration of outraged sensibility that she was forced to call in the principal, who tried to soothe me by suggesting that with longer togas no one would notice the legs and, besides, I should remember I had been commissioned to do figures (very admirable they were, too) which could stand up in chariots.

Aside from this one episode I remember nothing of those six years in the classroom but I do remember the afternoons out of doors, especially this particular afternoon in October. The sky was pale and the clouds were heavy and white and they moved so slowly, changed shape so slowly that one was quite hypnotized watching the castles become elephants, and the elephants swans, and the swans teachers. On this day Oliver and I unobtrusively slipped away from our game-playing classmates.

We walked quickly to the edge of the lawn, where a wooded cliff dropped nearly vertical to the river below. Here, hidden from the others by a row of evergreens, the river beneath us, we sat comfortably on the ground and I began to make up a story while Oliver listened eagerly, flatteringly.

It was he who noticed the robin first. "Look," he said, interrupting me, pointing at something in the grass. I looked and saw the bird. One of its wings had been broken and it fluttered feebly, still trying to fly. We went over and examined it carefully. Both wary of touching it for fear of an unexpected sting or bite or sinister germs.

"What'll we do?" I asked. One always had to do something about everything that came one's way.

Oliver shook his head; he was no use. "It's hurt bad." We watched the robin as it fluttered in a small circle on the ground. It made a small piping sound.

"Maybe we ought to take it home." But Oliver shook his head: "It's hurt too bad. It's not going to live long and anyway we wouldn't know what to do."

"Maybe we should get some witch hazel or something," I suggested; but since this meant approaching the authorities of the school, we decided against doctoring.

I have forgotten whose idea it was first. I hope it was Oliver's. We decided the robin must be put out of its misery; it must be killed. The decision was made easily enough but when it came to the actual execution we were not only uninventive but frightened.

Thinking of a picture I had seen of Saint Stephen, I suggested the robin be killed with a stone. Oliver took the first stone (I'm almost certain it was Oliver) and dropped it directly on top of the creature, but the stone fell to one side and the bird, still alive, fluttered its wings and gasped. Then *I* took a stone and dropped it and now, horribly, there was blood on the wings that fluttered in the bright air, that fanned the dead leaves on the ground.

Then we grew frightened and angry and we took more stones and threw them as hard as we could at the robin, anything to stop the motion of those wings and the sound of pain. The stones fell one upon another until the bird was covered except for its head . . . and still it was not dead: it would not die. Oliver (I am sure now it was Oliver) finally took a very large stone and smashed it as hard as he could on top of the pyramid, finishing the tomb. Then we listened carefully: there were no more sounds from within.

We stood for a long time, not looking at one another, the pile of stones between us. No sound but the distant shouts of our classmates playing on the lawn. The sun shone brilliantly; nothing had changed in the world but suddenly, without a word and at the same moment, we both began to cry.

1948

A MOMENT OF GREEN LAUREL

▼

My absentmindedness seems to have only to do with places;
I have little difficulty in recalling either names or faces and
I usually get to appointments on time although, even in
this, I've become a bit careless lately.

Last week I arrived for an appointment not only at the
wrong hour but at the wrong address, a somewhat disturb-
ing experience. But now the Treasury Building was straight
ahead and I was relieved that I could still find my way so
easily through the streets of Washington, a city I'd not lived
in for many years.

Thousands of people crowded the sidewalks, for this was
Inauguration Day and all were eager to watch the new president ride in state to the Capitol for the inaugural ceremony. The crowd was in a gala mood though the sky was
dull, promising rain.

With difficulty, I crossed the street to Willard's Hotel. At
the curb I was stopped by the pillar of some Midwestern

community, a pillar now wreathed in alcohol. In one hand he carried a small banner and in the other a bottle of whiskey with no label (I did not then guess the significance of this detail). "Things going change in this town. Take it from me." Gracefully, I took it from him and, avoiding the bottle proffered, moved as quickly as I could to the hotel entrance, and went inside.

Willard's has two lobbies: one on the F Street side and one on the Pennsylvania Avenue side, parallel to it; the lobbies are connected by a carpeted, mirrored, marbled corridor, where I was able to find a sofa to sit on that I might comfortably observe the hundreds of people who now passed from street to avenue, all hurrying, all delighted.

Out of loyalty to our elegant Washington society, I decided these noisy passersby must be from out of town: thick businessmen with rimless glasses, Southwesterners with Stetsons and boots, New York ladies in silver fox . . . all political and all, for one reason or another, well-pleased with the new president. Some carried whiskey flasks, I noticed: the first I'd seen since I was a child and Prohibition was, in theory, law. Now, apparently, flasks had come back, as the advertisers would say.

A political personage sat down beside me, his right buttock, a bony one, glancing off my thigh as he squeezed a place for himself on the sofa. He wiggled about, making more room for himself. I scowled, unnoticed.

"You sure get mighty tired standing around," he said at large, stumbling on truth. I agreed. He was Southern and he talked to me and from time to time I nodded with discreet half-attention, pretending to look for someone, hoping to excuse thereby my inattention. I even squinted nearsightedly as though a familiar face had suddenly appeared among strangers. Then one did. I saw my grand-

father, white-haired and ruddy-faced, approach with a
political colleague. He was smiling at something the other
was saying. As they passed in front of me, I heard my
grandfather say: "He knows as well as you do what I think
of gold . . ."

By the time I'd got to my feet, upsetting the Southerner,
the ghost was gone. My stomach contracted nervously; it
had been someone else, of course. I have always had a habit
of looking for likenesses. I will often notice a young boy
and think: why there's so-and-so! he was in school with me.
Then I'd recall that my acquaintance would be a grown
man by now, no longer fourteen. Nevertheless, disturbed
by this vision of my dead grandfather, I got to my feet and
went into the Pennsylvania Avenue lobby. Here, among
palms and portraits of the new president, more politicians
and hangers-on celebrated the great moment with noise,
whiskey, and thunderous goodwill.

"Come on up," said a woman beside me. She was blond,
well dressed, a little drunk, and in a friendly mood. "We've
got a suite upstairs. We're having a party. We're going to
watch the parade. . . . Emily!" And Emily joined us too and
we all went up in the elevator together.

The suite was two rooms hired weeks in advance for this
day. The party had already begun: thirty or forty men and
women, young officeholders for the most part, although
there were, I soon discovered, some native Washingtonians
too: parasitic figures to the business of government.

I was given a glass of champagne and left alone. My hostess and Emily, arm in arm, broke through circle after circle,
penetrating to the center of the party. I could hear their
laughter long after they had vanished.

I moved slowly about the room. It was like a dance and I
wished for the sake of appearances that I had found a partner. There is something profoundly negative about stand-

ing alone on the outskirts of a group where everyone has arrived, like animals in a Noah's Ark, in twos, and departs in twos. I thought of floods.

I finished the champagne, wondering idly why I knew no one in the room. The city's changed, I thought; I'd been away ten years, a long time. I crossed the room to the window and looked out at the parade, which had begun. Loudspeakers at each street corner made the inaugural address audible but unintelligible. Something had gone wrong with the synchronization and the loudspeakers echoed one another dismally, confusing the presidential voice. The woman next to me remarked, "It doesn't make any sense."

I looked at her and saw to my surprise that it was my mother who had spoken. "What're you doing here?" I asked.

"What am I . . . ?" She looked puzzled. "Dorothy . . . you know Dorothy, don't you? asked . . ." There was too much noise and I didn't hear the rest of this sentence.

"But I thought you were going to stay home today?" She looked at me oddly and I realized she hadn't heard me. Conversation was now impossible. People shoved us, gave us drinks, greeted her enthusiastically. As I watched her I wondered, as I often do, at all the people she knows. It was apparent that during the many years I have been away from Washington, a whole new group had come to town and she knew them all.

"How long've you been here?" she asked brightly.

"I got here just a few minutes ago."

"No, I mean how long . . ." But a large cavalry officer came between us. Isolated by his enormous, uniformed back, I looked out the window.

The sky was pale. Night loitered behind the dome of the Capitol, where the president, with unusual resonance for him, had just finished his address. Below my window, soldiers were marching and the mob which lined both sides of the avenue murmured at their ordered progress.

"How do you like it?" my mother asked, pitching her voice above the noise of the room; the cavalry officer had gone.

"Just like all the others we've seen."

"I meant Washington."

I paused. We had been through this so many times before. "Well, you know what I think. . . ."

"I know . . . ?"

"I meant it's just as dull as it always was." Then I thought she said: "How long did you live here before?" But since there was now so much confusion in the room I was not positive. I cleared my throat; men separated us. She was looking, I thought, extremely handsome. I hadn't seen her look so fine in years.

But now something unusual was happening outside. The noise of the crowd increased its volume like a radio being turned up or like an approaching earthquake, which, in earthquake countries, can always be heard minutes in advance: a distant rumbling as the ground ripples in ever-widening circles from the disturbed center. Responding to this urgent sound, the people in the room pushed against the windows and looked out just as the president passed beneath us in an open car. He lifted his top hat and waved it. Then he was gone and the shouting died away.

"Are you going back to the house?" I asked, turning to my mother. We were together again, circled by Air Corps officers.

She frowned vaguely. "I suppose I'll see you later . . . sometime," she added, and before I could answer, a squad of women, wearing paper hats and blowing horns, divided the room with the fury of their passage, and I took that wise moment to leave the party, narrowly avoiding the gift of a paper hat.

I wondered, as I walked back to the hotel, why my mother had been at that party. I realize that she knows a good many people nowadays that I don't know: people who've come to town in the years I have been away, traveling farther and further from Washington, without regret or longing, always conscious, however, that nostalgia for place may yet occur in time. My family is a sentimental one and more and more I tend to believe in the heredity of behavior. I shall probably be very moved one day at the thought of spring (or autumn) in Rock Creek Park, where most of my childhood was spent, in a gray stone house on a hill, bordered by a steep lawn, by maple and oak trees, among hills evenly crossed by the rock-littered, iron-brown Rock Creek, whose bright course winds through those green woods.

As I walked, I contemplated the election and the inauguration, which meant much less to me than I publicly pretended. I have a conviction that individuals have little to do with state affairs, that governments are essentially filing systems which in time break down for lack of cabinet space, clerks, typewriters, paper, and, perhaps, faith in order. More and more I find it difficult to take public matters seriously: a definite schizoid tendency, as a psychologist friend of mine would say, placing me figuratively in a gray rubber sack, where, cut off from the world outside, I might regard with neither pleasure nor dismay the interior of my private realm, complacent at having escaped so neatly, so thoroughly.

I was now on the outskirts of Rock Creek Park. Obeying an impulse, I turned into the Park and walked down to Broad Branch Road, past Pierce's Mill . . . named for that good president who gave Hawthorne a consulate.

As I walked, day ended. The planet Venus, a circle of silver in a green sky, pierced the edge of the evening while the wintry woods darkened about me and in the stillness the regular sound of my footsteps striking the pavement was like the rhythmic beating of a giant stone heart.

At last I came to the hill where, at the top of a serpentine drive, our old house stood, a solid gray house, owned now by strangers. I was about to continue on, when a young boy crossed the road, coming from the creek.

He was half-grown with silver-blond hair and dark eyes. In his arms he carried several branches of laurel. When he saw me, he stopped. Then, magically, the streetlamps went on, ending twilight, shadowing our faces.

"You live up there?"

"Yes." His voice was light, not yet changed. He moved the green branches from one arm to the other, tentatively, as though undecided whether to stay and talk or to go home. "It's my grandfather's house."

"Have you lived there long?"

"Most of my life. You know my grandfather?"

I said I did not. "But I used to live in that house, too . . . when I was about your age. *My* grandfather built it thirty years ago."

"No, I don't think so. *Mine* built it a long time ago: when I was born."

I smiled, not questioning this. "How old are you?" I asked.

"Twelve," he said, embarrassed he was not older. In the unshaded white light, his hair glittered like metal.

Then I asked the traditional questions about school: adults and children meet always as foreigners with a limited common vocabulary and mutual distrust. I should have liked to talk to him as an equal, I thought: my eyes on the green only, not on silver or on brown skin. There was a directness about him which is rare among children, who usually are not only careful but often downright political in their dealings with the larger people. I asked questions by rote: "What do you like best in school?"

"Reading. My grandfather has a big library . . ."

"In the attic," I said, remembering my own childhood.

"Yes, in the attic," he said, wonderingly. "How did you know?"

"We kept books there, too, thousands of them."

"So do we. I like the history ones."

"And the Arabian Nights."

He looked surprised. "Yes. How did you know?"

I nodded, looking at him directly for the first time: a square brown face between silver hair and green laurel, a beardless, smooth face, uncomplicated by lines or dry skin or broken veins or by character, which, once formed, like a poison in the blood, corrupts the face. The streetlamp was directly overhead revealing the familiar skull. We looked at one another and I knew I should say something, ask yet another question but I could not and so we stood until at last, to stop this silence, I repeated: "Do you like school?"

"No. You live in Washington?"

"I used to . . . when I lived up there." I indicated the hill. "Before the war."

"That was a long time ago," said the boy, frowning, and time, I remembered, depends on how old one is: ten years, nothing to me now, was all his life.

"Yes, a long time ago."

He shifted his weight from one foot to the other. "Where do you live?"

"In New York . . . sometimes. Have you been there?"

"Oh, yes. I don't like it."

I smiled, remembering as a child the prejudice Washington people had for New York. "What are you going to do with these?" I asked, touching a branch of laurel. "Make wreaths the way the Romans did?" I remembered an illustrated Victorian edition of Livy in which all the heroes wore Apollo's laurel.

He looked at me with surprise; then he smiled. "Yes, I do that sometimes."

Nothing has changed, I thought, and the terror began.

"I have to go," he said, stepping out of the circle of electric light.

"Yes, it's time for dinner."

From the top of the hill a woman's voice called a name which made us both start.

"I have to go," he said again. "Good-bye."

"Good-bye."

I watched him as he clambered straight up the hill and across the lawn, not following the paved driveway. I continued to watch until the front door opened and he stepped into the yellow light. Then, as I walked away, down the road between the dark evening hills, I wondered if I should ever recall an old encounter with a stranger who had asked me odd questions about our house, and about the green laurel which I carried in my arms.

1949

THE ZENNER TROPHY

▼

I

"I understand that Sawyer left early this morning, before anyone had a chance to talk with him, before the faculty met." The Principal was appropriately grave.

"That's correct, sir," said Mr. Beckman. "And according to his adviser he left most of his clothes behind," he added, as though by a very close examination of all detail he might somehow avoid the crisis. He had been at the School less than a year, and although he'd faced any number of trying situations at other schools he was by no means prepared to handle a disaster as vast as this one.

Fortunately, the Principal was a rock. In twenty years he had become the School or rather the School had been reshaped in his own image, to the delight of everyone except the faculty old guard. When he spoke he was able to do so with total knowledge and total authority; not only could he quote the entire constitution of this century-old academy but he could also make cogent analogies between today and yesterday, this century and the last. Rather like an Arab sage, thought Mr. Beckman, as the principal made a precise and intelligent comparison between the present crisis and an earlier one for, like the Arab philosophers, he assembled the main facts and then produced . . . from memory, not from reason . . . a relevant antique text which gave him his solution, shaped by precedent and the cumulative wisdom of an old institution.

Such an efficient man, thought Mr. Beckman, nodding intelligently, not listening, too much absorbed by his sincere appreciation of this splendid human being who had saved him the year before from Saint Timothy's, where he'd been an underpaid history instructor with nothing to look forward to but a future of dim discomfort, of dining hall dinners (cold tuna fish, brown lettuce, potato chips, and canned peas) made edible only by the frequent, the ritualistic use of a richly carved pepper mill given him by the parents of a subnormal pupil he had befriended. But the previous spring his luck had changed; he was offered a summer job tutoring a boy at Oyster Bay. He had accepted the assignment, enjoyed the summer and the company of the boy's uncle, who, by a fortunate coincidence, was the Principal himself. . . . And here I am, thought Mr. Beckman complacently, crossing his legs and leaning forward, tuning in again, as it were, on his chief.

"And so, Mr. Beckman, you can see that this distasteful business is not by any means unfamiliar. We have faced it squarely in the past and no doubt we will have to face it again in the future, as squarely, alas." He paused, allowing that classical epithet of sorrow, that stylized expression of grief to represent his attitude toward not only this particu-

lar instance of viciousness but toward all moral lapses, in
school and out.

"I see what you mean, sir. Even at Saint Timothy's there
was a similar case . . ."

"I know, Mr. Beckman, I know," interrupted the Principal. "It is the specter of all schools and the ruin of some; but
not ours, Mr. Beckman, not ours." The Principal smiled
proudly up at the portrait of himself over the mock fireplace. It was a good portrait, painted in the Sargent
manner, idealized but recognizable. The Principal gazed at
his own portrait, as though drawing strength from this official version of himself, strength from the confident knowledge that this work would hang for generations in the
chapel of the School, a decorative symbol of the reign of the
thirteenth Principal, a likeness which would impress everyone with the distinguished arrangement of the features: a
large, strong nose, a firm, lipless mouth, white brows, and a
full head of hair. In every respect it was the face of a man of
power (that the body was small and fat made no difference,
for it was hidden by academic robes). Then, sustained by
this vision of his own posterity, the Principal returned to his
vexing problem, or, as it soon developed, Mr. Beckman's
vexing problem.

"You have seen, sir, the speed with which the School has
acted." Mr. Beckman nodded, wondering if anyone since
Dr. Johnson had so achieved the knack of making the ordi-
narily respectful *sir* sound a cozy diminutive. "We have
always moved quickly in these matters. The . . . revelation
was made last night. By ten o'clock this morning the
faculty, a majority of the faculty at least, had met and acted.
That's quick action. Even *you* must admit that."

Mr. Beckman admitted that it was very quick indeed: the
"even *you*" was the Principal's little joke, for he liked to

pretend that Mr. Beckman was a critical and supercilious outsider, a spy from the church academies, eager to find fault with this sternly Protestant school.

"Now Sawyer, it seems, has preferred to leave before his fate was made known to him. A cowardly flight but on the whole sensible for there could have been no doubt in his mind as to what our decision would be: by leaving, he has saved us a certain embarrassment. I've written his parents already." He paused as though expecting some word of approbation from Mr. Beckman; none came, for Mr. Beckman was now studying the portrait and wondering to himself what future generations would say when they saw it in the chapel: "Who was that ape?" The irreverent thought amused him and he faced the original of the painting with a smile which the Principal interpreted as applause. Nodding abruptly as though both to acknowledge and silence a cheering crowd, the Principal continued. "I believe I have presented the case quite dispassionately. I feel that the facts speak for themselves, as facts will, and that it would be gratuitous of me to make further comments. The responsibility is no longer mine but theirs. *Sawyer is no longer one of us.* Flynn, however, presents a more difficult problem."

"You mean because he *hasn't* left?"

The Principal shook his head and he looked, thought Mr. Beckman, somewhat anxious. "No, although I must say it might have helped matters if he'd gone when the other did. But that's not the trouble."

"The Trophy?"

"Exactly. The Carl F. Zenner Award for clean sportsmanship, our highest honor. He was, if you remember, an extremely popular choice."

"I certainly do remember. The boys cheered him for hours in chapel. I thought they'd never stop."

The Principal nodded glumly. "Fortunately, the trophy

itself is not presented until Commencement Day; we have at least a week in which to consider what's to be done. Flynn of course can't have it now. I must say I wish we hadn't made the announcement so far in advance . . . but it's done and that's that and we'll have to make the best of it. I favor reawarding it, but the Athletics Director tells me Flynn was the only possible choice . . . our finest athlete." He paused. "Do you remember the day he pitched against Exeter? Marvelous! Quite a good-looking boy, too. But I'm afraid I never knew him well." The Principal was, in every way, the modern head of a great school: aloof, majestic, concerned only with the more abstract theories of education as well as the unrelenting, Grail-like quest for endowments. He had met very few of his youthful charges. In any case, after thirty years, one boy tends to be very like another.

"Yes, he was a fine athlete," agreed Mr. Beckman and he wondered how he might extricate his chief from this dilemma. The problem was partly his since the boy had been his advisee. Each boy had an official adviser among the faculty. The duties of these advisers, however, were somewhat ill-defined; they were generally thought to be responsible for the academic careers of their advisees but actually they were policemen, commissioned to keep order in the dormitories. The boy, Flynn, had been one of Mr. Beckman's charges and until now he had been his dormitory's chief ornament; he was the best athlete the school had produced in over a decade; so celebrated was he, in fact, that Mr. Beckman had been somewhat shy with him and consequently had not come to know him well.

"We must keep this from the students," said the Principal, suddenly, looking at Mr. Beckman as though he suspected him of giddiness, of talebearing.

"I quite agree, sir, but I'm afraid that they'll find out

sooner or later. I mean it's not just as if Flynn were an ordinary student. He's one of the heroes of the School. When the boys discover he isn't going to graduate they'll wonder."

"I realize that there will be talk but I see no reason for us to reveal the true cause of the young man's separation from this institution." The operative verb puzzled Mr. Beckman until he remembered that the Principal had been, for a year or two during the war, a colonel in Washington and that he could still turn a military phrase with the best of the younger faculty men who had also served in the war.

"But *what* are we to say?" Mr. Beckman persisted. "We shall have to give some excuse."

"There is no occasion, Mr. Beckman, for us *ever* to give excuses," said the Principal in a cool star-chamber voice. "Besides, Commencement is only a week away and I am sure that if we all maintain a discreet silence the business will soon be forgotten. The only complication, as I've mentioned before, involves the Zenner Trophy. At the moment I'm tempted not to give it at all this year, but of course we'll have to see what our faculty committee digs up. . . . Anyway that has nothing to do with the business at hand, which, specifically, concerns the expulsion of Flynn, an unpleasant task traditionally performed by the Dean. In his absence, and he is absent, the sad duty must be performed by the faculty adviser involved."

"Not by the Principal?"

"*Never* by the Principal," said that officer, constructing a pile of papers in front of him as though to barricade himself even more securely against the sordid life of the School.

"I see. I don't suppose there is any chance of keeping him on? I mean of letting him graduate next week?" He felt that it was his duty to make this suggestion.

"Of course not! How could you suggest such a thing

after what's happened? There were two witnesses and both were faculty members. Had there been only *one* witness we might perhaps . . ." The Principal paused, contemplating collusion . . . to no avail. He returned quickly to his original position, remarking that the morality of the thing was perfectly clear and that the crime and the punishment were both well-known and that there wouldn't have been this much discussion if it had not been for that damned award. "No, the boy has been expelled and that's that. I've already written to his parents."

"Did you tell them what has happened? in detail?"

"I did," said the Principal firmly. "After all, he's their son and they should know everything. I wouldn't be doing my duty if I did not tell them."

"Rather hard on him, don't you think?"

"Are *you* defending him?" The Principal reduced Mr. Beckman's momentary disaffection to total compliance with a single glance from agate eyes, eyes which had so often quelled student revolts, bullied the faculty, extorted endowments from the most brutal of millionaires.

"No, sir . . . I only thought . . ." That was the end of that, thought Mr. Beckman gloomily, mumbling himself back into favor again.

"Very good," said the Principal rising, ending the audience. "You'll talk to him. Tell him that the faculty has unanimously expelled him and that the Zenner Trophy will be given to someone else. You might also mention the sorrow with which I personally learned of his . . . activities and that I do not condemn him too much; rather, I pity him. It is a terrible handicap not to know right from wrong in such matters."

"I shall tell him that, sir."

"Good. . . . Just what sort of young man is he? I've seen him play ball many times, of course . . . a real champion . . .

but I never got to know him. On the few occasions when we did meet he seemed perfectly . . . well-adjusted. He comes from a good home, too. Odd that he should be such a marvelous athlete, all things considered."

"Yes, a marvelous athlete," repeated Mr. Beckman. This was apparently to be Flynn's epitaph; he tried to translate it into Latin but failed, unable to remember the word for athlete.

"You never noticed anything unusual about him, did you? Any clue which might, in retrospect, explain what has happened."

"No, sir. I'm sorry to say that I noticed nothing at all."

"Well, it's no fault of yours, or of the School's. These things will happen." The Principal sighed. Then: "Drop by my office around five . . . if it's convenient."

II

The morning was marvelously clear and bright and Mr. Beckman's weak eyes watered as he crossed the lawn of the quadrangle, a vivid area of green in the solemn light of noon. Students greeted him politely and he responded vaguely, not seeing them, his eyes not yet accustomed to the day. He blundered accurately across the quadrangle to the library, where he stood a moment, blinking, until at last he could see that it was indeed a lovely day and that the School looked most handsome.

The main buildings bordered the vast green lawn of the quadrangle, a lawn marked with numerous graveled paths, designed with considerable geometric ingenuity to allow, its architect had mistakenly supposed, for any possible crossing a student might want to make. Of the buildings on the quadrangle, the Administration Hall was the handsomest and the oldest; it was nearly old enough to be in fact what it was in facsimile: a Colonial affair of red brick with a clock tower and bell, a bell which irritated Mr. Beckman unreasonably. It rang at five minutes to every hour as well as on the hour from morning chapel until the last evening class. The bell rang now. Eleven o'clock. He had exactly one hour in which to "separate" Flynn from the school he had so brilliantly adorned. A warm wind stirred the lilacs and, suddenly, he was frightened at what he had to do. He was not equipped to deal with mysteries. He had very early chosen the bland familiar for his domain and he had never before ventured into the dangerous interior of another's life: now, in a few moments, he must sack a temple, sow foreign earth with salt, and rend a mystery. Half-shutting his eyes against the blaze of sun, Mr. Beckman made his way to the rose-brick senior dormitory where Flynn and he both lived. Inside the building, he proceeded down the wax-smelling corridor, his tongue dry, his hands cold, panic insecurely leashed. At Flynn's door, he stopped. He knocked softly. Receiving no answer, he turned the knob and opened the door, praying the boy was gone.

Flynn had not gone. He was sitting on the edge of his bed, an open suitcase on the floor in front of him. He stood up when Mr. Beckman entered.

"Am I out?" he asked.

"Yes." That was quick. For a moment Mr. Beckman considered flight.

"I figured that would happen." The boy sat down on the bed again. Mr. Beckman wondered what he should say next. Since nothing occurred to him, he seated himself at the desk by the window and assumed an expression of grave sympathy. The boy continued to pack his suitcase. A long moment of silence stretched taut Mr. Beckman's nerves. At last, he broke the silence.

"The Principal wanted me to tell you he is very sorry about what's happened."

"Well, you tell him I'm sorry too," said Flynn, looking up from his packing and, to Mr. Beckman's surprise, he was grinning. He seemed not at all shaken, Mr. Beckman remarked with wonder, examining him carefully. The eighteen-year-old Flynn was a well-constructed man of middle height, muscular but not burly like the other athletes; his freckled face was amiable and quite mature, his eyes dark blue; his hair, of no particular color, was worn short, in a crew cut. During the winter his hair had been longer and Mr. Beckman recalled that it had been quite curly, like the head of the young Dionysus.

He looked about the room, at the banners on the walls and at the calendar of partly dressed girls, one for each month. In a corner was piled athletic equipment: football helmet, shoulder pads, sweat-marked jerseys, shorts, tennis racket . . . the tools of a serious career rather than the playthings of an energetic boy. No, he would never have known, never.

There was another long pause, but this time Mr. Beckman was more at ease even as he sensed his own position becoming less and less secure. "I suppose," he said, "that you'll go on to college now."

"Yes, I suppose I will. I got all the credits I need from high school, and the university back home wants me to play ball. I won't have any trouble getting in . . . will I?"

"Oh, no. No trouble at all, I'm sure."

"*They* don't plan to make any trouble for me, do they?"

"Who do you mean by 'they'?"

"The School. They aren't going to write the university or anything like that, are they?"

"Oh, Heavens no!" Mr. Beckman was relieved to have

some good news, no matter how negative. "Except for expelling you, they are doing nothing at all. Of course . . ." He paused, noticing that the other looked very grim.

"Of course what?"

"They have written your parents."

"Written my parents *what*?"

"The . . . the whole business. It's customary, you understand. The Principal wrote the letter himself, today, this morning, as a matter of fact," he added precisely, addressing his attention, as he always did in a crisis, to the periphery of the situation, to the incidental detail in the hopes that he might yet avoid involvement. But it was no use.

"Well, I'll be damned!" Flynn sat up straight, his large square hands clenched into two useful and dangerous-looking fists. Mr. Beckman trembled. "So he went and wrote everything, did he . . ." He stopped and hit the bed with his fist; the springs creaked. It was all very dramatic and Mr. Beckman sat up straight in his chair, raising one hand as though to defend himself.

"You must remember," he said, his voice trembling, "that the Principal was only doing his duty. You *were* caught, you know, and you *were* expelled. Don't you feel your parents deserve some sort of explanation?"

"No, I don't. Not like that, anyway. It's bad enough being kicked out without having that dumb bastard go and upset them. It's no way of getting back at me: I earn my own way. I can go to any school I want on a scholarship. Or I can turn pro tomorrow and make ten times the money that fool Principal makes. But why, I want to know, does somebody who doesn't even know me go out of his way to make such a mess for my family?"

"I'm sure it's not a deliberate persecution," said Mr. Beckman dryly. "And you should have thought of all that

when . . . when you did what you did. There *are* certain
rules of conduct, you know, which must be obeyed and you
obviously forgot . . ."

"Oh, shut up!"

Mr. Beckman had a dizzy sense that he was falling; only
with great effort did he get to his feet, saying, shakily, "If
you're going to take that tone with me, Flynn, I see no
point in . . ."

"I'm sorry. I didn't mean it. Come on, sit down." And
Mr. Beckman sat down, his authority gone. He could no
longer predict the direction this conversation would take
and he was actually relieved that the initiative was no
longer his.

"You see how I feel, don't you?"

"Yes," said Mr. Beckman. "I do." And unhappily he did.
Not only was he sympathetic: he was partisan, hopelessly
identified with the other. He shuddered at the thought of
the meeting between son and parents and he tried to think
of what would happen . . . would she have a stroke? would
she weep? "If there is anything I might do . . ." he began.

Flynn smiled. "No, I don't think there's anything to be
done, thanks. I guess it was probably too much to expect
. . . I mean that they'd keep it quiet. But what about the rest
of the school? Is the Principal going to get up in chapel and
tell the whole story?"

"Oh, no. His plan is to say nothing at all to the students.
He's instructed the faculty to keep absolutely quiet."

"Well, that's good news but you know they're going to
be wondering why Sawyer and I didn't graduate, why we
left just a week before Commencement." He paused; then:
"What're they going to do about the Trophy?"

"I don't know. Since they can't give it to you they're in
rather a spot: if they reward it, that will draw attention to
the fact you've been expelled. I have a hunch they won't

give it at all this year." And Mr. Beckman chuckled, totally aligned against the School which until an hour ago he had so much admired and had so sincerely longed to serve.

"I guess that's their worry now," said Flynn. "Were they pretty shocked?"

"Who?"

"The faculty. You know: all the ones who knew me, like the coaches I worked with. What did they say?"

"No one said much of anything. I think they were all surprised. I mean you were just about the last person anyone would have expected to be involved . . . like this. I'm afraid *I* was rather surprised, too," he added shyly, waiting.

But Flynn only snorted and looked out the window at the tower of the Administration Building, red brick against blue sky. At last he said: "I guess there *is* something wrong with me, Mr. Beckman, because I can't for the life of me see what business it is of anyone else what I do."

This was not at all what Mr. Beckman had anticipated; identified as he was with Flynn, he still found it difficult to accept the curious amorality of this attitude. He took a firm line. "You must realize," he said, as gently as possible, "that we are all guided by a system of conduct formulated and refined by many centuries. Should this system, or any important part of it, be destroyed, the whole complex structure of civilization would collapse." Yet even as he said these familiar words, he realized that they were, in this case at least, irrelevant and he noticed dispassionately that Flynn was not listening to him. He was standing over his athletic equipment, tossing the pieces he didn't want into a far corner of the room. Mr. Beckman enjoyed watching him move, for he never struck an ugly or a self-conscious attitude. "And so you see," he concluded to the boy's back, "that when you do something as basically wrong as what you've done, you'll have all of organized society down on you and you'll be punished."

"Maybe so." Flynn straightened up, holding his armor, his weapons in his hands. "But I still don't see why what I want to do should ever be anybody's business except my own . . . after all it doesn't affect anybody else, does it?" Noisily, he dumped the equipment into the open suitcase. Then he sat down on the bed again and looked at Mr. Beckman. "You know I'd really like to get my hands on those two," he said abruptly, scowling.

"They were only doing their duty. They had to report you."

"I suppose I should have known they were suspicious in the first place . . . when I saw them last night, before I went up to Sawyer's room. They were hanging around the common room, whispering. Sawyer thought there was something going on but I said so what."

"And you were caught."

"Yes." He blushed and looked away. He seemed for the first time very young; Mr. Beckman was compassionate.

"I gather," he said slowly, allowing the other to regain his composure, "that Sawyer went home?"

Flynn shook his head. "No, he's over at the Inn, waiting for me. I figured they might want to question us and I thought I'd better be the one who did the talking. He went over there first thing this morning."

"What sort of boy is Sawyer? I don't think I've seen him around."

Flynn looked at him with surprise. "Of course you've seen him. He's on the track team. He's the best sprinter we got."

"Oh yes, of course." Mr. Beckman had not gone to any of the track meets. He had found that after he'd attended the football and the baseball games that he didn't very much want to see the swimming team or the track team or even the School's celebrated basketball team.

"He's too small to play football, and besides, he hasn't got the right temperament for a football player," said Flynn professionally. "He blows up too easily and he doesn't work out on a team . . ."

"I see. And you've been good friends for a long time?"

"Yes," said Flynn and he shut the suitcase with a snap.

"Where do you think you'll go now?" asked Mr. Beckman, obscurely anxious to prolong this interview.

"Back home and it's not going to be much fun. I just hope my mother doesn't have a relapse or anything like that."

"Where will Sawyer go?"

"Oh, he's coming on to the university with me. He's got a high school diploma, too. He won't have any trouble getting in."

"So then you aren't really very discouraged by all of this?"

"Why? I don't like what's happened but then I don't see what I can do about it now."

"You're very sensible. I'm afraid that if I'd been in your place I would have been most upset."

"But you *wouldn't* have been in my place, would you, Mr. Beckman?" Flynn smiled.

"No, no, I don't suppose so," said Mr. Beckman, aware that he had been abandoned long ago and that there was no one he could turn to now, no one he could confide in. He realized that he was quite alone and he hated Flynn for reminding him of the long and tedious journey ahead, down an endless, chalk-smelling corridor where each forward step took him ever farther away from this briefly glimpsed design within a lilac day.

The bell rang. He stood up. It was time to go to class. "I suppose you'll be leaving for Boston on the next train?"

Flynn nodded. "Yes, I've got to take some books back to the library first; after that, I'll pick up Sawyer at the Inn. Then we go."

"Well, good luck." Mr. Beckman paused. "I'm not so sure that, after all, any of this matters very much," he said, in a last effort to console himself as well as the other.

"No, I don't suppose it does either." Flynn was gentle. "You've been very nice about this . . ."

"Don't mention it. By the way, if you like, I'll return any library books for you."

"Thanks a lot." Flynn took three books from the top of the desk and handed them to him.

Mr. Beckman hesitated. "Do you ever get to Boston? I mean do you think you'll come into town much after you enter the university?"

"Sure, I suppose so. I'll let you know and we might get together some weekend."

"I should like that. Well, good-bye." They shook hands and Mr. Beckman left the room, already late for class. Outside, he glanced at the titles of the books he was carrying: one was a volume of historical documents (required reading) and one was a mystery story. The third was a volume of Keats. Dazzled by sunlight, he crossed the quadrangle, aware there was nothing left that he could do.

1950

ERLINDA AND MR. COFFIN

▼

I am a gentlewoman in middle life and I have resided for a number of years at Key West, Florida, in a house which is a mere stone's throw from the naval station where the presidents visit.

Before I recount, as nearly as I am able, what happened that terrible night at the Theater-in-the-Egg, I feel that I should first give you some idea of myself and the circumstances to which Providence has seen fit to reduce me. I came originally from a Carolina family not much blessed with this world's goods but whose lineage, if I may make the boast in all modesty, is of the highest. There is a saying that no legislature of the state could ever convene without the presence of a Slocum (my family name) in the Lower House, a lofty heritage you must concede and one which has done much to sustain me in my widowhood.

In olden times my social activities in this island city were multifarious, but since 1929 I have drawn in my horns, as it

were, surrendering all my high offices in the various organi-
zations with which our city abounds to one Marina
Henderson, wife of our local shrimp magnate and a cultural
force to be reckoned with in these parts not only because
her means are ample but because our celebrated Theater-in-
the-Egg is the child of her teeming imagination: she is its
Managing Directress, Star, and sometime Authoress. Her
productions have been uniformly well regarded since the
proceeds go to charity. Then, too, the unorthodox arrangement of the theater's interior has occasioned much interested comment for the action, such as it is, takes place on an
oval platform ("the yolk") about which the audience sits
restively in camp chairs. There is no curtain of course and so
the actors are forced to rush in and out, from lobby to yolk,
traversing the aisles at a great rate.

Marina and I are good friends, however, even though we
do not forgather as often as we once did: she now goes
with a somewhat faster set than I, seeking out those of the
winter residents who share her advanced views, while I keep
to the small circle that I have known lo! these many years,
since 1910, in fact, when I came to Key West from South
Carolina, accompanied by my new husband, Mr. Bellamy
Craig, who had accepted a position of some trust earlier
that year with a bank which was to fail in '29, the year of his
decease. But of course no such premonition marred our
happiness when we set out, bag and baggage, to make our
way to Key West.

I do not need to say that Mr. Craig was in every sense a
gentleman, a devoted husband, and though our union was
never fulfilled by the longed-for arrival of little ones we
managed, nonetheless, to have a happy home, one which
was to end all too soon as I have intimated, for when he
passed on in '29 I was left with but the tiniest of incomes, a
mere pittance from my maternal grandmother in Carolina,

and the house. Mr. Craig had unfortunately been forced, shortly before his death, to jettison his insurance policy, so I could not even clutch at that straw when my hour came.

I debated whether to go into business or to establish a refined luncheon room or to seek a position with some established business house. I was not long in doubt, however, as to what course I should pursue. For, not being desirous of living anywhere but in my own home, I determined, with some success, financially at least, to reorganize the house so that it might afford me an income through the distasteful but necessary expediency of giving shelter to paying guests.

Since the house is a commodious one, I have not done badly through the years and, in time, I have accustomed myself to this humiliating situation; then, too, I was sustained secretly by the vivid memory of my grandmother Arabella Stuart Slocum of Wayne County, who, when reduced from great wealth to penury by the War, maintained herself and children, widow that she was, by taking in laundry, mostly flat work, but still laundry. I will confess to you that there were times at night when I sat alone in my room, hearkening to the heavy breathing of my guests, that I saw myself as a modern Arabella, living, as did she, in the face of adversity, inspired still by those high ideals we, she and I and all the Slocums, have held in common reverence since time immemorial in Wayne County.

And yet, in spite of every adversity, I should have said until recently that I had "won through," that in twenty years as innkeeper I had not once been faced with any ugliness, that I had been remarkably fortunate in my selection of paying guests, recruiting them, as I did, from the ranks of those who have reached "the age of discretion," as we used to say. But all of this must now be in the past tense, alas.

Late one Sunday morning, three months ago, I was in

the parlor attempting with very little success to tune the piano. I used to be quite expert at tuning but my ear is no longer true and I was, I confess, experiencing a certain frustration when the ringing of the doorbell interrupted my labors. Expecting certain of my late husband's relatives who had promised to break bread with me that day, I hastened to answer the door. It was not they, however: instead a tall thin gentleman in middle life, wearing the long short trousers affected over in Bermuda, stood upon my threshold and begged admittance.

As was my wont, I ushered him into the parlor, where we sat down on the two Victorian plush chairs Grandmother Craig left me in her will. I asked him in what way I might be of service to him and he intimated that rumor had it I entertained guests on a paying basis. I told him that he had not been misinformed and that, by chance, I had one empty room left, which he asked to see.

The room pleased him and, if I say so myself, it is attractively furnished with original copies of Chippendale and Regency, bought many years ago when, in the full flush of our prosperity, Mr. Craig and I furnished our nest with objects not only useful but ornamental. There are two big windows in this room: one on the south and the other on the west. From the south window there is a fine view of the ocean, only partly obliterated by a structure of pink stucco called the "New Arcadia Motel."

"This will do very well," said Mr. Coffin (he had very soon confided his name to me). But then he paused and I did not dare to meet his gaze for I thought that he was about to mention the root of all evil and, as always, I was ill at ease for I have never been able to enact the role of businesswoman without a certain shame, a distress which oftentimes communicates itself to the person with whom I must

deal, causing no end of confusion for us both. But it was
not of money that he wished to speak. If only it had been!
If only we had gone no further in our dealings with one
another. "To call back yesterday," as the poet observed,
"bid time return!" But it was not to be and wishing cannot
change the past. He spoke then of *her*.

"You see, Mrs. Craig, I must tell you that I am not
alone." Was it his English accent which gave me a sense of
false security? created a fool's paradise wherein I was to
dwell blissfully until the rude awakening? I cannot tell.
Suffice it to say I trusted him.

"Not alone?" I queried. "Have you some companion
who travels with you? a gentleman?"

"No, Mrs. Craig, a young lady, my ward . . . a Miss
Lopez."

"But I fear, Mr. Coffin, that I have only the one room
free at the moment."

"Oh, she can stay with me, Mrs. Craig, in this room. You
see, she is only eight." Both of us had a good laugh and my
suspicions, such as they had been, were instantly allayed. He
asked me if I could find him a cot and I said of course, nothing could be more simple; and then, correctly estimating
the value of the room from the sign on the door, he gave
me a week's rent in cash, demonstrating such delicacy of
feeling by his silence at this juncture that I found myself
much prejudiced in his favor. We parted then on excellent
terms and I instructed my girl-of-all-work to place a cot in
the room and to dust carefully. I even had her supply him
with the better bath towels, after which I went in to dinner
with my cousins, who had meanwhile arrived, ravenously
hungry.

Not until the next morning did I see Mr. Coffin's ward.
She was seated in the parlor looking at an old copy of *Vogue*.

"Good morning," she said and, as I entered the room, she rose and curtsied, very prettily I must admit. "I am Erlinda Lopez, the ward of Mr. Coffin."

"I am Mrs. Bellamy Craig, your hostess," I answered with equal ceremony.

"Do you mind if I look at your magazines?"

"Certainly not," I said, containing all the while my surprise not only at her good manners and grown-up ways, but also at the unexpected fact that Miss Lopez was of an unmistakable dusky hue, in short a Dark Latin. Now I must say that although I am in many ways typical of my age and class I have no great prejudice on the subject of race. Our family, even in their slaveholding days, were always good to their people and once as a child when I allowed the forbidden word *nigger* to pass my lips I was forced to submit to a thorough oral cleansing by my mother, with a cake of strong soap. Yet I am, after all, a Southern woman and I do not choose to receive people of color in my own home: call it intolerant, old-fashioned, or what you will, it is the way I am. Imagine then what thoughts coursed through my startled brain! What was I to do? Having accepted a week's rent, was I not morally obligated to maintain both Mr. Coffin and his ward in my house? At least until the week was up? In an agony of indecision, I left the parlor and went straight to Mr. Coffin. He received me cordially.

"Have you met Erlinda yet, Mrs. Craig?"

"I have indeed, Mr. Coffin."

"I think her quite intelligent. She speaks French, Spanish, and English fluently and she has a reading knowledge of Italian."

"A gifted child I am sure but *really*, Mr. Coffin . . ."

"Really what, Mrs. Craig?"

"I mean I am not *blind*. How can she be your ward? She

is . . . colored!" I had said it and I was relieved: the fat was
in the fire; there was no turning back.

"Many people are, Mrs. Craig."

"I am aware of that, Mr. Coffin, but I had not assumed
that your ward was to be counted among that number."

"Then, Mrs. Craig, if it offends your sensibilities, we will
seek lodgings elsewhere." Oh, what insane impulse made
me reject this gesture of his? What flurry of noblesse oblige
in my breast caused me suddenly to refuse even to entertain
such a contingency! I do not know; suffice it to say, I ended
by bidding him remain with his ward as long as he should
care to reside beneath my roof, on a paying basis.

When the first week was up I must confess that I was
more pleased than not with my reckless decision for,
although I did not mention to my friends that I was giving
shelter to a person of color, I found Erlinda, nonetheless, to
be possessed of considerable charm and personality and I
spent at least an hour every day in her company, at first from
a sense of duty but, finally, from a very real pleasure in her
conversation, which, when I recall it now (the pleasure, I
mean), causes my cheeks to burn with shame.

I discovered in our talks that she was, as I had suspected,
an orphan and that she had traveled extensively in Europe
and Latin America, wintering in Amalfi, summering in
Venice, and so on. Not of course that I for one moment
believed these stories but they were so charming and indicated such a fund of information that I was only too pleased
to listen to her descriptions of the Lido, and her recitations
from Dante, in flawless Italian or what I took to be Italian
since I have never studied other tongues. But, as I have said,
I took her tales with the proverbial grain of salt and, from
time to time, I chatted with Mr. Coffin, gleaning from him
. . . as much as I was able without appearing to pry . . . the
story of Erlinda's life.

She was the child of a Cuban prizefighter who had toured Europe many times, taking Erlinda with him on his trips, showering her with every luxury and engaging tutors for her instruction, with a particular emphasis on languages, world literature, and deportment. Her mother had died a few months after Erlinda was born. Mr. Coffin, it seems, had known the prizefighter for several years and since he, Mr. Coffin, was English, a friendship between them was possible. They were, I gathered, very close and since Mr. Coffin had independent means they were able to travel together about Europe, Mr. Coffin eventually assuming responsibility for Erlinda's education.

This idyllic existence ended abruptly a year ago, when Lopez was killed in the ring by a Sicilian named Balbo. It appears that this Balbo was not a sportsman and that shortly before the fight he had contrived to secrete a section of lead pipe in his right boxing glove, enabling him to crush Lopez's skull in the first round. Needless to say the scandal which ensued was great. Balbo was declared middleweight champion of Sicily and Mr. Coffin, after protesting to the authorities, who turned a deaf ear to him, departed, taking Erlinda with him.

As my friends will testify, I am easily moved by a tale of misfortune and, for a time, I took this motherless tyke to my heart. I taught her portions of the Bible, which she had not studied before (Mr. Coffin, I gather, was a freethinker), and she showed me the scrapbooks she and Mr. Coffin had kept of her father's career as a pugilist . . . and a handsome young man he was, if photographs are to be believed.

Consequently, when a new week rolled around and the period of probation, as it were, was up, I extended them the hospitality of my home indefinitely; soon a pattern of existence took shape. Mr. Coffin would spend most of his days looking for shells (he was a collector and, I am assured by certain authorities, the discoverer of a new type of pink-lipped conch), while Erlinda would remain indoors, reading, playing the piano, or chatting with me about one thing or the other. She won my heart and not only mine but those of my friends, who had soon discovered, as friends will, the unusual combination I was sheltering. But my fears were proved to be groundless, a little to my surprise, for the ladies of my acquaintance are not noted for their tolerance: yet Erlinda enchanted them all with her conversation and saucy ways. Especially Marina Henderson, who was not only immediately attracted to Erlinda personally but, and this I must say startled me, professed to see in the child thespian qualities of the highest order.

"Mark my words, Louise Craig," she said to me one afternoon when we were sitting in the parlor waiting for Erlinda, who had gone upstairs to fetch one of the scrapbooks, "that child will be a magnificent actress. Have you listened to her voice?"

"Since I have been constantly in her company for nearly three weeks I could hardly *not* have heard it," I responded with some acerbity.

"I mean its timbre. The inflection . . . it's like velvet, I tell you!"

"But how can she be an actress in this country when . . . well, let us say the opportunities open to one of her . . . characteristics are limited to occasional brief appearances as a lady's maid?"

"That's beside the point," said Marina, and she rattled on as she always does when something new has hit her fancy, ignoring all difficulties, courting disaster with a fine show of high spirits and bad judgment.

"Perhaps the child has no intention of exploiting her dramatic gifts?" I suggested, unconsciously wishing to avert disaster.

"Nonsense," said Marina, staring at herself in the tilted Victorian mirror over the fireplace, admiring that remarkable red hair of hers, which changes its shade from season to season, from decade to decade, like the leaves in autumn. "I shall talk to her about it this afternoon."

"You have something in mind then? some role?"

"I have," said Marina slyly.

"Not . . . ?"

"Yes!" Needless to say I was astonished. For several months our island city had been agog with rumors concerning Marina's latest work, an adaptation of that fine old classic *Camille*, executed in blank verse and containing easily the finest part for an actress within memory, the title role. Competition for this magnificent part had been keen but the demands of the role were so great that Marina had hesitated to entrust it to any of the regular stars, including herself.

"But this will never do!" I exclaimed; my objections were cut short, however, by the appearance of Erlinda and when next I spoke the deed was done and Erlinda Lopez had been assigned the stellar role in Marina Henderson's *Camille*, based on the novel by Dumas and the screenplay by Miss Zoë Akins.

It is curious, now that I think of it, how everyone accepted as a matter of course that Erlinda should interpret an adult Caucasian woman from Paris whose private life was not what it should have been. I can only say, in this regard, that those who heard her read for the part, and I was one of them, were absolutely stunned by the emotions she brought to those risqué lines, as well as by the thrilling quality of her voice, which, in the words of Mr. Hamish the newspaperman, was "golden." That she was only eight and not much over three feet tall disturbed no one for, as Marina said, it is *presence* which matters on the stage, even

in the Theater-in-the-Egg: makeup and lighting would do
the rest. The only difficulty, as we saw it, was the somewhat
ticklish problem of race, but since this is a small community
with certain recognized social arbiters, good form prevents
the majority from questioning too finely the decisions of
our leaders, and as Marina occupies a position of peculiar
eminence among us there was, as far as I know, no grum-
bling against her bold choice. Marina herself, by far our
most accomplished actress, certainly our most indefatigable
one, assigned herself the minor role of Camille's confidante
Cecile. Knowing Marina as I do, I was somewhat startled
that she had allowed the stellar role to go to someone else,
but then recalling that she was, after all, directress and
authoress, I could see that she would undoubtedly have
been forced to spread herself too thin had she undertaken
such an arduous task.

Now I do not know precisely what went on during the
rehearsals. I was never invited to attend them and although
I felt I had some connection with the production, Erlinda
having been my discovery in the first place, I made no
demur and sought in no way to interfere. Word came to me,
however, that Erlinda was magnificent.

I was seated in the parlor one afternoon with Mr. Coffin,
sewing some lace on a tea gown our young star was to wear
in the first scene, when Erlinda burst into the room.

"What is the matter, child?" I asked as she hastened to
bury her head in her guardian's lap, great sobs racking her
tiny frame.

"Marina!" came the muffled complaint. "Marina Henderson is a ——!" Shocked as I was by the child's cruel obser-
vation, I could not but, in my heart of hearts, agree that
there was some truth to this crushing estimate of my old
friend's character. Nonetheless, it was my duty to defend
her and I did, as best I could, recounting relevant episodes

from her life to substantiate my defense. But before I could even get to the quite interesting story of how she happened to marry Mr. Henderson, I was cut short by a tirade of abuse against my oldest friend, an attack inspired, it soon developed, by a quarrel they had had over Erlinda's interpretation of her part, a quarrel which had ended in Marina's assumption of the role of Camille while presenting Erlinda with the terrible choice of either withdrawing from the company entirely or else accepting the role of Cecile, hitherto played by the authoress herself.

Needless to say we were all in a state of uproar for twenty-four hours. Erlinda would neither eat nor sleep. According to Mr. Coffin she paced the floor all night, or at least when he had slipped off to the Land of Nod she was still pacing and when he awakened early the next morning she was seated bitterly by the window, haggard and exhausted, the bedclothes on her cot undisturbed.

I counseled caution, knowing the influence Marina has in this town, and my advice was duly followed when, with broken heart but proud step, Erlinda returned to the boards in the part of Cecile. Had I but known the fruit of my counsel I would have torn my tongue out by the roots rather than advise Erlinda as I did. But what is done is done. In my defense, I can only say that I acted from ignorance and not from malice.

The opening night saw as brilliant an assemblage as you could hope to see in Key West. The cream of our local society was there as well as several of the president's retinue and a real playwright from New York. You have probably heard many conflicting stories about that night. Everyone in the state of Florida now claims to have been present and, to hear the stories some of the people who were there tell, you would think they had been a hundred miles away from the theater that fateful night. In any event, *I* was there in my white mesh over peacock blue foundation, carrying the imitation egret fan that I have had for twenty years, an anniversary gift from Mr. Craig.

Mr. Coffin and I sat together, both of us excited to fever pitch by the long-awaited debut of our young star. The audience, too, seemed to have sensed that something remarkable was about to happen for when, in the middle of the first scene, Erlinda appeared in a gown of orchid-colored tulle, they applauded loudly.

▲   ▲   ▲

As we took our seats for the fifth and final act we were both aware that Erlinda had triumphed. Not even in the movies have I ever seen such a performance! Or heard such a magnificent voice! Poor Marina sounded like a Memphis frump by comparison and it was obvious to all who knew our authoress that she was in a rage at being outshone in her own production.

Now, in the last act of Marina's *Camille* there is a particularly beautiful and touching scene where Camille is lying on a chaise longue, wearing a flowing negligee of white rayon. There is a table beside her on which is set a silver candelabra, containing six lighted tapers, a bowl of paper camellias, and some Kleenex. The scene began something like this.

"Oh, will he never come? Tell me, sweet Cecile, do you not see his carriage approaching from the window?" Cecile (Erlinda) pretends to look out a window and answers, "There is no one in the street but a little old man selling the evening newspapers." The language, as you see, is poetic and much the best writing Marina has done to date. Then there is a point in the action, the great moment of the play, when Camille (that's not the character's real name, I understand, but Marina called her that so as not to confuse the audience), after a realistic fit of coughing, rises up on her elbow and exclaims, "Cecile! It grows dark. He has not come. Light more tapers, do you hear me? I need more light!"

Then it happened. Erlinda picked up the candelabra and held it aloft for a moment, a superhuman effort since it was larger than she; then, taking aim, she hurled it at Marina, who was instantly ignited. Pandemonium broke loose in the theater! Marina, a pillar of fire, streaked down the aisle and into the night: she was subdued at last in the street by two policemen, who managed to put out the blaze, after which they removed her to the hospital, where she now resides, undergoing at this moment her twenty-fourth skin graft.

Erlinda remained on the stage long enough to give *her* reading of Camille's great scene, which, according to those few who were close enough to hear it, was indeed splendid. Then, the scene finished, she left the theater, and before either Mr. Coffin or I could get to her, she was arrested on a charge of assault and battery, and incarcerated.

My story, however, is not yet ended. Had this been all I might have said: let bygones be bygones. The miscreant is only a child and Marina *did* do her an injury, but during the subsequent investigation it was revealed to a shocked public that Erlinda had been legally married to Mr. Coffin in the Reformed Eritrean Church of Cuba several months before and a medical examination proved, or so the defense claims, that Erlinda is actually forty-one years old, a dwarf, the mother and not the daughter of the pugilist Lopez. To date the attendant legal complications have not yet been unraveled to the court's satisfaction.

Fortunately, at this time, I was able to avail myself of a much needed vacation in Carolina, where I resided with kin in Wayne County until the trouble in Key West had abated somewhat.

I now visit Marina regularly and she is beginning to look more or less like her old self, even though her hair and eyebrows are gone for good and she will have to wear a wig when she finally rises from her bed of pain. Only once has she made any reference to Erlinda in my presence and that was shortly after my return from the north when she remarked that the child had been temperamentally all wrong for the part of Camille and that if she had it to do over again, everything considered, she would still have fired her.

1951

PAGES FROM AN ABANDONED JOURNAL

▼

I

April 30, 1948
After last night, I was sure they wouldn't want to see me again but evidently I was wrong because this morning I had a call from Steven . . . he spells it with a *v* . . . asking me if I would like to come to a party at Elliott Magren's apartment in the Rue du Bac. I should have said no but I didn't. It's funny: when I make up my mind *not* to do something I always end up by doing it, like meeting Magren, like seeing any of these people again, especially after last night. Well, I guess it's an experience. What was it Pascal wrote? I don't remember what Pascal wrote . . . another sign of weakness: I should look it up when I don't remember . . . the book is right here on the table but the thought of leafing through all those pages is discouraging so I pass on.

Anyway, now that I'm in Paris I've got to learn to be

more adaptable and I do think, all in all, I've handled myself pretty well . . . until last night in the bar when I told everybody off. I certainly never thought I'd see Steven again . . . that's why I was so surprised to get his call this morning. Is he still hopeful after what I said? I can't see how. I was *ruthlessly* honest. I said I wasn't interested, that I didn't mind what other people did, etc., just as long as they left me alone, that I was getting married in the fall when I got back to the States (WRITE HELEN), and that I don't go in for any of that, never did and never will. I also told him in no uncertain terms that it's very embarrassing for a grown man to be treated like some idiot girl surrounded by a bunch of seedy, middle-aged Don Juans trying to get their hooks into her . . . him. Anyway, I really let him have it before I left. Later, I felt silly but I was glad to go on record like that once and for all: now we know where we stand and if they're willing to accept me on *my* terms, the way I am, then there's no reason why I can't see them sometimes. That's really why I agreed to meet Magren, who sounds very interesting from what everybody says, and everybody talks a lot about him, at least in those circles, which must be the largest and busiest circles in Paris this spring. Well, I shouldn't complain: this is the Bohemian life I wanted to see. It's just that there aren't many girls around, for fairly obvious reasons. In fact, except for running into Hilda Devendorf at American Express yesterday, I haven't seen an American girl to talk to in the three weeks I've been here.

My day: after the phone call from Steven, I worked for two and a half hours on Nero and the Civil Wars . . . I wish sometimes I'd picked a smaller subject for a doctorate, not that I don't like the period but having to learn German to read a lot of books all based on sources available to anybody is depressing: I could do the whole thing from Tacitus but that would be cheating, no bibliography, no footnotes, no scholastic quarrels to record and judge between. Then, though the day was cloudy, I took a long walk across the river to the Tuileries, where the gardens looked fine. Just as I was turning home into the Rue de l'Université it started to rain and I got wet. At the desk Madame Revenel told me Hilda had called. I called her back and she said she was going to Deauville on Friday to visit some people who own a hotel and why didn't I go too? I said I might and wrote down her address. She's a nice girl. We were in high school together back in Toledo: I lost track of her when I went to Columbia.

Had dinner here in the dining room (veal, french fried potatoes, salad, and something like a pie but very good . . . I like the way Madame Revenel cooks). She talked to me all through dinner, very fast, which is good because the faster she goes the less chance you have to translate in your head. The only other people in the dining room were the Harvard professor and his wife. They both read while they ate. He's supposed to be somebody important in the English Department but I've never heard of him . . . Paris is like that: everybody's supposed to be somebody important only you've never heard of them. The Harvard professor was reading a mystery story and his wife was reading a life of Alexander Pope. . . .

I got to the Rue du Bac around ten-thirty. Steven opened the door, yelling: "The beautiful Peter!" This was about what I expected. Anyway, I got into the room quickly . . . if they're drunk they're apt to try to kiss you and there was no point in getting off on the wrong foot again . . . but luckily he didn't try. He showed me through the apartment, four big rooms one opening off another . . . here and there an old chair was propped against a wall and that was all the furniture there was till we got to the last room, where, on a big bed with a torn canopy, Elliott Magren lay, fully dressed, propped up by pillows. All the lamps had red shades. Over the bed was a painting of a nude man, the work of a famous painter I'd never heard of (read Berenson!).

There were about a dozen men in the room, most of them middle-aged and wearing expensive narrow suits. I recognized one or two of them from last night. They nodded to me but made no fuss. Steven introduced me to Elliott, who didn't move from the bed when he shook hands; instead he pulled me down beside him. He had a surprisingly powerful grip, considering how pale and slender he is. He told Steven to make me a drink. Then he gave me a long serious look and asked me if I wanted a pipe of opium. I said I didn't take drugs and he said nothing, which was unusual: as a rule they give you a speech about how good it is for you or else they start defending themselves against what they feel is moral censure. Personally, I don't mind what other people do. As a matter of fact, I think all this is very interesting and I sometimes wonder what the gang back in Toledo would think if they could've seen me in a Left Bank Paris apartment with a male prostitute who takes drugs. I thought of those college boys who sent T. S. Eliot the record "You've Come a Long Way from St. Louis."

Before I describe what happened, I'd better write down what I've heard about Magren since he is already a legend in Europe, at least in these circles. First of all, he is not very handsome. I don't know what I'd expected but something glamorous, like a movie star. He is about five foot ten and weighs about a hundred sixty pounds. He has dark straight hair that falls over his forehead; his eyes are black. The two sides of his face don't match, like Oscar Wilde's, though the effect is not as disagreeable as Wilde's face must've been from the photographs. Because of drugs, he is unnaturally pale. His voice is deep and his accent is still Southern; he hasn't picked up that phony English accent so many Americans do after five minutes over here. He was born in Galveston, Texas, about thirty-six years ago. When he was sixteen he was picked up on the beach by a German baron, who took him to Berlin with him. (I always wonder about details in a story like this: what did his parents say about a stranger walking off with their son? was there a scene? did they know what was going on?) Elliott then spent several years in Berlin during the twenties, which were the great days, or what these people recall now as the great days . . . I gather the German boys were affectionate: it all sounds pretty disgusting. Then Elliott had a fight with the Baron and he walked, with no money, nothing but the clothes he was wearing, from Berlin to Munich. On the outskirts of Munich, a big car stopped and the chauffeur said that the owner of the car would like to give him a lift. The owner turned out to be a millionaire shipowner from Egypt, very fat and old. He was intrigued with Elliott and he took him on a yachting tour of the Mediterranean. But Elliott couldn't stand him and when the ship got to Naples, Elliott and a Greek sailor skipped ship together after first stealing two thousand dollars from the Egyptian's stateroom. They went to Capri, where they moved into the most expensive hotel and had a wonderful time until the money ran out and the sailor deserted Elliott for a rich American woman. Elliott was about to be taken off to jail for not paying his bill when Lord Glenellen, who was just checking into the hotel, saw him and told the police to let him go, that *he* would pay his bill . . . here again: how would Glenellen know that it would be worth his while to help this stranger? I mean you can't tell by looking at him that Elliott is queer. Suppose he hadn't been? Well, maybe that soldier I met on Okinawa the night of the hurricane was right: they can always tell about each other, like Freemasons. Glenellen kept Elliott for a number of years. They went to England together and Elliott rose higher and higher in aristocratic circles until he met the late King Basil, who was then a Prince. Basil fell in love with him and Elliott went to live with him until Basil became king. They didn't see much of each other after that because the war started and Elliott went to California to live. Basil died during the war, leaving Elliott a small trust fund, which is what he lives on now. In California, Elliott got interested in Vedanta and tried to stop taking drugs and lead a quiet . . . if not a normal . . . life. People say he was all right for several years but when the war ended he couldn't resist going back to Europe. Now he does nothing but smoke opium, his courtesan life pretty much over. This has been a long account but I'm glad I got it all down because the story is an interesting one and I've heard so many bits and pieces of it since I got here that it helps clarify many things just writing this down in my journal. . . . It is now past four o'clock and I've got a hangover already from the party but I'm going to finish, just as discipline. I never seem to finish anything, which is a bad sign, God knows.

While I was sitting with Elliott on the bed, Steven brought him his opium pipe, a long painted wooden affair with a metal chimney. Elliott inhaled deeply, holding the smoke in his lungs as long as he could; then he exhaled the pale medicinal-scented smoke, and started to talk. I can't remember a word he said. I was aware, though, that this was probably the most brilliant conversation I'd ever heard. It might have been the setting, which was certainly provocative, or maybe I'd inhaled some of the opium, which put me in a receptive mood but, no matter the cause, I sat listening to him, fascinated, not wanting him to stop. As he talked, he kept his eyes shut and I suddenly realized why the lampshades were red: the eyes of drug addicts are hypersensitive to light; whenever he opened his eyes he would blink painfully and the tears would streak his face, glistening like small watery rubies in the red light. He told me about himself, pretending to be a modern Candide, simple and bewildered but actually he must have been quite different, more calculating, more resourceful. Then he asked me about myself and I couldn't tell if he was really interested or not because his eyes were shut and it's odd talking to someone who won't look at you. I told him about Ohio and high school and the university and now Columbia and the doctorate I'm trying to get in History and the fact I want to teach, to marry Helen . . . but as I talked I couldn't help but think how dull my life must sound to Elliott. I cut it short. I couldn't compete with him . . . and didn't want to. Then he asked me if I'd see him some evening, alone, and I said I would like to but . . . and this was completely spur of the moment . . . I said I was going down to Deauville the next day, with a girl. I wasn't sure he'd heard any of this because at that moment Steven pulled me off the bed and tried to make me dance with him, which I wouldn't do, to the amusement of the others. Then Elliott went to sleep so I sat and talked for a while with an interior decorator from New York and, as usual, I was floored by the amount these people know: painting, music, literature, architecture . . . where do they learn it all? I sit like a complete idiot, supposedly educated, almost a Ph.D., while they talk circles around me: Fragonard, Boucher, Leonore Fini, Gropius, Sacheverell Sitwell, Ronald Firbank, Jean Genet, Jean Giono, Jean Cocteau, Jean Brown's body lies a'mouldering in Robert Graves. God damn them all. I have the worst headache and outside it's dawn. Remember to write Helen, call Hilda about Deauville, study German two hours tomorrow instead of one, start boning up on Latin again, read Berenson, get a book on modern art (what book?), read Firbank. . . .

II

May 21, 1948
Another fight with Hilda. This time about religion. She's a Christian Scientist. It all started when she saw me taking two aspirins this morning because of last night's hangover. She gave me a lecture on Christ–Scientist and we had a long fight about God on the beach (which was wonderful today, not too many people, not too hot). Hilda looked more than ever like a great golden seal. She is a nice girl but like so many who go to Bennington feels she must continually be alert to the life about her. I think tonight we'll go to bed together. Remember to get suntan oil, change money at hotel, finish Berenson, study German grammar! See if there's a Firbank in a paper edition.

May 22, 1948
It wasn't very successful last night. Hilda kept talking all the time, which slows me down, also she is a good deal softer than she looks and it was like sinking into a feather mattress. I don't think she has bones, only elastic webbing. Well, maybe it'll be better tonight. She seemed pleased but then I think she likes the idea better than the actual thing. She told me she had her first affair at fourteen. We had another argument about God. I told her the evidence was slight, etc. but she said evidence had nothing to do with faith. She told me a long story about how her mother had cancer last year but wouldn't see a doctor and the cancer went away. I

didn't have the heart to tell her that Mother's days are unpleasantly numbered. We had a wonderful dinner at that place on the sea, lobster, *moules*. Write Helen.

May 24, 1948
A fight with Hilda, this time about Helen, whom she hardly knows. She felt that Helen was pretentious. I said who isn't? She said many people weren't. I said name me one. She said *she* wasn't pretentious. I then told her all the pretentious things she'd said in the past week starting with that discussion about the importance of an aristocracy and ending with atonalism. She then told me all the pretentious things I'd said, things I either didn't remember saying or she had twisted around. I got so angry I stalked out of her room and didn't go back: just as well. Having sex with her is about the dullest pastime I can think of. I went to my room and read Tacitus in Latin, for practice.

My sunburn is better but I think I've picked up some kind of liver trouble. Hope it's not jaundice: a burning feeling right where the liver is.

May 25, 1948
Hilda very cool this morning when we met on the beach. Beautiful day. We sat on the sand a good yard between us, and I kept thinking how fat she's going to be in a few years, only fit for childbearing. I also thought happily of those agonizing "painless" childbirths she'd have to endure because of Christian Science. We were just beginning to quarrel about the pronunciation of a French word when Elliott Magren appeared . . . the last person in the world I expected to see at bright noon on that beach. He was walking slowly, wearing sunglasses and a pair of crimson trunks. I noticed with surprise how smooth and youthful his body was, like a boy. I don't know what I'd expected: something

gaunt and hollowed out I suppose, wasted by drugs. He came up to me as though he'd expected to meet me right where I was. We shook hands and I introduced him to Hilda, who fortunately missed the point to him from the very beginning. He was as charming as ever. It seems he had to come to Deauville alone . . . he hated the sun but liked the beach . . . and, in answer to the golden Hilda's inevitable question, no, he was not married. I wanted to tell her everything, just to see what would happen, to break for a moment that beaming complacency, but I didn't . . .

May 27, 1948
Well, this afternoon Hilda decided it was time to go back to Paris. I carried her bag to the station and we didn't quarrel once. She was pensive but I didn't offer the usual small change for her thoughts. She didn't mention Elliott and I have no idea how much she suspects; in any case, it's none of her business, none of mine either. I think, though, I was nearly as shocked as she was when he came back to the hotel this morning with that fourteen-year-old boy. We were sitting on the terrace having coffee when Elliott, who must've gotten up very early, appeared with this boy. Elliott even introduced him to us and the little devil wasn't faintly embarrassed, assuming, I guess, that we were interested in him, too. Then Elliott whisked him off to his room and, as Hilda and I sat in complete silence, we could hear from Elliott's room on the first floor the hoarse sound of the boy's laughter. Not long after, Hilda decided to go back to Paris.

Wrote a long letter to Helen, studied Latin grammar. . . . I'm more afraid of my Latin than of anything else in either the written or the orals: can't seem to concentrate, can't retain all those irregular verbs. Well, I've come this far. I'll probably get through all right.

May 28, 1948

This morning I knocked on Elliott's door around eleven o'clock. He'd asked me to pick him up on my way to the beach. When he shouted come in! I did and found both Elliott and the boy on the floor together, stark naked, putting together a Meccano set. Both were intent on building an intricate affair with wheels and pulleys, a blueprint between them. I excused myself hurriedly but Elliott told me to stay . . . they'd be finished in a moment. The boy, who was the color of a terra-cotta pot, gave me a wicked grin. Then Elliott, completely unself-conscious, jumped to his feet and pulled on a pair of trunks and a shirt. The boy dressed, too, and we went out on the beach, where the kid left us. I was blunt. I asked Elliott if this sort of thing wasn't very dangerous and he said yes it probably was but life was short and he was afraid of nothing, except drugs. He told me then that he had had an electrical shock treatment at a clinic shortly before I'd first met him. Now, at last, he was off opium and he hoped it was a permanent cure. He described the shock treatment, which sounded terrible. Part of his memory was gone: he could recall almost nothing of his childhood . . . yet he was blithe even about this: after all, he believed only in the present. . . . Then when I asked him if he always went in for young boys he said yes and he made a joke about how, having lost all memory of his own childhood, he would have to live out a new one with some boy.

May 29, 1948

I had a strange conversation with Elliott last night. André went home to his family at six and Elliott and I had an early dinner on the terrace. A beautiful evening: the sea green in the last light . . . a new moon. Eating fresh sole from the

Channel, I told Elliott all about Jimmy, told him things I myself had nearly forgotten, had wanted to forget. I told him how it had started at twelve and gone on, without plan or thought or even acknowledgment until, at seventeen, I went to the army and he to the Marines and a quick death. After the army, I met Helen and forgot him completely; his death, like Elliott's shock treatment, took with it all memory, a thousand summer days abandoned on a coral island. I can't think now why on earth I told Elliott about Jimmy, not that I'm ashamed but it was, after all, something intimate, something nearly forgotten . . . anyway, when I finished, I sat there in the dark, not daring to look at Elliott, shivering as all in a rush the warmth left the sand about us and I had that terrible feeling I always have when I realize too late I've said too much. Finally, Elliott spoke. He gave me a strange disjointed speech about life and duty to oneself and how the moment is all one has and how it is dishonorable to cheat oneself of that. . . . I'm not sure that he said anything very useful or very original but sitting there in the dark, listening, his words had a peculiar urgency for me and I felt, in a way, that I was listening to an oracle. . . .

June 1, 1948
Shortly before lunch, the police came and arrested Elliott. Luckily, I was down on the beach and missed the whole thing. . . . The hotel's in an uproar and the manager's behaving like a madman. It seems André stole Elliott's camera. His parents found it and asked him where he got it. He wouldn't tell. When they threatened him, he said Elliott gave him the camera and then, to make this story credible, he told them that Elliott had tried to seduce him. . . . The whole sordid business then proceeded logically: parents to

police . . . police to Elliott . . . arrest. I sat down shakily on the terrace and wondered what to do. I was . . . I am frightened. While I was sitting there, a gendarme came out on the terrace and told me Elliott wanted to see me, in prison. Meanwhile, the gendarme wanted to know what I knew about Mr. Magren. It was only too apparent what his opinion of *me* was: another *pédéraste américain*. My voice shook and my throat dried up as I told him I hardly knew Elliott . . . I'd only just met him . . . I knew nothing about his private life. The gendarme sighed and closed his notebook: the charges against Elliott were *très grave, très grave,* but I would be allowed to see him tomorrow morning. Then, realizing I was both nervous and uncooperative, the gendarme gave me the address of the jail and left. I went straight to my room and packed. I didn't think twice. All I wanted was to get away from Deauville, from Elliott, from the crime . . . and it *was* a crime, I'm sure of that. I was back in Paris in time for supper at the hotel.

June 4, 1948
Ran into Steven at the Café Flore and I asked him if there'd been any news of Elliott. Steven took the whole thing as a joke: yes, Elliott had called a mutual friend who was a lawyer and everything was all right. Money was spent; the charges were dropped and Elliott was staying on in Deauville for another week . . . doubtless, to be near André. I was shocked but relieved to hear this. I'm not proud of my cowardice but I didn't want to be drawn into something I hardly understood.

Caught a glimpse of Hilda with some college boy, laughing and chattering as they left the brasserie across the street. I stepped behind a kiosk, not wanting Hilda to see me. Write Helen. See the doctor about wax in ears, also liver. Get tickets for Roland Petit ballet.

III

December 26, 1953

The most hideous hangover! How I hate Christmas, especially this one. Started out last night at the Caprice, where the management gave a party, absolutely packed. The new room is quite stunning, to my surprise: black walls, white driftwood but not artsy-craftsy, a starlight effect for the ceiling . . . only the upholstery is really *mauvais goût*: tufted velveteen in SAFFRON! . . . but then Piggy has no sense of color and why somebody didn't stop him I'll never know. All the tired old faces were there. Everyone was going to the ballet except me and there was all the usual talk about who was sleeping with whom, such a bore . . . I mean who cares who . . . whom dancers sleep with? Though somebody did say that Niellsen was having an affair with Dr. Bruckner, which is something of a surprise considering what a mess there was at Fire Island last summer over just that. Anyway, I drank too many vodka martinis and, incidentally, met Robert Gammadge the English playwright, who isn't at all attractive though he made the biggest play for me. He's supposed to be quite dreary but makes tons of money. He was with that awful Dickie Mallory, whose whole life is devoted to meeting celebrities, even the wrong ones. Needless to say, he was in seventh heaven with his playwright in tow. I can't understand people like Dickie: what fun do they get out of always being second fiddle? After the Caprice I went over to Steven's new apartment on the river; it's in a remodeled tenement house and I must say it's fun and the Queen Anne desk I sold him looks perfect heaven in his living room. I'll say one thing for him: Steven is one of the few people who has the good sense simply to let a fine piece *go* in a room. There were quite a few people there and we had New York champagne, which is drinkable when you're already full of vodka. Needless to say, Steven pulled me off to one corner to ask about Bob. I wish people wouldn't be so sympathetic, not that they really are of course but they feel they must *pretend* to be: actually, they're only curious. I said Bob *seemed* all right when I saw him last month. I didn't go into any details though Steven did his best to worm the whole story out of me. Fortunately, I have a good grip on myself nowadays and I am able to talk about the breakup quite calmly. I always tell everybody I hope Bob will do well in his new business and that I like Sydney very much . . . actually, I hear things are going badly, that the shop is doing *no* business and that Bob is drinking again, which means he's busy cruising the streets and getting into trouble. Well, I'm out of it and any day now I'll meet somebody . . . though it's funny how seldom you see anyone who's really attractive. There was a nice young Swede at Steven's but I never did get his name and anyway he is being kept by that ribbon clerk from the Madison Avenue Store. After Steven's I went to a real brawl in the Village: a studio apartment, packed with people, dozens of new faces, too. I wish now I hadn't got so drunk because there were some really attractive people there. I was all set, I thought, to go home with one but the friend intervened at the last moment and it looked for a moment like there was going to be real trouble before our host separated us . . . I never did get the host's name. I think he's in advertising. So I ended up alone. Must call doctor about hepatitis pills, write Leonore Fini, check last month's invoices (re: missing Sheraton receipt), call Mrs. Blaine-Smith about sofa.

December 27, 1958
I finally had tea with Mrs. Blaine-Smith today . . . one of the most beautiful women I've ever met, so truly chic and well-dressed. . . . I'm hopelessly indebted to Steven for

bringing us together: she practically keeps the shop going. She had only six or seven people for tea, very much *en famille,* and I couldn't have been more surprised and pleased when she asked me to stay on. (I expect she knows what a discount I gave her on that Hepplewhite sofa.) Anyway, one of her guests was an Italian count who was terribly nice though unattractive. We sat next to each other on that delicious ottoman in the library and chatted about Europe after the war: what a time that was! I told him I hadn't been back since 1948 but even so we knew quite a few people in common. Then, as always, the name Elliott Magren was mentioned. He's practically a code word . . . if you know Elliott, well, you're on the inside and of course the Count (as I'd expected all along) knew Elliott and we exchanged bits of information about him, skirting carefully drugs and small boys because Mrs. Blaine-Smith though she knows everyone (and everything) *never* alludes to that sort of thing in any way, such a relief after so many of the queen bees you run into. Hilda, for instance, who married the maddest designer in Los Angeles and gives, I am told, the crudest parties with everyone drunk from morning till night. (Must stop drinking so much: nothing *after* dinner, that's the secret . . . especially with my liver.) We were discussing Elliott's apartment in the Rue du Bac and that marvelous Tchelitchew that hangs over his bed when a little Englishman, whose name I never did get, turned and said: did you know that Elliott Magren died last week? I must say it was stunning news, sitting in Mrs. Blaine-Smith's library so far, far away. . . . The Count was even more upset than I (could he have been one of Elliott's numerous admirers?) I couldn't help recalling then that terrible time at Deauville when Elliott was arrested and I had had to put up bail for him and hire a lawyer, all in French! Suddenly everything came back to me in a flood:

that summer, the affair with Hilda . . . and Helen (incidentally, just this morning got a Christmas card from Helen,
the first word in years: a photograph of her husband and
three ghastly children, all living in Toledo: well, I suppose
she's happy). But what an important summer that was, the
chrysalis burst at last, which, I think, prepared me for all
the bad luck later when I failed my doctorate and had to go
to work in Steven's office. . . . And now Elliott's dead.
Hard to believe someone you once knew is actually dead,
not like the war, where sudden absences in the roster were
taken for granted. The Englishman told us the whole story.
It seems Elliott was rounded up in a police raid on dope
addicts in which a number of very famous people were
caught, too. He was told to leave the country; so he piled
everything into two taxicabs and drove to the Gare St.
Lazare, where he took a train for Rome. He settled down
in a small apartment off the Via Veneto. Last fall he under-
went another series of shock treatment, administered by a
quack doctor who cured him of drugs but lost his memory
for him in the process. Aside from this, he was in good
health and looked as young as ever except that for some
reason he dyed his hair red . . . too mad! Then, last week,
he made a date to go to the opera with a friend. The friend
arrived . . . the door was open but, inside, there was no
Elliott. The friend was particularly annoyed because Elliott
often would not show up at all if, en route to an appointment, he happened to see someone desirable in the street.
I remember Elliott telling me once that his greatest pleasure was to follow a handsome stranger for hours on end
through the streets of a city. It was not so much the chase
which interested him as the identification he had with the
boy he followed: he would become the other, imitating his
gestures, his gait, becoming himself young, absorbed in a
boy's life. But Elliott had followed no one that day. The

friend finally found him face down in the bathroom, dead. When the autopsy was performed, it was discovered that Elliott had had a malformed heart, an extremely rare case, and he might have died as suddenly at any moment in his life . . . the drugs, the shock treatments, and so on had contributed nothing to his death. He was buried Christmas Day in the Protestant cemetery close to Shelley, in good company to the end. I must say I can't imagine him with red hair. . . . The Count asked me to have dinner with him tomorrow at the Colony (!) and I said I'd be delighted. Then Mrs. Blaine-Smith told the most devastating story about the Duchess of Windsor in Palm Beach.

Find out about Helen Gleason's sphinxes. Call Bob about the keys to the back closet. Return Steven's copy of *Valmouth*. *Find out the Count's name before dinner tomorrow.*

1956

THE LADIES IN THE LIBRARY

▼

(For Alice Bouverie)

I

He seldom saw his cousin Sybil and he was always ill at ease on those occasions when they did meet for she still represented the Family: a vague and now spent force which had been in a process of dissolution ever since his college days some twenty years earlier, diminishing not only as a force but as a fact until today only the two of them were left.

She lived in Baltimore and he lived in New York. Neither had married, a clear indication that nature had abandoned yet another experiment in eugenics. In other times he had occasionally tried to imagine himself as a father with numerous children in whose healthy veins his essence would be precipitated into future time, ensuring for him that posterity of blood which so appeals to those who briefly see eternity in man, but unfortunately neither the literal nor the metaphysical image ever concretized properly in his imagination, much less in life; and now, middle-aged, he assumed the conditions of his bachelor existence were fixed, the danger of serious change remote.

Sybil too had neglected to marry, and although she still made cozy allusions to weddings and Christmas parties, to Easter egg hunts and funerals, to all the beloved activities of a family's life, in actual fact she had consigned most human relationships to pleasant memory, devoting her life instead to dogs and cats, her dealings with these dependent creatures not unlike those she might have enjoyed with the children she never bore, with the family that had died. In a sense of course all things were nearly equal: she gave Christmas parties for the dogs and she made matches for the cats, arranging their destinies with the energy of a matriarch and, certainly, with better luck than matriarchs usually enjoy in the world of people.

We have nothing in common, he thought, as he waited for her in the Union Station, the dome of the Capitol like an elaborate dessert framed in the doorway. We would never have known one another if we had not been first cousins but then, to be precise, we do not *know* each other now. With a wetted forefinger he tried to paste back one corner of a curling Excelsior Hotel sticker which threatened to tear off the way the Continental, Paris, and the El Minzah, Tangier, had, leaving his suitcase messy with shreds of bright-colored paper making no design at all, none at all.

"Ah, there you are, Walter. I'm sorry if I'm late. But then I don't think I *am* late. Here, let my porter take your bag; he's a gem." The gem took his suitcase and as they walked to the train, she asked him about New York. But he had no intention of telling her anything about New York while she, he knew, had every intention of discussing Baltimore, the dogs and the cats, and then, more soon than late, she would talk about the Family, about that race of Virginia cavaliers, the Bragnets, who, except for the two of them, had seen fit to vanish in the first half of the twentieth century leaving no monument except the house they had built near Winchester so many, many years ago when the country was new and rich and their apple orchards were still saplings, without blossoms or fruit or history. The name of Bragnet on her lips was always strange and marvelous as though she were intoning, priestesslike, the secret name of a deity, a name which could blast trees, shatter stone, separate lovers, cause twins to be born joined, curdle cream, and, best of all, re-create the house of their common memory with the grace-ful, long-dead figures of those Bragnets who now lay in the dust of the Episcopal cemetery at Winchester.

But she was not herself today for even after they had taken their seats in the train and he had arranged their suit-cases on the rack overhead she did not pronounce the magic name. She wanted deliberately to mystify him, he decided irritably, and the only way he could retaliate was to ask no questions, to pretend that it made no difference to him that for the first time in twenty years he was returning to Winchester, at her inscrutable request.

"I've had such a busy time in Washington this week," said Sybil. "We had several really creative meetings of the Dog Society . . . oh, I know what you feel about our work. I've given up trying to convert you." She laughed heartily; she was blonde-gray, untidy, and as old, he recalled, as their splendid century but unlike the century not scarred at all. Sybil belonged to quite another time, to a world of serene country life where dogs mattered and horses were ridden, where men and women remained married despite all differences . . . a legendary age where emotion had been contained shrewdly by a formal manner which, in its turn, could only flourish in great houses, in high-ceilinged rooms with massive doors and bright brass. Sybil belonged to that world in spirit if not in fact and although she lived in a very small house in Baltimore her whole being suggested vast lawns and ordered gardens: boxwood, clipped and severe, muting the brilliance of roses; formal gardens set in wild uncharted country.

"I never knew that you knew Miss Mortimer," he said at last, forestalling a full report on the health and adventures of her animal friends in Baltimore.

"Oh, I've known her for years. As a matter of fact, I was in the house the day your mother decided to sell the place to her and I've always made it a point to keep in touch, because of the house."

Walter, at this point, was inclined to reminisce about the house (most conversations, it often seemed to him, were no more than competing monologues: a condition which he accepted as human and natural, a part of the universal strangeness) but Sybil had resolutely embarked upon Miss Mortimer: "A sweet, sweet woman. You'll adore her although people don't always, at least not at first. I'm not sure why. Perhaps because she *seems* sad and of course you never really know *what* she'll say or do . . . not that I mean she's eccentric: she's not one of those women who'll do anything for an effect. No, she's quite serious and she has her own little set in Winchester. . . . The Parker family are especially close to her. You remember the girls, don't you? the three sisters? They're all married now and all three live in Winchester . . . isn't that remarkable, keeping so close together? No, I'm really devoted to her. And I've told her so much about you. Why, she's even read one of your books. Anyway, we both decided that after all these years it was time you two got together."

Now it was out, he thought glumly. Sybil was trying to make a match, doubtless to get Bragnet House back into the family again. It was childishly clear: if he married Miss Mortimer and went to live at Bragnet, Sybil would once again have a marvelous big place to keep her dogs and cats. He looked at her suspiciously but she had again shifted the subject: she asked him about his life in New York, inquired graciously if he had written anything new.

"I'm always working." He hated to be asked what he was doing because the temptation to answer at length was so great. Briefly, he told her his plans for the season. And then, upon request, he named their mutual friends one by one and if she liked them he very subtly made them out worse than they were while if she disliked them he discovered heretofore unsuspected virtues in their characters. Neither took the ritual of this conversation very seriously; they were not half done when, like the sudden tolling of a bell, Sybil at last pronounced the name of Bragnet.

"We are the last," she said, with a rich melancholy pride, "you and I. Strange how a family dies out. There were so many Bragnets fifty years ago and now there are only two . . . and the house."

"Which is no longer ours."

"Your mother should never have sold it, never."

"It was too big for us," said Walter and then, before Sybil could embark on that line, he asked if there were to be other guests for the weekend.

"Only her nephew. He's supposed to be very bright. He's still in school. I suppose he'll inherit the house." She paused and Walter noticed she was uneasy, unlike her usual self. "Oh, you'll like her," she added, disjointedly. "I just know you will."

"Why *shouldn't* I?"

"Well, one's friends don't always like each other, do they? And she *is* a little difficult to know . . . rather unnerving at first: but that's only because she's shy."

"I promise not to be terrified."

"I'm sure you won't be." On that odd note the conversation lapsed and both for a long time studied the green countryside beyond the telephone poles which sped past with the regularity of pentameter in a blank verse tragedy.

II

As far as the eye could see to the south the apple trees grew in ordered ranks upon the rolling land, their leaves glittering green and new and their fruit green too, not yet ripe. Among the orchards, on a hill a mile removed from the asphalt highway, stood the lawn-circled house where Walter Bragnet was born and where his family had lived for so many generations in one long golden season of comfort, untouched by the wars, made rich by their orchards, and sustained from century to century by a proud serenity which was, his cousin Sybil maintained, inspired by the earth in these parts as well as by the rose-red brick house with its Greek Revival colonnade, the last tangible expression of the Bragnet family now reduced to two travelers who, with weekend valises, were deposited by a taxicab before the front door of their old home.

As he rang the doorbell, he wondered what he should feel or, more important, what he *did* feel but as usual he could not determine . . . he would have to wait until he could safely recall this scene in memory; only in the future could he ever discover what, if anything, he had felt: he existed almost entirely in recollection, a peculiarity of considerable value to him as a writer, though disastrous in his life since no event could touch him until it was safely past, until alone in bed at night he could experience in a rush all the emotions that he had been unable to feel at the appropriate time; then he would writhe, knowing it was again too late to act.

The door opened and they were admitted by a Negro in a white jacket, an acquaintance of Sybil's. They inquired solicitously of one another, as Walter followed them up the familiar staircase. The rooms were burdened with the same odor of musty linen, of roses, and of wood smoke which he remembered from his childhood. On the walls of the upstairs corridor hung the same Gillray prints which his grandfather had brought back from England; and, finally, the room to which he was shown was the one he had lived in for nearly eighteen years. He glanced sharply at Sybil, suspecting her of stage-managing; but she only looked at him blandly and remarked, "This used to be your room, didn't it?"

He nodded and followed the servant into his old room: a four-poster bed of pale scarred wood with no canopy, a fire-place with brass phoenixes to support the logs, and, amazingly enough, his books were still on the shelves of the bookcase where he had left them the day that he went off to college. He had always presumed that when his mother sold the house she'd given them away; obviously she had not and here they were: the Oz books, the Arabian Nights, Greek mythology. . . .

As he dressed for dinner, he walked about the room, touching the books but not taking them down, repelling with a certain pleasure whatever force it was that insisted he look at them, become even more involved in Sybil's obscure plot. If she thinks that I'll try to get the house back she's mistaken, he murmured to his own image in the mirror above the chest of drawers. He noticed that his face was flushed as though he had been drinking. It was the heat, he decided, as Sybil rapped on his door and then, before he could speak, proceeded briskly into the room, plain and unfashionable in gossamer gray and wearing yellow diamonds. "I thought we would go down together since you don't know her."

"Together by all means," he said genially, and together they went down the staircase, moving decorously, tactful among their common ghosts.

In the drawing room, Miss Mortimer came forward to meet them and Walter experienced an inexplicable panic; fortunately, Sybil began to talk. "Well, here he is!" she said, embracing her hostess. "I promised I'd bring him and I did!"

"And now he's here," said Miss Mortimer with a smile; her voice was low and he found that he had to be most attentive if he wanted to hear what she said, and he did want to hear, very much. She took his hand in her cool one and drew him over to a sofa. "You have no idea how happy I am to see you at last. Sybil has talked so much about you. I've asked her many times to bring you here but you never came." They sat down, side by side.

"I've been very busy," said Walter, blushing. He paused and then repeated, "I've been very busy." He looked at Sybil, mysteriously helpless; she gave him bright succor: from her wealth of small talk, she tossed a penny to Miss Mortimer: "Where is that nephew of yours? Where's Stephen?" And Miss Mortimer told them that her nephew would be along presently, that he had been riding all day; he had only just got home. "I am afraid at times I hardly understand him." She smiled at Walter.

"Is he so difficult?" Walter was becoming more used to her, to the situation. She was handsome with regular features, dark hair and eyes, only her mouth was bad, thin and forbidding. She was tall and she sat very straight beside him, her white hands folded in her lap.

"No, not difficult, just strange to me. Others are charmed by him. I expect he's going through a phase and of course when he's older I'll have more in common with him. At the moment he's almost too energetic. He rides horses; he writes poems."

Walter wondered if he would be asked to read the boy's poems, to advise him whether or not to pursue a career of letters. He began to rehearse in his mind his set speech on the vicissitudes of the literary life.

"Yes, Mr. Bragnet, he is at *that* stage. He even has a lady friend, a Winchester girl whom he sees every evening."

Walter looked at her with interest, wondering why she should want to discuss her nephew in such detail. There was something quite un-Virginian in her lack of reticence and he liked her a little more for this.

The nephew entered the room so quietly that Walter was not aware of him until he saw by Miss Mortimer's expression that there was someone behind him. He turned and then, as the boy approached, he rose and they shook hands. Miss Mortimer performed the introductions; then Stephen sat down in a chair between Sybil and Walter, closing the half-circle before the empty fireplace. Sybil asked him numerous questions while Walter listened to neither the questions nor the answers. The boy was uncommonly good-looking with blond hair and skin dark from the sun, the face not yet coarsened by the grain of a beard. Walter was reminded of himself at the same age, living in this house, coming home at vacation time. . . . He glanced suddenly at Miss Mortimer, who had been watching him; she nodded gravely as though she had divined his mood and wanted now to console him with truth rather than with pity: *she* knew how fine it was to be young, in this house. He wondered if he liked her any better for having understood.

Stephen was speaking: "I rode over to the Parker place this afternoon. . . ."

"Did Emily ride with you?" asked Miss Mortimer. Walter knew that Emily must be the summer beloved, traditional figure of green and yellow light.

"No, she didn't," said the boy curtly, looking at his aunt with bright cold eyes. "I went alone, and I saw old Mrs. Parker, who told me to tell you the girls will be over for lunch tomorrow."

"I'm so glad!" said Sybil. "I haven't seen them in years. You remember them, Walter?"

"Certainly." He recalled three sisters: Claudia, Alice, and . . . Laura? But they would hardly be girls now, he thought. They would be middle-aged strangers, inquisitive, tiresome. Restlessly, he shifted his position, faced Stephen more squarely, his back to Miss Mortimer. While Sybil recalled with wonder and pleasure how the girls had all managed to marry Winchester men, Stephen sat straight and polite, his brown fingers interlaced, his eyes on his aunt. Walter wondered why they disliked one another so openly. It was obvious to him that there could be little sympathy between two such dissimilar people; yet this open warfare seemed inappropriate considering the essential casualness of their relationship.

"I hope you'll show Mr. Bragnet some of your poems, Stephen. He's a writer, you know."

"Yes, I know," said Stephen smiling and Walter froze, aware that he was no longer admired, that his vogue had ended many years ago and that other writers now claimed the attention of the young and earnest.

"I should like to see them," said Walter, almost sincerely, enchanted with the boy's apparent ease, with his vitality;

and he admired Stephen even more when, with an implaca-
ble grace, he faced Miss Mortimer and said, "I never show
them to anyone." Then he turned quickly to Walter. "I
mean I don't like to have people read them because they
aren't very good and because they're private. You know
what I mean, don't you?"

"Indeed I do," began Walter.

"By the way," interrupted Miss Mortimer, "why don't
you ask Emily to come over for lunch tomorrow? You know
I want to meet her. It would be great fun."

"Yes, it would," said Stephen, ironically, cutting short
this flanking movement. "I'm sure she'd like to . . . but she
can't tomorrow. She wants so much to meet *you*," he
added, grinning.

"Well, another time." And Miss Mortimer serenely
accepted checkmate.

"My gracious, Stephen, aren't you awfully young to be
having a lady friend?" asked Sybil with that clumsy teasing
tone which she often used with the larger dogs. Walter
wondered if there were some way in which he might align
himself with Stephen against the two women. But his assis-
tance was not needed. Stephen laughed and said, "No, I
don't think I am." Then Miss Mortimer led them all into
the dining room, where paintings of colonial Bragnets still
hung upon the walls, rich by candlelight.

"We *must* get the family portraits away from you," said
Sybil.

III

The next day luncheon was dinner and though much too
elaborate, too heavy for a hot day, Walter ate greedily. He
had spent a restless night in the bed of his childhood and

now he was tired, exhausted from lack of sleep. The Parker sisters were a further nuisance. They irritated him unreasonably. Now middle-aged, they were resolutely jolly, and appallingly confident. After lunch, still gabbling, the sisters sat side by side on a sofa in the library . . . like judges, thought Walter, loosening his belt, feeling ill. He was wondering if he should go to his room for pills (he took many pills; his heart murmured) when Miss Mortimer turned to him and they talked intimately and at length of dreams, of a particular dream he had had the night before in which he had found himself in a black sea, drowning.

Miss Mortimer appeared youthful today, even desirable, and he wondered how he could have had such a disagreeable first impression of her. During lunch she had talked to him of his books and long before the overrich pudding had been served, he realized that she was not only intelligent but uncannily sensitive to mood, knowing when to praise, when to chide. He had not felt so easy with a new person in many years. She even divined his physical discomfort for, suddenly, she suggested he go to Stephen outside on the terrace, where she would join them presently. Both excused themselves and the Parker sisters, busy now with their knitting and their judgments, seemed not in the least annoyed, so perfectly at home were they, so used to one another's company. Even Sybil defected to observe the old stables.

The sun was hot, its light diffused by clouds; for a moment Walter stood on the terrace, dizzy and blind. Then Stephen spoke to him. "You escaped."

"Yes." The world righted itself and Walter saw the green lawn before him, bending toward orchards. "I escaped."

Stephen pulled two deck chairs together and they sat down. Walter was alarmed to find that he felt no better; could the sun be bad for him? His heart thumped irregularly. His pulses fluttered.

"You lived in this house, didn't you?"

Walter nodded. "I was about your age when I went away to college. While I was gone, my mother sold the place and we moved to Washington."

"Did you like living here?"

"Oh, very much: don't you?"

"I like the place itself," said the boy slowly. "I like to ride. . . ."

"But you don't like your aunt." He was suddenly too tired and too ill to keep to the periphery; it was easier to go to the center immediately.

"No, I don't like her, I never have." He smiled. "She says I'll understand her better when I'm older."

"Perhaps you will." Both were silent then. Neither chose to pursue this indiscreet, unchivalrous tack.

Stephen played idly with a large winged ant and Walter watched as the ant would climb the boy's thumb only to be pulled back, to begin again its laborious ascent. Little beads of perspiration gleamed on Stephen's brown forehead and his hair glittered in the sun. Finally, the ant escaped. "I'm going to take a walk. You want to come with me?"

"No, I had better stay here." Walter wanted to go but he did not dare. With a sudden, inexplicable sorrow, he watched the boy walk across the lawn. Not till he was out of sight did Walter shut his eyes and rest. Murmuring summer held him. Sharp sweet odor of new-cut grass; croaking of frogs in a distant pond. He was nearly asleep when he heard voices: the ladies in the library were discussing him. He knew that he should get up and walk away but he did not stir.

"He never married. I wonder why." Walter could identify none of the voices: the sisters spoke alike.

"Not the sort."

"I hate it when they have no children. Oh, I know it's sentimental . . ."

"Well, he has none and that's that, and we have our work to do. He's had a pleasant time."

"I should say so, and he missed all our wars. How did he manage that?"

"Heart condition."

"I suspect that *that's* our cue."

"Does he still write?"

"No, he seems to have given up."

"At fifty-one? That's rather early. Perhaps if he were to have another few years, an even sixty . . ."

"No! It *must* be now!"

They lowered their voices then and talked of knitting . . . one of them had found a knot in her yarn; they also talked of accidents and diseases and he listened less attentively, shaken by what he had heard, wondering if he might not still be dreaming: how could these women have known so much about his life? so many things not even his closest friends knew?

". . . run down by a cab in front of the Union Station."

"Oh, not that, not *that*!"

"Blood poisoning? A scratch? A fever . . . ?"

"Out of character. When in doubt, be obvious."

"The heart . . . *again?*"

"And why not? Why confect some elaborate plot when procedure is so clearly indicated? There's no reason to be bizarre."

"Very well: the heart . . . but when? Miss Mortimer is restless."

"Tomorrow on the train? as he lifts his suitcase to put it on the rack . . ."

"No, not another day. I mean, look . . . it's absolutely

strung out to the end. Besides, Miss Mortimer's already on the terrace, waiting for us, poor angel."

"I'm afraid I can't get this last knot undone."

"Then use scissors. Here."

He could neither speak nor move now. He was conscious of a massive constriction in his chest. As he gasped for breath, nearly blind in the sun, Miss Mortimer appeared to him over the edge of the receding world, and he saw that she was smiling, a summer flower in her gleaming hair, an expected darkness in her lovely eyes.

1950

ABOUT THE AUTHOR

GORE VIDAL was born in 1925 at the United States Military Academy, West Point. He wrote his first novel, *Williwaw*, in 1946, while he was in the army. His many subsequent novels include *Julian* (1964), *Myra Breckinridge* (1968), *Live from Golgotha* (1992), and his multivolume fictional chronicle of American history: *Burr* (1973), *Lincoln* (1984), *1876* (1976), *Empire* (1987), *Hollywood* (1990), and *Washington, D.C.* (1967). His collected essays, *United States: Essays 1952–1992*, won the National Book Award in 1993.

ABOUT THE TYPE

This book was set in Galliard, a typeface designed
by Matthew Carter for the Merganthaler Linotype
Company in 1978. Galliard is based on the
sixteenth-century typefaces of Robert Granjon.